D1074927

Death by
Chocolate
Marshmallow Pie

Center Point
Large Print

Also by Sarah Graves and available from
Center Point Large Print:

Death by Chocolate Chip Cupcake
Death by Chocolate Snickerdoodle
Death by Chocolate Frosted Doughnut
Death by Chocolate Malted Milkshake
Death by Chocolate Cherry Cheesecake

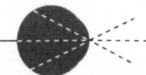

Death by Chocolate Marshmallow Pie

SARAH GRAVES

CENTER POINT LARGE PRINT
THORNDIKE, MAINE

This Center Point Large Print edition
is published in the year 2023 by arrangement with
Kensington Publishing Corp.

The text of this Large Print edition is unabridged.
In other aspects, this book may vary
from the original edition.
Printed in the United States of America
on permanent paper sourced using
environmentally responsible foresting methods.
Set in 16-point Times New Roman type.

ISBN: 978-1-63808-762-5

The Library of Congress has cataloged this record
under Library of Congress Control Number: 2023932205

One

"Oh, this is awful. One of us will just have to go over there and talk to him," said my friend Ellie White.

Frowning, she turned from the front bay window of our small chocolate-themed bakery, the Chocolate Moose, located on Water Street in the quaint island fishing village of Eastport, Maine.

"So who's it going to be?" she demanded.

"I'd rather stick pins in myself," I said as I put the final chocolate cookie onto a tray of them, then slid them into the cooler.

I hadn't met Brad Fairway, the new owner of the shop across the street from ours, and if his recent behavior was any clue, I didn't want to. Still, it was clear that something would have to be done.

"The nerve of that man," Ellie fumed, joining me behind the counter. Besides the cookies, I'd just finished stocking our glass-fronted display case with chocolate éclairs, fudge brownies, a chocolate-swirl cheesecake in a chocolate cookie–crumb crust, and . . .

You get the idea. Steps from the harbor, the Moose offered every kind of chocolate baked treat you could imagine, plus some you might not: chocolate-dipped bacon, for instance, and chocolate pretzels, both so edible that people had been known to make whole meals of them.

Not me, of course. Or hardly ever. Anyway . . .

Ellie slid a tray of her famously delicious chocolate macaroons into the cooler. I reached past her to filch one, popped it into my mouth, and bit down.

"Oh, good heavens." I managed around it as coconut, chocolate and the tart cherry jam in the middle all mingled gloriously. "Do I hear angels singing?"

The jam had been Ellie's idea. "Yes, well, our friend across the street had better hope that's who he hears when I get done with him," she said.

She closed the display case, carefully not slamming it, then grabbed the dustpan and broom and began sweeping angrily, never mind that I'd already done it not ten minutes ago. "Why, I've got half a mind to march over there right now and—"

"And what? Beat him up?" I went around behind her and put our eight black cast-iron chairs back in place around our four small cast-iron café tables. "You know you won't do any such thing," I added, setting out four small glass vases, each with a purple hyacinth bulb blooming in it.

"Not that you wouldn't, or couldn't," I conceded. The beating she delivered would only be verbal, but that might not matter. When Ellie got mad, she could deliver a truly top-notch scolding. "For one thing, we've still got to finish packing everything up for our table at the art fair later," I said.

Eastport's art fair, held each year in June, was a gloriously colorful and varied outdoor show of paintings, photographs, weaving, pottery, and other creations that local artists had been making in their studios all winter and spring. Ellie and I had promised we'd sell pastries and soft drinks in the parking lot by the fish pier where the fair was being held.

Now Ellie looked through the front window again, her eye catching something outside. "Darn, there's Harald Gleason," she sighed.

I followed her gaze, and sure enough, a tall, thin teenager in black jeans and a worn black concert T-shirt was out there loitering around the cars that were angle parked on the street.

"Kid's going to get himself in trouble someday," she said.

At fifteen, the gawky boy was all brains—he'd just graduated from high school, nearly two years early—but no common sense. Also, from what I'd heard, Harald's home life left plenty to be desired, but that wasn't the point right now.

"What's he doing, anyway?" I wondered aloud. Beyond the window, Harald sidled casually along, squinting from side to side and then glancing around to see if he'd been observed.

"Heaven knows," Ellie replied. "Statistical study of the ages and models of Eastport cars maybe? Or he's planning how to steal one?"

Harald was the type who could add columns of numbers in his head, fast. The last time he'd done a "statistical study," as he called them, he'd been twelve; it had been of the number of seagull landings on the Eastport dock hour by hour for a whole day.

So Ellie's first idea—some kind of research—wasn't out of the question, and I hoped it was something like that. But the way Harald kept eyeing the storefront doors he passed worried me, because Harald had also become fascinated with locks lately—picking them, mostly.

"You know Harald has never stolen anything," I said. "He just likes . . . Oh, I don't know. The challenge, I guess."

Harald himself had spent an hour explaining this to me recently, meanwhile surrounding several raspberry-chocolate scones and enough Pepsi to float a barge. He was a good kid, just confused by the amount of brainpower he'd been burdened with and unsure what to do with it.

I looked out once more. No Harald. "Anyway, he's gone."

"Mmm," Ellie said skeptically, but then she looked around at our shop and her face softened. With exposed redbrick walls, a vintage pressed-tin ceiling, and a century-old paddle-bladed fan

8

stirring the sweet-smelling air, the Chocolate Moose was a lot of work, but it was also a labor of love.

"And right now it's showtime." She unlocked the shop's front door and turned the CLOSED sign to OPEN. "But when I see that Brad Fairway guy, he'd better—" *Watch out,* her tone finished for her.

She'd have said it herself, but just then the silver bell over the shop door tinkled brightly and our first customer of the day bustled in.

"Oh, cheesecake!" Emily Prager said delightedly, approaching the display case. She was a tall, angular woman with steel-gray hair and ruddy cheeks, and today she was carrying a big straw bag over her freckled arm.

And Emily liked to talk, so this was my chance. Take the bull by the horns and so on. "I'll be right back," I said.

Outside, welcome warmth poured from the sky; after the winter we'd had, seventy degrees felt tropical. Around me, shopkeepers were planting more red and white geraniums in tubs and window boxes.

A police car slowed in front of me. The driver leaned over toward his open passenger-side window. "You ready for all this?" asked Bob Arnold. He was a big, bearish man, round faced and pink cheeked, with pale blue eyes, rosebud lips, and a deeply dimpled chin.

9

"All set." I waved toward the fish pier parking lot across the street from the hardware store. Tents, tables, and display racks were getting set up by volunteers; past them I could just glimpse the pink fringed awning over our own sales table fluttering in the breeze.

Meanwhile, the emptied vans and pickup trucks that had hauled all the artwork into the display area now began pulling out. Or trying. There were so many that a traffic jam had developed.

"That's my cue," Bob said, seeing the confusion, and when he'd gone, I finished crossing the street.

CHOCO'S! read the crisp black lettering on the brand-new front window. I stomped up the shop's granite steps and went inside, where the main room's vintage tin ceiling had been torn down, and finely milled woodwork, no-longer-trimmed windows and doors, and the venerable old horsehair-plaster walls had had foil wallpaper slapped onto them.

Slowly I turned, getting madder: brushed-steel countertops, hard molded plastic chairs, the once-gorgeous hardwood floor now covered by tiles made of imitation wood product.

"Hello?" I called out.

No answer. A mirror behind the counter showed my reflection—long, narrow face; dark eyes; short, dark hair—lit unflatteringly from above.

"Anyone here?"

Choco's display case held an assortment of cakes, cookies, brownies, muffins, doughnuts, pastries, pies . . . all items that the Moose sold, too, only Choco's prices were lower.

A lot lower.

"Hey! Anybody?" I drummed my fingertips impatiently on the steel countertop. The air in here was cool and still, redolent of pine-scented cleaning products but not of baking.

Nuts to this, I thought, turning to go.

But halfway to the door, I jumped as a loud burst of static erupted from behind the counter, followed by a man's voice. "Jake Tiptree?"

That's me, Jacobia Tiptree, Jake to my friends. "Who are you?" I demanded. "And where are you?"

"Brad Fairway. I'm in my office. You're on my security monitor," he said. "Talk to the mirror. That's where the camera is."

Yeah, talk to this, I thought and headed for the exit. "Do you know what slander is?" I called back over my shoulder.

It was what Ellie had been so mad about. "Because my lawyer does. I'll have her explain it to you if you want."

For unknown reasons, Brad Fairway had been harassing us since he'd first opened Choco's a couple of weeks earlier. At first, it was small stuff: coming into the Moose for some small chocolate item, then conspicuously dropping it

11

into a sidewalk trash bin after one bite, or shaking his head warningly at people who approached our door.

But now he'd gone too far, and if he thought he was going to get away with—

"Wait." This time the voice didn't come from a speaker. As I turned, a large man in a faded Hawaiian shirt and ragged cargo shorts stepped out from somewhere behind the counter. "Don't go away mad." His mouth smiled; his eyes didn't.

And I knew which part of his face I believed; owing to certain unfortunate events in my past, I'd met his type before. The more I looked, in fact, the more I thought . . . But no, it was too unlikely.

"You told Nan Porter that our flour has bugs in it," I accused as I stomped toward him. Nan was a longtime Chocolate Moose customer, and she'd reported this indignantly.

I kept closing in on Fairway, not dropping my gaze. The trick is to make them believe you'll walk right into them, and it worked like a charm. At the last minute he stepped back hastily.

"Come on, why would I say a thing like that?" Getting dusted back was a new experience for him, I could tell by the way his piggy little eyes didn't get friendlier.

And he still looked familiar. I hadn't seen him up close before; somehow it had always been Ellie who'd dealt with him at the Moose.

"I don't know," I snapped, trying to ignore

12

the alarms going off in my head. "Maybe the same reason you were bragging last night at the Crab that you're getting ready to put us out of business," I added.

The Crab was our local watering hole. The night before, Ellie's husband had been in there and had heard Fairway's half-in-the-bag blather. If that was all it was.

I pointed at the display-case items, with their unrealistically low prices prominently displayed. "That's why you're taking a loss on everything. Later you'll jack prices up. 'Cause you're a bully. A *lying* bully."

Rude, I know. But if you really want to find out what a person is made of, get right up in their face and make 'em mad.

Fairway's bullish shoulders moved up and down in a shrug under his bright shirt. "So?"

"So stop spreading rumors," I said, "that our dishwasher doesn't sterilize, our walnuts are rancid, our water's contaminated." And on and on. "Just cut it out," I repeated.

His turn to move forward. "Why? Because you say so?"

He got close enough so that I had to peer up at him. His small, slit-like eyes looked amused, and as if something unpleasant hunkered behind them.

And that was when I knew for sure who he was and where I'd seen him before.

13

"Correct," I managed finally, keeping my voice steady with an effort. "Because I say so. It's slander, and I can prove damages."

The local animal shelter's benefit dinner would be having its desserts catered by Choco's instead of the Moose this year, due to a story going around about our tainted ingredients. The shelter manager's apologetic call this morning was what had gotten Ellie's temper flaring just now.

"Damages," Fairway repeated sarcastically.

I wondered if I poked him in the chest with my index finger, would he grab it and bend it back? But at least he didn't recognize me.

"Why would I want to hurt you?" he asked, waving carelessly toward the Chocolate Moose. "That sad little dump," he said dismissively, then looked back at me. "People want new and shiny nowadays. You two're going to go broke no matter what, so if I wanted you gone, why wouldn't I just wait?"

My finger forgot about his chest and aimed toward his eye. It might even be worth getting the whole hand broken, I thought grimly as my elbow cocked back and the finger stiffened.

"Jake! What are you doing?" Ellie appeared suddenly outside the shop window, banged her knuckles insistently on it.

Fairway stood scowling at both of us as Ellie hurried in, wincing in distaste at Choco's new decorating scheme.

"Jake," she said sweetly, "we need you over in the shop." Taking my arm in a casual gesture, she squeezed it hard.

Like *What the hell are you doing?* hard.

"Sorry about this," she told Fairway while guiding me toward the door.

"Yeah, not a problem," he replied grudgingly, following us across the fake-wood floor, not chasing us, exactly.

Not quite. Ellie hustled me down the front steps, and when I looked back, Fairway's unfriendly gaze met mine. There was, thankfully, still no recognition in his eyes.

"Not a problem at all," he repeated before closing the door behind us. The OPEN sign in the window flipped over to CLOSED.

Yeah, you too, buddy, I thought.

"Where does he get his nerve?" Ellie demanded, still gripping my arm. "I want to go there and get some."

"You've got plenty of nerve," I said, stepping back fast, out of the way of a pickup truck with six wooden weaving looms rattling in its bed.

"Jake!" Ellie yanked me onto the sidewalk just as another car screeched by, narrowly missing me. From down the street, Bob Arnold glanced over and saw me nearly getting smushed. His shiny pink scalp reflected the morning sunshine as he shot me a look: *Watch it.*

"Anyway, you antagonized Fairway," Ellie said as we reached the opposite sidewalk. "You went over there and . . ."

When we went inside the Moose, my daughter-in-law, Mika, was getting ready to do bakery duty while we were at the art show. With her glossy black hair blunt cut just at chin level and a fresh white apron tied on over black slacks and a white shirt, she looked like a fashion model moonlighting as a shop clerk, only prettier.

"I didn't antagonize him half as much I wanted to," I said. Once upon a time I'd have thrown myself bodily at him, broken fingers be damned.

Ellie blew a breath out. "Jake, if I'd wanted to make things worse, I could've gone over there myself and—"

"Anything you'd like me to do while you're gone?" Mika cut in. Besides being my son's wonderful wife and the mom of my two gorgeous, terrifyingly smart grandchildren, she was a natural peacemaker.

"No thank you, dear," Ellie replied, turning down Mika's offer, her last word coming out *dee-yah,* the Maine way of saying it. "You just wait on customers and take phone orders and—"

"And if that guy from across the street comes in," I interrupted darkly, "feed him a poisoned cookie."

Ellie shot me a warning look, but of course I

wasn't serious. For one thing, I was pretty sure we didn't have any poison in the shop.

But later I wished I hadn't said it.

Ellie settled into her lawn chair under the pink fringed awning shading our art fair table. Around us, the vivid hues of watercolors, oil paintings, etchings, and pastels popped brilliantly, interspersed with displays of pottery, stitchery, and stained glass.

I pulled my chair up beside Ellie's. Out on the water, beyond the end of the fish pier, small whitecaps raced briskly, but here onshore the breeze felt sun kissed.

"I'm glad we have Mika to depend on," I said. "Someone we know well and can trust."

Mika and my son, Sam, and their children had shared my big old house with the rest of the family—my dad and stepmother; my husband, Wade Sorenson; and me—for nearly three years before finding their own place.

"Right," agreed Ellie. Then she added, "Uh-oh, here they come," as the first art fair visitors began circulating among the tents and booths around us.

Ellie sold two chocolate-cream cannolis to a couple dressed all in L.L.Bean. Tourists, definitely. I handed change to a fellow who'd already bitten into his mocha cupcake.

"And you?" Ellie's strawberry-blond curls

glinted red in the sun as she put two chocolate cream puffs into a white paper bakery bag and added two napkins.

Her thick-lashed eyes, the deep, dark blue of woodland violets, regarded me mildly. "How are you doing?"

"Me? What about me?" I asked innocently as a gaggle of ladies arrived at our table to try out our German chocolate cake.

"Well?" Ellie demanded again when they'd bought thick slices and moved on. "Something's been eating you since you were in Choco's."

I sighed deeply. "Okay. Remember how I've always said I hope no one from my deep, dark past ever moves to Eastport?"

Ellie put three chocolate dream bars into a bag for a skinny young fellow in a faded T-shirt and dungarees that had seen better days.

You wouldn't think from seeing him that his intricate beadwork was in museums around the world, but it was. With a pleasant grin and a mumbled thanks, he returned to his booth, where said beadwork was selling like crazy.

Unlike our baked goods. The few sales we'd made still left us with a tableful of sweets.

Ellie dumped a few small bills into our cashbox. "Yes, I've heard you say people from your past need to stay there, many times. But what's it got to do with . . . oh." She stopped as the explanation hit her. "You mean you . . . ?"

"Yup." I leaned back in my chair. "Brad Fairway. He's aged, and he's put on forty pounds or so. But back in the old days . . ."

Back then, I'm sorry to say, I'd been a money manager for guys whose large, illegal incomes arrived in manila envelopes. They were normal on the outside, these guys—that is, when they weren't killing people—but on the inside, they were . . . well, not nice.

Not even a little bit. And they'd needed somebody who was careful and trustworthy to handle all their money: to move it around, invest it and make it grow, and mostly to hide it so no IRS investigator or organized-crime cop could get a sniff of it. Someone like me, young and at the time without noticeable scruples, who could make a cash flow, a calculator, and a set of phony account books sing and dance like a talent-show contestant.

"I never knew his name. He came around where I worked," I said.

My office back then was a small, cluttered room at the rear of a shoe store in Queens. There I unsealed the cash, counted it, recorded it, and routed it through phony invoices and faked payments until all that dirty money was clean as a whistle again.

"Ohh," Ellie breathed. "So is he here on account of you?"

She knew enough about my past life to

understand that parts of it could still come back to bite me, even after all this time.

"I don't think so," I said. I'd been rattled earlier, but now I was calming down. "I doubt he ever noticed me back then, and I'm sure he didn't know me just now." Or if he had, his poker face was better than I recalled. "Only from now on you'd better deal with him," I said. "I'd rather not give his memory another chance to get jogged."

Ellie nodded agreement. "I'll go over there again later, soft-soap him a little. See if I can find out why he's being so . . ." Her final word rhymed with *hissy*.

"Bring over our old laptop, ask him if it's worth fixing," I suggested.

As I recalled, he'd had a string of electronics stores back in the city; maybe appealing to his knowledge might soften him up now.

Or not. I drank some coffee out of the go-cup I'd brought, and watched Harald Gleason slip easily among the crowds of fairgoers. I gathered he'd given up lurking on the sidewalk in favor of running errands for artists who were stuck at their sales tables and he was getting tipped for his trouble.

Like I said, he was smart, just not really well socialized. I hoped the boy found his way in life somehow, and then I forgot about him again.

"Just don't rile Fairway up any more than I already did," I added to Ellie. "I don't know what all other activities he might've gotten into since back then, but they probably weren't good."

Leg breaking, for instance, had been a specialty with some of those guys. And . . . other things.

"Don't worry," Ellie said. "I want to end his hostility, not encourage it." Unlike your performance with him earlier, she didn't add, but I knew she was thinking it.

"Fine. But if he gets mad again, leave before things escalate."

Birds of a feather, after all, and the last time I'd seen him, Brad Fairway had been flocking with the equivalent of velociraptors.

Still, on a day like today it was hard to worry about him for long. Down in the boat basin, lobster boats motored around, unloading their haul and heading out again.

"Pretty afternoon," Ellie remarked dreamily, turning her face up to the sun.

On the water, a flock of small sailboats tacked upwind, white sails billowing tautly, while beyond them the Campobello ferry chugged toward Canadian waters.

"And the artists seem happy," I said. The half dozen looms I'd seen earlier were set up nearby. The students seated at them bent to their work, while their instructor, a slim, fortyish blond woman named Babs Littrell, a visiting instructor at the Eastport Arts Center, moved cheerfully among them.

21

An hour later, when the students took a break, Babs Littrell stood talking with a slender young man in linen trousers and a loose white shirt, with leather huaraches on his feet. Silver medallions formed the band of his black felt hat.

He and Babs bent their heads together over his phone's screen, where colors moved in an animation of some kind. She looked pleased to be shown whatever it was, he not so much to be showing it, and when I looked over again, he was gone.

Then around twelve-thirty some local musicians with fiddles and banjos and a penny whistle began tuning up on the fish pier, and by the time Ellie had fetched us a pair of hot pork sandwiches from the lunch cart nearby, people were dancing.

Peppery-hot oil in small paper cups came with the sandwiches; the tender, spicy pork practically melted on contact with my teeth. As I devoured mine, the weaving students set their shuttles aside again and got up, then headed for the lunch cart, along with Babs Littrell.

Ellie frowned thoughtfully at our still unsold treats. Finally, she rose and went back to the lunch cart and spoke with the weaving instructor while pointing at our table.

"Sodas and desserts," she said, answering my unspoken question when she returned. "They can't buy them if they don't know they're here."

She was right. This time it wasn't Brad Fairway's dirty tricks obstructing us, but a large tent, full of brilliantly hand-painted silk jackets, trousers, and scarves, blocking people's view of us.

Now Ellie had advertised our presence, though, and ten minutes later, our tub of sodas and crushed ice held only slush, while not a crumb was left on our table.

"And that," said Ellie, dusting her hands together, "is that."

She folded our chairs while I emptied the cashbox, gathered stray napkins and bakery bags, and picked up litter. Then we started back toward the Chocolate Moose, and it was while we were passing the weaving area that I got my first look at what Babs Littrell had on her own loom.

"Oh," I heard myself saying. The fabric was nubbly in some places, smooth in others, colored in shades of blue, lime green, and purple flecked here and there with glimmers of gold. "I guess now I see how she's won all those prizes," I murmured.

Babs Littrell's summer residency at the arts center had been covered extensively in our local newspaper, the *Quoddy Tides*. Now I understood why. The cloth shimmered richly, looking almost alive. Standing there coveting it, I imagined how it might feel when draped over my shoulders: warm, magical.

"She's from where again? Iceland?" I asked.

The weaver's short-clipped blond hair was so pale, it was nearly white.

"Greenland," Ellie said as I made my way to where the artist sat.

"Will that be"—I gestured at the loom—"for sale?"

She smiled, pleased. "Yes, it will be. Do you like it?"

"Very much." I reached out. The fabric's edges were straight and tight, and its texture did not feel the least bit itchy. I loved it.

But a thing like this would be expensive. Babs Littrell seemed to sense my hesitation, and the reason for it.

"Why don't we let me get it done before we talk?" she suggested kindly. "Maybe we can come to some arrangement?"

"Thanks," I said, suspecting we wouldn't. Gorgeous weavings by world-renowned textile artists probably weren't in my budget, with or without a price break.

But as I rejoined Ellie, I reminded myself that if I'd wanted to be wealthy, I could've stayed back in the city, where selling my soul piece by piece had been making me richer than sin.

As we approached the Moose, through our front window I spied Mika sitting at one of the tables with a nutpick, shelling walnuts. The strains of a Bach string quartet floated out through the screen door.

She hadn't seen us. I backed away. "Let's walk up to my house and get your car?" I suggested to Ellie.

The morning had been so lovely, she'd parked at my place, and we'd walked down here together.

"Give Mika another hour?" Ellie asked. Of peace and quiet, she meant. With two young kids at home, Mika thought bakery sitting was practically a vacation.

So we walked back up Water Street, past the WaCo Diner, the Tides Institute, the Mexican restaurant, and the old redbrick Frontier Bank building, now housing a small recording studio called Downeast Sounds.

On our way up Key Street, we passed between small white clapboard houses with brick front walks laid out in the jack-on-jack pattern, now cemented with ancient moss.

Then at the top of the hill, my house came into view: a massive old white-clapboard dwelling with three full floors plus an attic, forty-eight wavy-glassed, double-hung windows with green shutters, three brick chimneys, and a workshop, where Wade restored rare and antique firearms.

I loved the old place, but my pleasure was marred today by the sight of peeling paint on the siding. The roof needed attention, and a downspout had blown loose, perhaps my least favorite home-repair job.

Out on the porch, my housekeeper-slash-stepmother, Bella Diamond, was shaking out rugs, her ropy arms working vigorously as she snapped pale clouds of dust into the air.

"Go talk to your father," she greeted me, her frizzy, henna-dyed hair blazing red in the early afternoon sun. "He's got a plan," she added, and the twist that she'd put on the final word let me know what she thought of it.

"Hi, Bella," said Ellie, wrapping her arms around the skinny old woman and drawing her close. Bella wore faded jeans, beat-up penny loafers, and a tattered gray sweatshirt with UMAINE on the front.

"Mmph," Bella replied, grudgingly allowing herself to be hugged. She had begun years earlier as my helper, had soon moved in with me and Sam, and had married my dad soon after he reappeared in my life.

"Your father wants to *move,*" she burst out suddenly. "To a nursing home, of all places." Rolling her big grape-green eyes, she made a shooing motion at me with one rawboned hand. "I can't get anywhere with him. You try."

"Sure," I said, not feeling optimistic about this. I'd heard that some men got less stubborn as they aged, but I'd never met any of them.

Pulling open the porch door, I let my other hand rest briefly on Bella's bony shoulder. She could be prickly, but she'd have stepped in front of a freight train for any one of us.

"Just talk to him," she said.

My kitchen had tall, bare windows, a scuffed hardwood floor, and high wooden wainscoting varnished the same dark burnt orange as the beadboard cabinets. A round wooden table with a green glass pitcher on it stood between the gas stove and the original old soapstone sink.

"Ellie!" my father said, looking up with a grin from his rocker by the woodstove in the corner. He spread his arms wide as she crossed to him and leaned to kiss his cheek.

"Jacob," she said affectionately, beaming at him. Then she wandered tactfully off into another room.

"Hi, Dad," I said.

Pink with recent scrubbing and shaving, he wore a green sweatshirt, navy blue fleece pants, and leather sandals.

"What's this about you wanting to move to the nursing home?"

"It's not a nursing home," he corrected me. "It's an assisted living facility. There's a big difference." His long gray hair was tied with a leather thong; a ruby stud that had been my late mother's gleamed red in his left earlobe.

"Dad, we've put in a stair chair," I reminded him.

It slid smoothly and quietly between the first and second floors at the turn of a knob, and now that it was here, no one in this house ever needed to climb stairs again. So far all we'd done with it was give the children rides, but surely it would be handy sooner or later.

"Your bathroom is so well equipped for mobility, you could lower yourself into the bathtub with a winch if you wanted," I went on. "As for your social life, you already spend so much time at the senior center, you might as well live there. So why a nursing home? I mean, assisted living?" I corrected myself hastily.

I wasn't even sure what it cost or how we could pay for it. But that wasn't the point. "And what about Bella?" I asked.

His face, spotted by age and wrinkled as a walnut, opened into a smile. "Oh, she'll come around. She's hard against it, but—"

"But nothing," I cut in. "She hates the idea, and so do I." I took a breath. "Dad, if your plan is to make more room in this house or save me trouble or anything like that, just know that I've had plenty of time away from you already, and I don't need more now."

His lips pursed. "Well, that's something, I suppose."

Darn. Now I'd hurt his feelings, reminding him of the years when I hadn't even known whether he was alive. He felt guilty about it, even though none of it had been his fault.

"I'm sorry," I said. "I just meant . . ." Damn. Why did this still have to be so hard sometimes?

But after a moment, his intelligent old eyes said he understood. "No sense pretending we're the average American family, is there?"

A laugh escaped me. He'd been a wholehearted radical activist, and then he had gotten framed for supposedly killing my mother and had gone on the run. From age three I had lived in orphanages, foster homes, and later on the street, which was where I had found out I was good with numbers.

I mean, really good.

"Yeah, you've got that right," I told him. "Ward Cleaver you ain't."

But then, "Jacobia, you'll need to trust me on this. Bella too."

"But—" I began.

He held up a lean, liver-spotted old hand. "My mind," said my elderly but still perfectly competent father, "is made up. And that's all there is to it."

Two

My name is Jacobia Tiptree, and when I first came to Maine, I had a twelve-year-old son, a car trunk stuffed with cash, and a head full of the clear, cold awareness that I could be shot dead at any moment and no one would ever find out who'd done it.

I'd been married to a brain surgeon whose history of infidelity was so well known that the nurses at his hospital called him Vlad the Impaler, the ones, that is, who weren't leaving bits of lacy black lingerie in his coat pockets and calling him at home.

Meanwhile, my son and his pals skipped school regularly to go shoplifting, jump subway turnstiles, and take whatever drugs they found in their parents' medicine chests, washing them down with the contents of their parents' liquor cabinets.

And I wasn't much better. Basically, I'd get cash from the shoe store into banks all over the city, in small amounts so no automated alarms would go off. With what didn't get laundered locally, I'd buy securities, precious metals, and real estate, a little at a time.

For this—and for keeping my mouth shut about it—I was paid ridiculously well. Hey, a girl with a talent for handling dirty money is a good pet to have, as somebody a lot smarter than me once put it.

But then one morning I woke up in the Manhattan penthouse that I shared with my sludge-dwelling slime toad of a husband and discovered that instead of attending a surgical convention, he was doing whatever with whomever at a hideaway in Vermont.

The girl with him, probably hoping I'd let him divorce me and marry her, had messaged me very late the night before to inform me of this. But hers wasn't the only news; the TV said my bosses at the shoe store had been nabbed, not for money laundering but for murders. Mob hits, they called them.

MASSACRE FOR HIRE! blared the *Post* when I ran downstairs to get it. My heart, what was left of it after the Vermont girl's charming missive, lurched up into my throat when I saw the front page. On top of all that, Sam hadn't been home for a few days, and it was him, even more than the possibility of the Feds being at my door any minute—

I didn't see how they'd locate me, or how anyone would, really. The shoe-store guys never knew my real name or address; back when I first started working for them, I hadn't even had an address.

Still, it was Sam and the idea of him finding

me all bloody on the floor that propelled me into what happened next.

"Mom," he protested when I'd tracked him to a dark, gritty games arcade, where he was hanging out with his friends.

"Never mind," I explained and seized him by the elbow, then muscled him out onto the street. "Car," I said crisply, urging him along.

I remember he was wearing green cargo pants, the cuffs puddling over scuffed black lace-up boots, and a black hoodie over a T-shirt screen-printed with the word *luck*. Or it rhymed with luck, anyway.

"In," I said, yanking open the car door.

He grumbled loudly, but he obeyed.

At our apartment: "Grab your stuff," I told him. "One duffel, no more. Hurry."

"Mom, what's going on?" he demanded. "I have a right to know why you're so . . ."

That rhyme again. "Don't use that tone with me, Sam. I'll tell you when we're in the car. You have five minutes."

I checked the phone again. No messages. That was good. Not that the cops generally alert you before they arrest you.

Shoe-store guys don't, either. The ones who weren't already in jail might show up, offering help, but if I took it, I was toast. The help they'd offer was permanent.

Thinking these things, I grabbed all the cash

in the apartment. It was a lot, and I had more in safety-deposit boxes around town. The wages of sin were pretty good, actually, and had been for a while.

Sam came out hauling his duffel bag plus a backpack.

"All right," I said grudgingly at his look of appeal.

He couldn't have loaded all that in five minutes. He must have already been planning to go somewhere, or maybe he'd been waiting for his mom to get her head on straight and get us both the hell out of Dodge.

I shepherded him toward the door, not sparing a look back at the view over Central Park or the terrace, with its Lily Pulitzer–cushioned wicker chairs under large, professionally cared-for potted trees.

I dropped my apartment keys on the hall table, locked the door from inside, and pushed Sam out, then slammed the door behind us.

"You still haven't told me what's going on," Sam complained when we got outside.

Across from us in the park, carriage horses waited patiently for the next batch of tourists to employ their top-hatted drivers.

"Backseat," I told Sam, glancing quickly up and down the crowded sidewalk. Coming down in the elevator, I'd been convinced we were going to step out into a fusillade.

But so far, so good. In crosstown traffic we took Fifty-Seventh Street to the bank holding my largest cash stash. When I came out, I threw four bulging shopping bags into the trunk of my husband's fancy new sports car, got back behind the wheel, and hit the gas.

Sam had caught a glimpse into one of the shopping bags. "Was that all money?" he whispered as we sailed up onto the FDR.

"Yep. See, I've been involved in some . . . activities."

It wasn't all the money, though. Not even close. It was all that I had time to grab up before we got out of here.

Hey, you win some, you lose some.

Sam surprised me by pulling a face. "I'm not stupid, Mom. I know you work for the mob, okay?"

I glanced in the rearview, where his face had once again taken on the bored, contemptuous expression I'd come to accept as normal. That and his dark, curly hair, hazel eyes, and long jaw were all so much like his father's, I nearly burst into tears.

"So is that why we're running?" Sam wanted to know. "Did they put out a hit on you or something?"

"Maybe not yet," I muttered. Then, louder, "Of course not. It's just that . . ."

How could I tell this poor kid that his dad was

a scoundrel *and* his mom was a criminal? "I do have some work trouble," I admitted.

That was putting it mildly. The cops liked to follow the money, and for that, they liked the bookkeeper to show them around. That was also the reason why my bosses would prefer I be unavailable.

Permanently unavailable.

"I got some news about your dad," I said, glancing back at Sam again. "Seems he's not at the convention, like he said he was."

I'd called the inn in Vermont to check.

"Instead, he took a young lady on a trip," I said. By now we were way uptown, passing under the Ninety-Sixth Street pedestrian bridge and heading toward the Bruckner. "A romantic trip," I added. We hit a pothole, and I bit my lip hard, letting the resulting tears slide down my face.

"Surprise, surprise," Sam said sarcastically. Then at my look, he added, "What? You're just figuring all this out?"

I sighed, meanwhile negotiating a ridiculously complex series of on-ramps and left-lane merges.

"No," I admitted when we were accelerating northward again. It was a very nice little sports car: five speeds forward, black ragtop, more power than a locomotive. I pictured Victor's face when he learned I had taken it. "No, I've known for a long time, actually."

I just hadn't realized that Sam knew, too.

"But the thing is . . ."

He must've heard the tears in my voice. "So, like, did he break your heart or something?" Not sounding concerned, which came as no shock. What with all the screaming and crying and wineglass throwing he'd grown up witnessing, his emotional armor must've been as thick as alligator hide.

Mine wasn't. "Yes," I managed. "Yes, he did break it." I swallowed hard. "That's not your problem, though. Not your fault."

He reached forward to pull a packet of tissues from the car's vestigial center console and passed a wad of them to me.

"Thanks." I blew hard. "The thing is, Sam, I really loved him. I mean, from the moment I met him." I had, too, truly, deeply.

Sam fell back onto the car's tiny rear seat. "Wow," he said, trying and, I supposed, failing to imagine this.

But Victor could charm the birds out of the trees when he wanted to, and he was good-looking, too. Plus, he was the kind of brain surgeon you went to when the others had told you to get your affairs in order, and he might even succeed in saving you where the others had not.

Sam didn't speak again until we had gotten at last onto the New England Thruway and were heading through Cos Cob. "People like what they like, you know," he said, echoing my thought. "They just do. They can't help it."

"I know," I said quickly. It was the conclusion that I'd come to, finally, too: that you can want all you want, but sometimes you can't get there from here.

"So we'll take a trip of our own," I said, trying to cheer Sam. "See new stuff, clear our heads," I said brightly.

Sam's answering look said, *Yeah, right,* but he didn't protest, only scrunched himself up in the tiny backseat and endured the ride.

Four hours later we hit the Maine Turnpike, and I just kept driving, waiting for something, anything, that would make me think taking an exit was better than just going on until we ran out of gas.

Finally, the low-fuel light did start blinking annoyingly, so we had to stop. The pump worked fine, the cashier was pleasant, and a man buying Swisher Sweets tipped his cap and said "Ma'am" to me on my way out, but I figured those things, especially all at once, were probably unusual and wouldn't happen again in a million years.

But then at the rest area, the air wasn't laden with noise and exhaust fumes, and the restroom was at least as clean as our bathroom at home. In the high, airy lobby, a display shelf held a collection of Maine crafts. I bought a map and a piece of carved maple in the shape of a lobster.

"Let's find some real food," Sam said, nose wrinkling at the lobster, so we did that and then wandered around Freeport for a while and stayed the night.

The next morning we were on the turnpike again, zooming toward Bangor, and then on Route 1, heading for the coast. That afternoon we crossed a long causeway onto an island where tall, pointed firs stabbed the sky. In the village, streets full of old clapboard houses led down to a boat-filled harbor.

There was a post office, a library, and a small downtown business district—hardware, marine supply, diner—but no gaming arcade, and I thought Sam would surely be bored out of his mind here.

But I was wrong.

"Wow," he breathed from the backseat when I pulled over near the harbor.

When I turned, he was already out of the car, on his way out to a concrete dock that made an L shape over the water. Soon he met a fisherman casting for mackerel, and the fisherman had a house to sell.

I tried explaining that I wasn't in the market, but the man was persuasive, Sam eyed me in appeal, and the house turned out to be an authentic 1823 white-clapboard Federal with a fireplace in every room.

Just one bathroom, and the kitchen dated back to the 1940s, but light from the wavy-glassed windows gleamed golden on the hardwood floors. From the open front door, I could see all the way downhill to the water and the Canadian island of Campobello across the bay.

"Mom." Sam came up behind me. He had already been through the whole house, had decided we were buying it, and had even chosen his room.

"Mom?" he repeated. It wasn't an appeal. It was advice, which I badly needed. What I didn't need was a massive old house that already resembled a sign reading SHOVEL MONEY IN HERE.

Still, I did need to lay low for a while, at least until I managed to get all that shoe-store stuff straightened out. And this seemed a fine solution: little known and very remote, Eastport, Maine, was approximately the last place anybody would look for me.

Meanwhile, the light in Sam's eyes was a kind I'd last seen when he was three and nobody had ruined his dreams yet. I didn't know why he liked Eastport so much, but in a leap of faith roughly akin to stepping out over a crevasse, I decided to take his advice.

The house came furnished; cutlery, dishes, and brand-new, still-in-the-wrapping mattresses, furniture, pots and pans, and linens were all included. There was even a coffeemaker, and the power and water were turned on.

"I guess you were ready for someone to come

along," I said as I counted out cash from the car trunk onto the kitchen table.

"Ayuh," said the man, whose frizzly gray hair stuck out from his navy watch cap. His hands, battered and scarred, searched the pockets of his denim jacket.

"So, let's do the transaction." The bills in the bag were all hundreds; each bundle held fifty of them. I counted out ten of the bundles plus half of one more, marveling at the exotically low price of the real estate here.

The man scrawled a bill of sale on some notebook paper he had found in one of the pockets. Sam watched as if loaves and fishes were being multiplied. Finally, the fisherman ruffled Sam's hair in a way that if I'd tried it, I'd have lost a finger.

"There ya go, young fella. You 'n' your mom have bought yourselves a fine old house. Keep you warm in the winter." *Wintah,* the Maine way of saying it. "Now, you give me a call," he added to me, "if you need anything, or anything goes wrong."

"Thanks," I said, and we shook on it, whereupon Sam laughed in a way I hadn't heard in a while, then ran back upstairs to get settled into his new room.

"I don't know what's come over him," I said, feeling as if I was in a dream. Nobody bought houses on the spur of the moment like this.

"Eastport came over him," said the man. "Takes some people that way." He stuffed the cash into his jacket and zipped it. "I'll stop by next week sometime with the paperwork, get the deed to you and so on," he said.

And that was that. The fisherman went off down the front walk, while I stood wondering what in the world I'd just gotten myself into.

I sat down dazedly at the round wooden table in the bright, old-fashioned kitchen. Around me, the house was silent except for the thud and rumble of Sam moving furniture in his new room.

It occurred to me then that I might be doing something similar, but with my life. One thing was for sure: there was still some arranging to do, to make sure I was not going to get rubbed out. But if things went the way I hoped, I'd never have to see the shoe-store guys again or anyone associated with them.

And fifteen years later, I hadn't, not until Brad Fairway showed up and started trying to put the Chocolate Moose out of business.

Which was when all hell broke loose.

My phone rang at just past nine o'clock on the evening of the art fair's first day.

"Jake?" Ellie's voice was tremulous, and that was so unusual that I shut the door to the phone alcove and sat down on the wooden folding chair we kept in there.

"What?" Through the closed door I heard Bella moving around in the kitchen, preparing to go to bed.

"Jake, can you come down here? To the Moose?" Ellie asked.

Bella snapped the light out and padded up the hall stairs. My dad was already upstairs, and Wade had settled in the parlor, in front of the Red Sox game on TV.

"Just come," Ellie said urgently.

Downtown Eastport was like a graveyard, with only a few cars still parked outside the Happy Crab restaurant. In the fish pier's parking lot, a teardrop trailer with a dim light burning inside said that someone was watching over the art fair displays.

Tarps draped the artwork against the late evening damp. A chilly gray fog drifting in off the bay haloed the streetlamps in yellow and muffled the foghorns moaning out there on the dark water.

Then Ellie came hurrying toward me, her eyes wide and her lips a tight, scared line. Behind her, light from the Moose's windows spilled out onto the sidewalk.

The lights were on inside Choco's, too. Probably Brad Fairway was in there right now, I thought grimly, cooking up new ways to ruin us.

"Thank goodness you're here," Ellie said shakily when she reached me. She waved at our bakery competitor's establishment. "I want you to see for yourself what I saw in there a few minutes ago."

"In Choco's? What were you doing there? I thought—"

I'd thought she would wait until morning, at least. Or that she might even decide not to do it at all. Certainly he'd made clear there was no point to any further discussion. And now that I'd recognized him, I was fine with that. We'd find some other way to end his harassment.

"Also, I know why he was trying to drive us out of business," Ellie said. She was calming down a little. "George . . ."

In Eastport, Ellie's husband, George Valentine, was the man you called if you had bats in your attic, birds' nests in your chimney, or porch steps that were threatening to collapse into toothpicks at the next opportunity.

"George was at city hall today," Ellie said. "For a building permit or something, I don't know."

Sometimes the attics required more than bat eviction. Same with chimneys. And porches . . . Don't even get me going about those. So George pulled building permits practically every other week.

"And George says he heard that Brad Fairway bought the buildings on either side of us. Either side of the Chocolate Moose, I mean."

I felt my eyebrows go up. "Wow." I knew that

the buildings, one still housing a florist and one a dog groomer's called Woofster's, had been for sale. But it had been so long since anyone had even looked that I'd stopped thinking there'd be a buyer.

"And that's not all," said Ellie. "He hired an architect. To tear down all three buildings, ours included, and build . . ." She drew in a shaky breath. "He was going to build condos," she finished.

The fog thickened to mist, beading in my eyelashes and dampening my cheeks. As I brushed away the moisture, what she'd said hit me. Not the part about the buildings. The other part.

"Wait a minute. What do you mean, he *was* going to . . . ?"

Just then Bob Arnold's black squad car turned slowly onto Water Street. His index finger lifted off the steering wheel in greeting as he rolled past us, brake lights flaring by the tarp-draped displays clustered in the parking lot's gloom. Then he drove on.

"Come on," Ellie said, urging me up the steps toward Choco's front door.

I turned the knob; it was unlocked.

"It was that way when I got here," she said as we went in. "I'd called him and told him I was coming and that he'd better be here when I arrived. That was right after I found out what he meant to do."

At night, Choco's shiny walls, white tiled floor, and steel-and-glass interior made it look like the kind of place where you could get yourself cryogenically frozen. I followed Ellie down a short hallway to where a door marked PRIVATE led into a small office.

In the office were a walnut desk, a leather chair, a small TV monitor showing four grainy black-and-white views of the outer shop area, a dead body . . .

"Oh," I said.

The body lay on the floor by the desk, arms flung out and legs bent, as if perhaps it had slumped sideways and fallen onto the brown polypropylene stubble of the room's indoor-outdoor carpet.

Centered in the body's forehead was a dark red hole about as big as the end of my little finger. I crouched to peer down and sideways, and as I expected, the exit wound was bigger.

Much bigger. As was the amount of bright, fresh physical evidence thickly painted onto the Sheetrocked wall directly behind the chair.

"You found him just like this?" I asked Ellie.

It was Brad Fairway, wearing the same sweatshirt and cargo shorts I'd seen him in earlier. His once-florid face was now fish-belly white, his mouth stretched in an unhappy grimace of terminal surprise.

"Yes," said Ellie. "I came in and called for him

a few times, then went looking. When I got back here, I found . . ."

Yeah. This. I turned to her. "Okay. It's all going to be okay. We'll go find Bob Arnold. He's probably still downtown here somewhere, and . . . But, listen, you didn't move anything? Or touch anything?"

Not that I thought she would. Over the years, Ellie White and I had been involved in a number of Eastport murder investigations, so we knew the drill. But . . .

"I touched *him,*" she said, eyeing her hands queasily, and now I saw that they were smeared with red. "I didn't know he was dead, so I crouched and put my hand on his neck to feel for a pulse. But there was—" She stopped, remembering. Like I said, it was a big exit wound. "And now," she went on, "I can't wash them, can I? Not until . . ."

I guess she must have thought Bob Arnold should see them first.

"Yeah, no," I said. "Forget it. I'm not letting you sit around that way."

The door to a small bathroom just off the office stood open; no doubt there was a sink. But then it occurred to me that if she washed here, she might contaminate evidence that was already in the sink's trap. And while I was puzzling over what we should do about that, Bob Arnold walked in.

"Anyone here?" he called from out in the main shop area.

"Bob," I called back to him, "in here."

He appeared in the office doorway, still in his cop clothes and wearing his duty belt with his sidearm on it. "Lights on, door wide open," he began, "at this hour of the—" He spotted Brad Fairway. "Huh," he said.

Unsnapping his sidearm's safety strap with one practiced hand, he got his phone out of his uniform's breast pocket with the other. "Yeah, dispatch, get the state cops on the line, will you? I need a couple of officers downtown, an ambulance, too."

He listened. "Yeah, no sirens. Guy's in no hurry."

In Maine, homicides belong to the state cops except in Bangor and Portland; they have their own investigators.

Bob put the phone away, meanwhile eyeing Ellie's hands. "Okay," he said tiredly. "First of all, are you two all right?" He took in our emphatic nods. "Good. Now, what happened here?" He eyed Ellie's hands again. "And how'd you get so bloodied up?" he finished to Ellie.

"I found him. I called Jake," she said shakily. "That's it."

It wasn't like Ellie to be unnerved. In my opinion, she'd gotten way too good a look at what was left of the back of Brad Fairway's head.

And at what had exited it. She waved helplessly at the body. "I found him like this."

Bob waved us out into the hall, then shooed us along to the front area of the shop, where the counter and display cases were. Suddenly the bright fluorescent lights looked pretty good to me, although now I could hear clearly that one of them was buzzing. Everything felt too vivid, sharp edged, and yet somehow unreal.

"I called Jake," Ellie repeated, frowning down at her stained hands. "I tried to help him," she added. "But he was . . ."

"Take your time," Bob said patiently, then turned as behind him the front door swung open.

I glanced over in surprise; it was too soon for state cops to have gotten here and too late for bakery customers.

"What's going on?" a high, faintly accented voice demanded. "I saw the police car. What's wrong?"

It was Babs Littrell, the textile artist from the fair's weaving demonstration. Wearing a dark hoodie over faded dungarees and sneakers, she shoved a hand back through her clipped-short platinum hair and looked around anxiously.

"A man has passed away," Bob said. "Brad Fairway. You know him?"

Her mouth fell open. "Brad? You mean he . . . ?"

She tottered across the shop's shiny white tiled floor to one of the stools at the counter and hoisted herself onto it. "Oh my God," she uttered softly.

In the mirror behind the counter, her lean face looked haggard. The harsh overhead lights showed the crow's-feet at the corners of her eyes and a barely-there softening at her jawline.

It was as if sudden sorrow had aged her already. Or worry. At any rate something about her expression didn't sit right with me. I eased over to her while Bob got on the phone again and Ellie waited for him.

"I'm so sorry," I said. "Was he a friend of yours?"

"What happened?" Babs asked, not looking up.

Not answering my question, either. I side-stepped in return. "I'm not sure. Possibly an accident."

I didn't think so. In fact, I could practically see it happening: someone walks right in—because Fairway had left the door open for Ellie—and strolls back to Fairway's office. Fairway looks up, probably thinking that Ellie must have arrived, and *boom,* no more Brad Fairway.

Exit murderer, enter Ellie, and you know the rest. Bob put his phone away again and approached Babs, while Ellie went outside to sit on the steps.

I followed and sat next to her, took my jacket off and put it around her. She was trembling, and she still hadn't washed her hands.

"This is silly," she said quietly. "I've seen bodies before."

Me too. Over the years we'd both had some experiences, in fact. A mummified body's finger broke off in my hand once, and I'll never forget the time Ellie fished a boot out of the bay and found a sock in it, and the sock had a foot in it.

"It was just so sudden," she said. "All the blood and . . ."

Right, and the look on his face had been no picnic, either. Shivering, she pulled the jacket tighter around herself as somewhere out on the water a foghorn moaned hauntingly and a bell buoy clanged a reply.

"At least no condos will go up where the Moose was," I said. And whatever "bad old days" trouble Fairway might've ended up making for me, he wouldn't be making it now, would he?

Ellie laughed faintly, which I thought was a good sign. But then she sniffled, which I didn't.

"Come on." I got up. "We're going across the street to the Moose, where it's warm. If Bob needs anything more from us, he can—"

"Come and get it," I'd have said. Instead, Bob came out to us.

"Okay, listen," he said, "this is going to take some time. The state guys are in Cherryfield right now, finishing up with a domestic. You're sure you're both okay?"

I peered in through Choco's big front window.

Babs still slumped at the counter, her face buried in her hands. Under the blue hoodie, her shoulders moved convulsively.

"Ellie, I'll call you in the morning. We'll set up an interview," Bob said. "State cops'll be here by then, and they'll want to hear how you found him. No sense you having to tell it twice."

Beside me, Ellie was still shivering hard, and her lips had that bluish look, like she was chilled to the bone. I was about to lead her away when Babs Littrell came out of Choco's, too.

In the drizzly gloom of the late-night street, I couldn't tell for sure what her expression conveyed. If I'd had to guess, though, I'd have said she looked terrified.

Three

The next morning, when I came downstairs, two things set my alarm bells ringing right off the bat.

First, my son, Sam, was at the breakfast table, eating bacon and eggs, which was fine by itself. But he had his own house to eat them in, and a wife and two children to keep him company while he did it, so what was he doing here?

"Hi, Ma," he said, looking up. But his eyes didn't meet mine.

"Hi, Sam," I replied, letting it pass for now. Ellie had insisted on going straight back to her own house the night before, and I'd stayed with her for a while, so I'd been out late.

And now I hadn't even had my coffee yet. This, however, didn't prevent my noticing the two large paper shopping bags crammed full of stuff in the back hall, or the fact that Bella was stomping around the kitchen grouchily.

"Fine. Let him go," she was muttering. "He'll find out. Hah!" She slapped a dish towel onto its hook.

I'd just gotten my nerve up sufficiently to ask Bella what was wrong when I heard the unmistakable hum of my father's electric stair chair descending. Then he appeared, carrying yet another shopping bag.

"That's enough for now," he said, dropping it by the first two in the hall.

"Dad—" I began, but a sharply honked car horn from outside on the street interrupted me, and a minute later a very large young man in a white shirt and pants came in.

"All ready, Mr. Tiptree?" he boomed cheerfully. He had a square head, blocky jaw, muscular build. Smiling, he looked as if he could probably crack walnuts with those big white choppers of his.

"Oh, he's ready, all right," Bella fumed, shaking a blizzard of scouring powder into the sink. "Ready for the funny farm, if you ask me." She attacked the sink with a scrubber sponge. "Not that anyone wants *my* opinion," she added under her breath.

"Now, Bella," said my father. He wore loose gray trousers, a dark green sweatshirt, and sandals on his feet, even though the morning air out there was chilly, or so I gathered from the quilted jacket draped on the back of Sam's chair.

"You'll see it's the best thing," my dad said, coming to put his arm around Bella, while the big man in nursing garb waited patiently. "You've just got to trust me on this," said my father, at which Bella turned a flat, tight-lipped look on him and pulled away.

"Humph," she said expressively.

Unfazed, he returned to the hallway and hoisted

a shopping bag; his large helper took the other two easily.

"See you later," my dad said and went out.

I sat at the table, stunned. "I can't believe it," I said. "He's really going?"

"So he says," Bella snapped. Now she was rinsing the scoured sink with steaming water from the teakettle. In her view, unkilled germs were the cause of most of the problems in the world, and hot soap and water a good part of the solution.

But not for this problem.

"He says he's getting old," Bella spat. "Wants to get accustomed to the place well ahead of time, he says, while he's still got all his faculties."

Sam looked up. "Makes sense," he opined. "Harder to adjust to new surroundings if you're already confused, wouldn't you think?"

Bella stared at him as if he'd just turned into a strange bug. "How about a person lives life in their own home until they can't anymore? And *then* move somewhere. Why is *that* not a good plan?" Then, astonishingly for Bella, she pressed her chapped, bony hands tightly to her face and fled the room.

I went after her. "Bella? Bella, listen, you don't have to—"

"Don't follow me!" she cried, already halfway up the stairs by the time I reached the front hall. The electric stair chair sat looking forlorn at the bottom of its track. "I mean it. Just let me alone!" she cried.

Back in the kitchen, I found Sam looking contrite. "What'd I say?" he asked, standing at the sink, doing his dishes.

"Nothing. Bella's upset with your grandfather, that's all."

I sat down again with my coffee. "He never was much of a one for just letting things happen," I told Sam. "He always has a plan."

For my mother, for the three of us . . . but that was a long time ago. I swept the thought aside.

"Not that they always work out," I added. My mother's murder had swept all my dad's plans aside, too.

Sam finished the dishes and hung the dishcloth carefully just the way Bella liked it, stretched out over the faucet so it would dry.

"But that's all I said," he pointed out.

"Right, but Bella wasn't at all in the right mood to hear it. I gather she doesn't agree, and maybe she feels . . . abandoned."

Sam dried his hands on a paper towel. Germs on the dish towel were another of Bella's . . . Well, let's just call them "intense dislikes."

"He's coming back, though, isn't he?" Sam asked.

I got up. "As far as I know." I'd gotten a peek into those first two bags in the hall. "It looked to me like he only took his cribbage board, his chess pieces, and the jigsaw puzzles that he was so in love with last year . . . stuff for the social room, maybe."

Still, now that he'd started, I knew my father was sure to go on moving things, then moving himself. It was another of his longtime tendencies, not leaving anything unfinished.

"Sam," I began as he pulled on his quilted jacket, wanting to ask him if everything was all right at home. But he must have known this, because when he turned, his face was already closed to the question.

"Ma. I'm fine, okay? Don't worry," he said as he went out. Then, from the front of the house, I heard Bella padding downstairs again.

"Bella?"

In the kitchen she blew her nose hard, then splashed her face at the sink. "I don't," she pronounced crisply, "want to talk about it."

I might've tried persuading her, but just then Ellie arrived to pick me up. It was time for the two of us to go downtown and open the Chocolate Moose, and I wasn't even dressed yet.

Out in the driveway, I gaped in surprise at the sight of my car, which had been in storage all the previous winter, gleaming in the sunshine.

"Sam must've brought it and forgot to mention it." I walked around the little sports car, a 1974 Fiat 124 Sport Spider with an apricot paint job, black ragtop, and the classic Italian body, like the Mazda Miata but old-school cool.

"He left the top down," Ellie remarked. "We could drive to the shop in it right now." She liked zipping around in the Fiat almost as much as I did.

"Mmm. The top is stuck down," I said regretfully. "It's an old car. The top's metal frame needs cleaning and lubricating and one of the latches replaced," I said.

Fortunately, there was a good-sized tarp in the shed. Until I got the top fixed, I could just cover the little vehicle when it rained, I decided.

"Let me take it out for a test-drive by myself before we use it," I said, turning toward Ellie's car.

"You just want to go faster than I'm going to like," she said as we headed downtown in her car, and it was true. My idea of a test-drive involved about sixty miles per hour more than hers did, among other things.

Then I brought Ellie up to speed on what was going on with my dad. "The good news is, he has not lost his mind," I said.

I supposed we could have rehashed Brad Fairway's murder. But at the time I still had no idea that it was any of our concern.

"Is your dad . . . entirely rational?" Ellie asked.

It was the first thing I'd thought of, too, that maybe he'd noticed his grip on his faculties loosening, and now he was trying to arrange things for himself while he still could.

"As far as I can tell, he's as sharp as he ever was," I said. Which was pretty sharp. Back in his youth, he was an old-style radical whose specialty was bombs, but with a twist: if you wanted to blow up some evil-doing billionaire's big black limousine, he was your man.

But not with the billionaire in it. Bloodshed was off-limits. Later, when he fled with cops in pursuit (for my mom's death, not the bombs), the score was Dad four, Limos zero, and no one had been hurt.

"Maybe he knows something you don't know," said Ellie, pulling into one of the angled parking spots in front of the Moose.

The early sun had vanished; now a brisk wind blowing in off the gray, choppy waters of Passamaquoddy Bay snapped the flags in front of the Coast Guard station.

"Maybe," I said. Then another thought occurred to me. "Listen, have you still got that twenty-two pistol in there?"

After our last Eastport snooping episode, during which we'd found out too late that we needed weapons—a howitzer and a rocket launcher would have been just right, plus plenty of ammo—Ellie had bought the pistol from Wade and had practiced extensively with it.

But I hadn't seen it lately, and if she'd put it

somewhere else, I wanted to know about it before I reached for it. Not that I expected to, but that was what I'd thought about the howitzer and the rocket launcher, too.

"Yep," she replied as we got out of the car. "It's in there, all locked up. I figure as long as I have it, we won't need it."

Down in the boat basin, fishing vessels rigged for lobstering creaked and groaned as their bumpers moved against the dock platforms. Across the street, two sheriff's cars and the state mobile forensics van were lined up against the curb in front of Choco's.

We climbed out of the car and went into the Moose. Inside, the sweet-smelling air was still and cool. Ellie started the coffeemaker while I went around turning things on. Lights, fan, radio, credit card reader . . . I raised the shade on our big front bay window and stopped, struck by a new thought.

"You don't suppose he's sick and hiding it from us, do you?"

If my father thought taking care of him would create more work for the rest of us, I could see him doing something about it.

Ellie came out of the kitchen with a big bag of marshmallows in her hand and started to answer, but I stopped her as movement across the street caught my attention.

It was Bob Arnold, stomping out of Choco's.

On the sidewalk he paused, looking over at our shop, as if trying to come to a decision.

"Come on, Bob," I murmured. "We want to hear the latest."

"No, we don't," Ellie said firmly. I looked at her in surprise.

"I barely got to sleep last night. All I could see when I closed my eyes was Brad Fairway with that hole in his forehead," I told her.

She held up the marshmallows. "Meanwhile, d'you suppose we could do something with these?" she asked, changing the subject. "A pie maybe?"

I turned from the window. "Marshmallows! How . . . interesting."

Personally, I would rather toast cotton balls over a campfire, since unlike marshmallows, they burn up almost completely, so you don't have to eat them.

"Good way to waste a perfectly decent pie-crust," I added, but she wasn't listening.

"Maybe chocolate cream," she mused, frowning at the marshmallow bag, which unfortunately was full of marshmallows. Then: "I know. We'll make one and try feeding it to the artists. For free. We'll give out slices and then ask them if they—"

"That's not a test. Starving artists will eat anything," I said.

Ellie went to the window. A few minutes ago,

the fish pier parking lot had been full of creative types busily pulling down tarps, opening tents, and setting up tables.

"Do you see Babs Littrell anywhere?" Her looms had all still been there this morning, but there'd been no sign of her.

"No. I hope she's okay," I replied. "Were they friends, do you suppose? Or maybe more?" A shudder went through me at the memory of his big, beefy face. "He didn't seem like her type." Turning our door's sign from CLOSED to OPEN, I went on, "Not that he seemed like anyone's."

Ellie looked down thoughtfully at the marsh-mallows once more. "Broil them," she said to herself decisively, then tore the bag open and popped a whole one into her mouth, just as the little silver bell over the door tinkled.

Ellie chewed hastily. Then she said, "Good morning!" through the dusting of powdered sugar on her lips.

The day's first customer was a pretty girl in her twenties, tall and slim and with the sweetness of a child still in her face. Her skin was smooth and porcelain pale; her fine cap of light brown curls held neatly back with bobby pins.

"May I please have two large coffees, black? And two of those, please." She pointed into our display case. "Whatever they are. Wow, they look yummy."

She wore light tan slacks with a pink striped belt

and a white blouse with pink satin embroidery on the pocket. DORY, it read.

She saw me looking. "That's me." She smiled. "I'm Dory Sloan, Babs Littrell's personal assistant."

"Babs Littrell has an assistant?" I blurted as behind me Ellie poured the coffees. Then:

"I'm sorry," I said, oddly flustered by the girl. "That didn't come out the way I meant it. I mean, I thought artists were . . ."

"Poor?" Dory smiled, showing small, beautifully kept teeth. "The starving-artist thing?" She shrugged agreeably. "Some are, I guess. Babs says she's been lucky, but I think it's talent plus a lot of hard work."

As I handed over the coffees, Dory's gray eyes met mine, and I got the strong sense that her mild presentation notwithstanding, there was steel in that slender frame of hers.

"She's awfully upset about Mr. Fairway," Dory went on. "We've been living in his guest cottage, but now that's probably going to end."

She sighed regretfully. "Babs wasn't planning on having to move. She says it's good for her creativity there, and it will cost money." To move, she meant. "And she might not be starving, but it's not like she's rolling in cash. I feel bad for her," Dory finished.

Fascinating. "You like Babs Littrell pretty well, do you?"

"I do," Dory answered eagerly. "She's so good about teaching me things. She takes her time and doesn't talk down to me. I'm a fabric artist, too." Her nails were unpolished, trimmed to thin half-moons. A Timex was on her wrist, and she wore no makeup.

"I'd better run," she said, glancing at the wristwatch. "Babs is over there setting up, and she'll want help. Thanks!" She managed the door without dropping her purchases. The little silver bell tinkled sweetly over her head as she went out.

"What a pleasant young woman," Ellie said into the silence that followed. Across the street the evidence techs' van was still parked outside Choco's.

"I had about a million questions I wanted to ask," I said. "Like how Babs Littrell wound up staying in Fairway's guest cottage, and what specifically Babs told Dory last night, after he got shot."

"Jake," Ellie said, "just because it happened right there"—she gestured toward Choco's—"that doesn't mean we've got any business snooping around in it. Whatever 'it' is."

"Right," I said, more firmly than I felt. Fairway getting killed only hours after I'd recognized him felt a little too cause and effect for my liking, and although our shared mob connections were probably just coincidence, I didn't like them very much, either. For one thing, they reminded me of what a complete jerk I used to be.

Then two more customers came in, and then a few more, all of them wearing lapel stickers identifying them as art fair participants. In the next hour, half the angel food cake and then the other half got sold, while the chocolate chip cookies and macaroons and the chocolate éclairs all practically walked out the door by themselves.

When the rush was over, I refilled the display case with things that Mika had baked the day before, while she'd been tending the shop. But first, of course, I had to test them.

Biting into a chocolate dream bar, I found tart raspberry jelly atop a tender graham-cracker crust. The next layer was vanilla cream, bright with homemade vanilla extract; and finally, a layer of bittersweet chocolate covered the whole thing, just hard enough to have a gentle crack to it when you bit it.

Yes, I know this is different from what I described earlier. But Mika was a genius and improved on our recipes each time she baked for us. I was filching another one just to make sure they were all that ravishingly good when Bob Arnold burst in, jangling the little silver bell so hard that it fell to the floor.

"What's wrong?" I asked, hurrying to pick it up. Bob didn't have steam coming out of his ears . . . not quite. But his face was red, his nostrils were flared, and his hands were clenched into fists that wanted to punch somebody.

"Where is she?" he grated out, and when Ellie appeared from the kitchen, he went on. "You didn't tell me you handled the weapon."

"Last night?" She squinted at him. "Bob, I never even saw any weapon, much less handled one. What makes you think I did?"

Head tipped, he eyed her. "For starters, the fact that the gun that the evidence guys just found belongs to you, if I'm not mistaken. Or, anyway, it's got your name etched into the grip."

His words hung in the shop's sweet-smelling air while I looked over at Ellie and she looked back at me. She did own a gun like that; Wade had done the decorative bit of etching for her. But—

"The glove compartment," we both said at once.

Rushing past Bob, we hurried outside, where Ellie got into her car on the passenger side and unlocked the glove box, where, of course, she'd had the weapon secured. Ellie was all about gun safes, trigger locks, and responsibility and proper gun handling. She'd have—

"Gone," she said.

I peered in past her. The open glove box held her registration and insurance card and a small flashlight.

Nothing more.

She looked up at me in dismay. "Jake, it was here. Right here, but now it's . . ."

Gone.

"It was there," Ellie repeated minutes later inside the Moose.

I'd sat her down and brought her some coffee. Bob Arnold sat across from her.

"Okay, go back a little," said Bob. "Wade sold you the gun."

My husband, he meant, who repairs firearms and has a collection of his own. Ellie had, of course, gone to him when she wanted a hand-gun.

"He had a twenty-two pistol he thought would be good for me," she said, "so we went to the target range, I tried it, it felt good to me, and then I bought it." She let out a shaky breath. "This is bad, isn't it?"

"Let's not get ahead of ourselves," said Bob. "When's the last time you fired the weapon?"

She looked a little embarrassed. "Not for a long time. I thought I'd practice more, but I haven't in . . . oh, a few months now."

"Okay," said Bob. "That's fine. But, Ellie, here's the thing. As it stands now, it looks like Brad Fairway was shot with your weapon, and you found his body." He frowned. "You say he knew you were coming to see him, that on the phone you and he had arranged—"

I broke in. "What do you mean, she says? That's what happened. Why are you—"

He held up a silencing hand, not looking at me. "Hold on, Jake. I'm just making sure I've got it right."

"It's okay," Ellie said quietly. "I told Fairway we should talk over our problems, see if we couldn't find some compromise." She turned to Bob. "He was making a nuisance of himself, and then I found out he was planning to—"

I raised a silencing hand. "Probably we don't need to get into those details," I suggested gently.

She caught my drift and shut up.

Bob sighed heavily as across the street, the evidence techs' van drove away and a black, unmarked hearse slid in to take its place.

"Okay, but here's the trouble," Bob said, sounding like a doctor who was about to describe how big the tumor had already gotten and how many vital organs it had invaded. "No one else knew you called Fairway or that you were going to meet him. You could've surprised him, shot him . . ."

Her chin lifted stubbornly. "I didn't. It's not what happened."

"Got splattered and then messed yourself up more, so you could say blood got on you when you were trying to help him," Bob continued.

She shook her head stubbornly. "I went there to

67

talk to him. Bob, he wanted our building, to tear it down and build residential units."

I personally didn't think it was necessary for her to supply a reason why she might've killed him. But she had, and now in a single morning we'd gone from bagged marshmallows to the murder trifecta: motive, method, opportunity.

Across the street, two men in sports coats came out of Choco's.

"Bob," I began, "you don't really think they suspect it was Ellie who killed him, do you? Why, she couldn't even—"

"Swat a fly," I'd have finished, but instead, a real fly that had flown in when Bob entered began pestering her. Hardly even looking at it, she clapped the buzzing insect right out of the air, and it dropped to the table, dead.

"Never mind," I finished as she plucked it up by a wing and took it to the kitchen. I heard the tap in the handwashing sink go on.

Bob was at the door. "Jake, she needs a lawyer."

My heart sank. Outside, the detectives were getting into their car. "But you know she didn't do it, right?" I hazarded.

Right about then, I'd have really liked hearing him say so. But . . .

"The state guys'll want to talk to Ellie," he replied. "You, too, probably. I don't know when."

He went out just as Ellie came back, looking

bemused. "So now I'm a suspect?" she said, as if testing the idea. "In . . . a *murder?*"

"Okay, now, don't panic," I told her. "Obviously, the idea is ridiculous, but we'll get you a lawyer, and it'll all get worked out."

Her eyes widened in alarm. "You really think I need . . ."

I'd thought so even before Bob advised it, because of the gun. It had apparently been used in a deadly crime, after all, and so far, we couldn't explain that.

"But right now," I said briskly, "the best thing for you is for us to get back to work. With Choco's gone, I expect we'll be acquiring even more customers."

Her shoulders straightened; she rose from her chair. "You're right," she pronounced. "This will work out. I mean, how can it not?"

Because she hadn't done it, she meant, which I thought showed a truly laudable degree of faith in the criminal justice system as it currently existed.

"So I shouldn't dwell on it," she said as she carried her cup to the kitchen, where she pulled on an apron and stuffed her hair up into a paper hair cover. "Especially since I still have that chocolate marshmallow pie to figure out," she finished.

Oh, great, I thought. Still, it must've been important to her if even being suspected of murder hadn't wiped it out of her head.

"Yeah, what's with that, anyway?" I asked. "Did you find a great recipe you want to try or something?"

"No, but Lee wants one for her birthday the day after tomorrow," Ellie said, "so now I've got to figure one out."

Lee was Ellie's daughter, born by surprise on my kitchen floor twelve years and eleven and three quarters months earlier.

She pulled out a mixing bowl, a Pyrex pie dish, and the notebook in which she tracked her progress through recipes she was inventing.

"How about if we start with chocolate short-bread for the crust?" I offered. Maybe I didn't enjoy marshmallows, to put it mildly, but I enjoyed working with Ellie, and I did want to help.

Her face smoothed with concentration as her hands moved swiftly and accurately among the pie ingredients she'd assembled. "Shortbread sounds good," she said. "You get out the butter and start softening it, why don't you? And I'll melt some chocolate."

Her enthusiasm made marshmallows sound not quite so gluey and sweet. As I worked alongside her, though, I couldn't help realizing again that Bob was absolutely right: she needed a lawyer, the sooner the better. I knew one, too, but it was almost noon. No doubt he'd be out at some courthouse-adjacent lunch spot, eating and schmoozing.

So instead, I got the butter out and a saucepan down and turned on the stove, and then the phone rang.

"Jake?" It was Bella, sounding upset. "Come home quick."

Anxiety pierced me. "What's wrong?"

"It's your father. He's gone. I've been looking all over, but . . ."

Ellie looked questioningly at me, concern on her face.

"He's not at the assisted living home, and he's not anywhere else I could think of, either. Jake, I can't find him!"

Four

After an hour of increasingly desperate searching, I walked back to the house and found my father in a lawn chair out back, hidden by a massive lilac bush.

"Dad!" I dropped to the grass beside him, feeling like I'd just run a marathon. Nothing raises my heart rate like hunting for an old man who is smart, stubborn, and as independent as a hog on ice, but who also could've fallen into the bay and drowned. "I've been looking all over for you," I told him. "Bella's inside losing her . . . marbles," I added, editing myself swiftly.

My dad smiled serenely. "Hello, Jacobia." He handed me a silver flask; I knocked back a jolt of the single malt Scotch it turned out to be full of. It was smoky tasting and aromatic.

I'd earned it. A robin lit briefly on a branch overhead, sending out a sweet-smelling burst of lilac perfume.

"Anyway, I'm glad I finally found you," I said as a rap on the kitchen window across the lawn made me turn. Bella's face showed; I pointed at the hidden lawn chair and flashed her a victory sign.

My dad sighed contentedly, the flask now tucked away somewhere. It seemed that he'd needed a holiday from all of us, and who could argue with that?

"So, what's new?" he asked mildly, and I hadn't meant to tell him, but relief at having found him—and that big swallow of Scotch, probably—made the whole thing tumble out.

"Ellie's suspected of murder," I said, and I followed this with a recounting of Brad Fairway's harassment tactics against us, our efforts to talk with him, and his violent death, after which Ellie discovered his body, plus the whole gun thing. "And that's how my day's gone so far," I told my dad, not adding that an hour spent running around looking for him hadn't helped.

He put his head back against the chair's plastic webbing, his wrinkly old eyelids dropping like draperies over his eyes. Around us the scent of lilacs joined the perfume of freshly cut grass.

"Anything else?" he inquired finally, clearly intuiting that I'd left something out. Have I mentioned yet that my father could read me like a large-print newspaper?

"I knew Fairway back in the city," I admitted. "Well," I amended, "not *knew* him. But I recognized him from there yesterday. I don't think he knew me, though, and even if he did, I can't see how that would be enough to get him murdered."

My dad's eyes stayed closed and he didn't comment on Fairway or on my checkered past.

73

"Don't really see many coincidences in the wild," was all he said.

My thought, too, unfortunately. Still, people did run into people they hadn't seen in years in Eastport; sometimes they even bought houses not far from each other without knowing until afterward. So it could happen, I told myself yet again.

"So where'd you go?" I shifted topics. His eyes were open now. I'd searched the yard earlier; he hadn't been here then.

He shrugged. "Took a stroll around the block. Must've missed you." Then: "Cops'll be questioning Ellie, then, will they?"

So much for trying to change the subject. "Yes. Bob Arnold is trying to keep us informed, but there's a limit to what he can say and do."

Because he was a cop himself, I meant. I got up, feeling the lawn's dampness on the seat of my pants, and I was halfway back to the house when he spoke again.

"Are you doing anything about it?"

About Ellie, he meant.

"Maybe. I'm not sure. It might still all blow over," I answered hopefully.

He considered this. Then: "One," he recited, "the dirty tricks Fairway was running against you to drive you out of business, and his plan to get rid of your building." His head tipped thoughtfully. "Two, Ellie's handgun, used in the crime."

I saw where he was going with this. Bella rapped the window again, this time impatiently.

"Dad, I—"

"Three, she made the appointment to see him, but she didn't tell anyone about it."

I felt my shoulders sag. "I know it looks—"

"Bad," I was about to say, but before I could, he started toward me across the lawn. For a skinny little old guy who used a walking stick and who strongly resembled a garden gnome, he was surprisingly fast.

"As for you and Ellie looking into it . . . ," he began as we moved toward the house. He teetered a little as we crossed the uneven lawn, but I resisted the impulse to take his arm. He wouldn't have liked it.

Then he stopped and turned slowly to me, and the look in his eyes seemed the oldest thing about him just then: the hard knowledge, borne of experience, that things didn't always work out for the best. That sometimes instead they worked out very poorly, indeed.

"As for you and Ellie looking into it all," he said, "my advice is that you start now, before it's too late."

I'd thought the brief sales rush we'd had earlier might be a fluke, but when I got back to the Chocolate Moose, it was mobbed.

"They've discovered us," Ellie told me a little

wildly between waiting on incoming customers and clearing up after departing ones. There was a line out the door, and the café chairs weren't even getting a chance to cool off before the next people were sitting in them.

I grabbed an apron, pulled on a hair cover, and hurried to the kitchen to start more coffee and move two dozen unbaked chocolate chip cookies from the cooler into the oven. Next, I hurriedly did a bunch of dishes and took out a bag of trash, and then the shop phone rang.

Ellie answered. "Mmm-hmm," she said, listening. "Five, you say. In ten minutes. Plenty of . . . yes."

I stepped out of the kitchen; the ravenous hordes had departed for now. But the shop was chaos: crumpled napkins, chairs every which way, a tray of cups headed for the dishwasher but not yet in it. . . .

Also, we were clean out of cookies and éclairs, and the pastry and cake situations were not much better.

Just then a faint, sweet aroma wafted worrisomely to my nostrils. Mystified, I glanced around and glimpsed pale gray vapors drifting out of the kitchen.

"Dear heavens," I heard myself saying as I realized what they were.

"Ten minutes," Ellie repeated agreeably into the phone, her eyes narrowing with the kind of purely Ellie-like determination that meant I should either get out of her way or get trampled.

"I forgot to set the oven timer," I exclaimed, hurling myself back into the kitchen, only to confront clouds of smoke billowing from the oven. In it, the cookies were charred lumps; they'd been baking for half an hour.

Fine, I told myself, carefully not screaming my head off or tearing my hair out. *Everybody burns cookies now and then. Just scrape them into the trash, run some water on the tray, and—*

Ellie appeared in the doorway, sniffing. "What burned?" Wisps of strawberry-blond hair stuck out from her hair cover, her apron hung askew, and a smear of chocolate under her nose resembled a suddenly sprouted mustache.

"Never mind." The list of baked things I'd burnt or ruined—for a thrill, try mistaking baking powder for cornstarch—at the Moose was available on a need-to-know basis, and she didn't.

Grabbing a fresh trash bag, I charged out to where the tables were a litter of cake crumbs, cookie fragments, and dessert plates. Behind me came Ellie with broom and dustpan, a dampened hand towel, and a bottle of spray cleaner.

"Who was on the phone?" I asked, beginning to clear the first table.

"Party of five, here in ten minutes," she replied, sweeping.

I stopped. "What? But . . . what will we serve?" I waved behind me, to where a lonely slice of German chocolate cake, its coconut topping beginning to shrivel, was all that remained in the display case.

"Go across the street," Ellie said decisively, still sweeping. "I saw an unopened box of something in the cooler last night."

I gaped at her. "To Choco's? Are you kidding?" No police officers or vehicles were there, but it was the scene of a crime in which Ellie was a suspect, for heaven's sake.

Also, and more to the point for my purposes, it was locked.

Ellie dug in her apron pocket. "Remember before Choco's, when the antique shop was in there?" Her hand reappeared, clutching something. "I've still got the key." She handed me her key ring and a flashlight from our utility drawer. "The owners went on vacation, and I fed the cat, remember? And they told me to keep the key for next time."

"Oh," I said reluctantly.

But Ellie was adamant, and of course she still had the key. Ellie had been wearing the same pair of sunglasses for twenty years, while my record was about twenty days.

"Go on," she urged, shooing me with her hands. "Unless you want five customers to have to share one slice of stale cake."

In the doorway I hesitated. "Store-bought pastry, though?"

"It'll be fine, Jake, trust me. Entenmann's raspberry-cheese Danish, I think it was, and if we put a little ice cream on it and drizzled it with our special chocolate sauce . . ."

The sauce was simple: chocolate, sugar, butter, vanilla. Stir it forever in a double boiler, and voilà!

Or viola, as Sam liked to say.

"So I'll warm the sauce, and you grab that Danish," she said. "The key fits the door around back. And hurry. They'll be here soon."

So finally, I pocketed the key. The store-bought pastry would indeed solve our problem, and there didn't seem to be anyone, official or otherwise, in or around Choco's just now. But . . .

"But what if I get caught in there?" I said, and Ellie gave me a look from beneath lowered eyelids.

"Don't get caught in there," she said.

Outside, people looked happily amazed to be wearing T-shirts and sneakers instead of parkas and boots. Warmth poured from the sky, where pale azure had firmly replaced winter's hard, dark blue.

I crossed Water Street between chattering tourists and art fair visitors making their way among locals intent on their daily errands. None paid any attention to me beyond a few pleasant hellos, I was relieved to note, and although Bob Arnold stood at the entrance to the fish pier parking lot, waving a panel truck out and a pickup truck in, his back was safely turned to me.

Alongside the Choco's building, an alley ran down to an asphalt-paved path leading along the waterfront. I turned onto the path and followed it to a battered but still serviceable-looking steel door.

Sticking the key in the lock, I tried to look as if I belonged here. Then I slipped inside.

Stupid, I know. But I was really very worried about Ellie. If the state cops wanted to talk to her about finding Fairway's body, I'd have expected them to get in touch with her by now.

Instead, crickets. And whoever said, "No news is good news" had it wrong, in my opinion. I slammed the steel door to Choco's cellar behind me, then snapped on the flashlight. A weak yellow gleam issued from it, followed by nothing.

Drat. In the darkness I felt around for anything solid, mostly in hopes of not walking face-first into it. Somewhere around here there had to be a set of stairs leading up to—

"Ouch!" The yelp escaped me. I'd backed into a wooden post with what felt like a nail sticking out of it. Trying to remember when I'd last had a tetanus shot, I felt my way forward again: door *there,* door handle *there.* . . .

Creeping along, I met no more potential death traps, and with any luck, there'd be a light switch by the stairs. If this, in fact, was the way to the stairs, I thought, and not, say, to an open pit where a nineteenth-century cistern used to be.

There . . . My hand found the switch. The dangling yellow bulb's pallid glow lit a set of wooden steps; now all I had to do was climb them and open the old wooden door at the top.

But as I climbed, an unwanted memory of Brad Fairway's face, with the small, dark hole in its forehead, rose up. Suddenly that old wooden door, so still and silent and *waiting,* somehow, was terrifying to me.

Surely someone stood on the other side, waiting. . . .

Stop that, I told myself. My hand on the railing felt slick and shaky. My other hand was free for the doorknob. Or to punch something.

But then, from upstairs came a *thump.* Softly, but I'd heard it, and somehow this solid belief in my own perceptions dissolved all my qualms and quickened my step.

The doorknob moved easily. The door didn't. Either a dead bolt or a slide bolt was on the other side, I imagined.

Then it did open, swinging away from me smoothly and without fanfare, as if I hadn't been shoving uselessly against it just moments ago.

Grimly, I stepped through into a hallway. Light came through a window somewhere, so it wasn't quite as dark here as it had been in the cellar.

But it was still plenty gloomy. Cursing the me who had foolishly neglected to check her flashlight batteries, I moved down the dim hall until I found another door, then stepped into the small office where Ellie had found Brad Fairway's body.

Early afternoon light streamed through a single window high in the wall. I winced at the stains on the carpet where he'd been lying and on the wall behind him.

A flicker of movement on Fairway's still active security monitor caught my attention. Mounted on his desk, its four screens took in the shop's front door, the display cases, and the steel counter.

Nothing moved in any of them now. The flicker, if I'd really seen it, had been in the front-door screen's view. Hesitantly I pressed the BACK button on the device's control panel, but nothing happened.

Then I noticed the open flap on the side of the monitor. Inside, there'd been a memory card. I knew this because Ellie and I had considered a security camera for the Moose, but after a discussion, we'd spent the money on a new stand mixer instead.

Without the card, the camera's video still went to the monitor, but the monitor couldn't save it, and that meant I couldn't replay it. Probably the cops had taken the card, I thought. Maybe it even showed Fairway's killer. In that case, Ellie would be off the hook.

But that was not why I'd come. Grimly, I marched out to get the badly needed pastry and grabbed it, then stopped as a sudden memory of that movement on the security monitor made my neck hairs prickle.

Or something did. "O-kay," I murmured aloud into the silence, abruptly deciding to get the heck out of here right this instant, if not sooner. But I couldn't flee out the front door, in case Bob Arnold was out there. I'd almost rather meet the killer; at least I could use the Entenmann's box as a weapon.

But with Bob, there'd be no hitting, only yelling. And possibly jailing. This was a crime scene, and I was tampering with it or, at the very least, trespassing in it.

Sucking in an anxious breath, I spun around, ready to run for the cellar stairway, but instead I slammed smack into Bob's remarkably solid midsection.

"Bob, I . . ."

His grip on my arm was firm, and his face looked as if molten lava might spew from it at any moment. "I don't want to hear it," he said. "I just really don't want to hear it."

After letting go, he strode angrily past the cluttered little room where Brad Fairway had breathed his last, yanked the cellar door open, and motioned sharply.

"Go," he told me in a voice like doom, then followed me down. We crossed the old cellar, ancient wooden beams above, dirt floor below. The door I'd come in through stood wide open.

"Outside," Bob grated at me. "And when you get there, don't you move a goddamned inch."

By now it was early afternoon, with thin fog drifting low over the water, though the sky above was still blue. At the art fair in the parking lot, fiddles and flutes played a jolly tune.

"Bob, I can explain," I said, waving the boxful of pastry in the general direction of the Moose.

No answer. We went up the alley alongside Choco's to the street, where he lifted a brusque, traffic-stopping wave as we crossed.

From inside the Moose, Ellie gazed anxiously at me through the window. Our party of five, all white-haired ladies, was still getting settled at a table.

Bob smiled and waved through the window at the ladies and at Ellie. "Go on. Take it in there," he told me, with a gesture at the pastry box I carried. "That's what you wanted it for, isn't it?"

Relief touched me. Bob connected dots better

and faster than anyone I knew. So surely he would figure out soon that I hadn't been—

"But stay where I can see you," he added in a voice that reminded me clearly of who was the police officer here and who wasn't. "And if you're not out again in two minutes, I'm coming in after you."

Over the years, Bob and I had become pretty good friends. I'd helped his ex-wife out of a situation that could've taken away her law license. He'd kept a much younger Sam out of the drunk tank more times than I could remember, and he'd stood by him, too, at court appearances and so on.

So I was pretty sure he wouldn't rat me out on the "sneaking into Choco's" thing if he could avoid it. But I worried that maybe this time he couldn't avoid it, as I sat across from him at his desk in the cop shop, as he always called it.

The office, recently remodeled, still smelled like fresh drywall compound and carpet adhesive, overlaid with the reek of coffee slowly cooking itself to a black tar-like syrup on the Mr. Coffee hot plate in the corner.

Bob put his hands flat on his desk. "Jake, I'm not gonna lie to you here. This is serious. Those homicide guys aren't fooling around, and they're looking hard at Ellie."

"Bob, we were in a jam, and I thought that

since the evidence techs had already been in there, I could . . ."

"Oh, you did, did you? What if they have to go back? Did you think of that? Even worse, you're best friends with a suspect. But you thought everyone would know you didn't mean any harm?"

What I'd thought was that no one would know about it at all, but I couldn't say that. "Well, when you put it that way . . ."

"There's no way to put it that doesn't make it look like you were over there where you shouldn't be, doing something you shouldn't do."

Correctamundo, as Sam would've put it.

"Now, I could call the state guys," Bob went on, "tell them what's happened, and let them deal with it." He paused, tenting his fingers. "Or I could just use my own judgment about what those guys do and don't need to know right now."

"That," I ventured quietly, "sounds like a great idea."

His pale blue gaze skewered me. "Yeah, I'll bet it does." He looked down at his hands. "The thing is," he went on, "if this all ends up in a courtroom, I'll get called to testify. About any run-ins I might've had with Brad Fairway, or maybe about the building's security. Had there been any break-ins and so on?"

The message was clear: under oath, he would tell the truth, and then he and I would both be in the soup, right along with Ellie.

"Yes, but ideally that won't happen," I said. And then, because I wanted very badly to change the subject, I asked, "They've got that memory card from the Choco's security setup? The homicide cops do?"

Bob made a sour face and got up. "Oh, yeah, they've got it." He walked to the office window. "And you didn't get this information from me, understand?" he said, parting the vertical blinds to look out into the parking lot. "But they've got it, they've played it, and there's nobody on it but customers. And after that, just you, me, and Ellie and that artist lady who came in all shook up, Babs Littrell."

He moved toward the door; I followed. Beyond the lobby's glass enclosure, afternoon sunshine glinted off the cars parked out there.

I went out. Bob's voice followed. "By the way, Jake, next time you decide to try sneaking into a place, try to remember to pull the door closed behind you."

A sliver of ice went through me as I realized he'd spotted the door to Choco's cellar hanging open and that was how he'd known I was in there, or that someone was, anyway.

I turned back just as an expression I couldn't identify vanished from his face. "I did close it," I said.

Five

Back at the Moose, I found Ellie in the kitchen crushing graham crackers with a rolling pin.

"We can try a crumb crust for the marshmallow pie in case the shortbread doesn't work out, don't you think?" she asked.

I thought leaving the marshmallows out altogether would be even better, but that wasn't what Ellie's daughter wanted for her birthday, so I kept quiet about it.

Instead, I told her, "Bob said there's nothing on Choco's security camera. So whoever killed Fairway probably got in through the cellar, like I did."

Ellie kept working the rolling pin over the cracker crumbs, not commenting on what I'd said. Until she revealed, "A state police detective called while you were gone."

So that was what had her unnerved. "Oh, terrific," I replied, recalling what else Bob had said. That they were serious about her. "They want to talk in person?"

I'd phoned my Portland friend early that morning. He did real estate law, but he had pals in criminal defense, and he'd promised to call a few of them for me.

"They do," Ellie replied. "The one who

called said they've both got to testify in a court case today and part of tomorrow. I should stay available, he said."

She sighed and went back to her test run on the pie. I stayed out front, waiting on customers for the rest of the afternoon. While I'd been out committing felonies and talking with Bob Arnold, she'd baked more cookies and some cranberry-chocolate scones, so I had plenty to sell.

"Here we go," she said proudly, bringing the cooled pie out to the front counter at last.

"Oh, how . . . interesting looking," I said. Ellie's graham-cracker crust had come out beautifully as usual, but the marshmallows on top had collapsed and the liquidy result had browned only slightly. Wincing, I imagined that sugary glop between my teeth.

"Here," said Ellie, handing me a slice on a paper plate.

I forked up a bite and chewed dutifully, whereupon the gluey sweetness clung to my teeth and coated my tongue while the chocolate flavor got lost entirely. I swished coffee around in my mouth, trying to dislodge the half-solid marshmallow lumps still stuck to my molars.

"Oh, Ellie, I'm sorry," I said when I could speak again, and she must have agreed.

Nodding resignedly, she carried the pie dish back to the kitchen and emptied it into the trash.

"How can s'mores taste so good and this be so bad?" she sighed frustratedly.

I didn't exactly agree with the "s'mores taste good" proposition, but it did give me an idea. "Proportions maybe? S'mores have almost as much graham cracker as marshmallow, you know. Also, the chocolate's darker."

And when s'mores get made, there's usually the whole campfire-under-the-stars scene to distract you from your jaws being glued shut and your blood-sugar level skyrocketing so high that your eyeballs are spinning like a cartoon character's.

I glanced at the clock. Somehow it had gotten to be nearly four. In the golden afternoon light now filling the street, the art fair attendees were pulling on sweaters and hoodies as they headed toward parked cars.

"Will Lee and George be home for dinner?" I asked Ellie.

She shook her head, writing intently in her test recipe–results notebook. "Uh-uh," she said. "Lee's at a track meet in Houlton. They'll eat on the way. George'll be at the port authority meeting until late, and they're having pizza sent in."

A plan began forming in my mind. "Let's you and I go out for supper, then? We can talk more about the marshmallow pie Lee wants."

Wade would be at the port authority, too, I knew, and I thought that Bella and my dad could probably use an evening alone to get back on each other's good side.

Ellie brightened at the prospect. "I guess I should make the most of my freedom while I've got it, right?" she joked.

The deck at the brewery overlooked the harbor, the boat basin now full of tubby little fishing vessels all rigged for lobster hauling, and the bay. Across the blue water, Campobello lay on the horizon like a long bar of gold.

Minutes after we reached our table, two personal-sized eggplant pizzas with sausage, mushrooms, and feta cheese arrived, along with two schooners of the brewery's excellent pale ale.

For a while we ate in silence, tired and hungry and ready to not think about anything at all. But finally, we got down to the business of the day, which had turned out to be figuring out some way to keep Ellie from going to jail.

"So Bob Arnold is on our side," Ellie concluded when I'd reported on my chat with him.

"Of course he is," I replied, "but he's in an awkward position." I stopped as the server brought back my change and departed again. "Because what if he does end up testifying at a trial? Then what?" I finished.

We had coffee, then began gathering our things. The sun had fallen far enough to put the deck into chilly shade, and when we reached the street, the sky was milky with approaching fog. Down the street, in the fish pier parking lot, Babs Littrell's looms still stood, blue tarped against the damp.

"I'll call my lawyer friend back tonight," I promised Ellie. "She might've found a lawyer for you."

Preferably one who ate prosecutors for lunch with no ketchup, I thought as we got into Ellie's car. Then a crazy notion struck me.

"Let me drive," I said, and when Ellie had switched places with me, I backed out and turned left onto Washington Street.

"I thought we'd just take a little cruise out to Brad Fairway's place," I said as we headed out of town, past the barbershop, the nail salon, and the firehouse. "Just to get the lay of the land," I said.

Which was not entirely true, but I was winging it. Right now, I knew that I wanted a look at the place where Brad Fairway had lived, but I wouldn't find out until I got there whether or not I wanted more.

In the oncoming evening, with the sun an orange ball on the western horizon, we swung into the long curve at Carrying Place Cove, then took an unmarked uphill turn. The tree-lined road narrowed and darkened in deep shade; small branches scraped the car until ahead, a faint glow flickered intermittently through a stand of birches.

I switched off the headlights; Ellie looked

sideways at me but said nothing. After another fifty yards I shut the engine off, too, and we rolled silently around a pine needle–carpeted circle drive to the front of a house.

"Wow," Ellie said softly. Fairway's place was an aggressively modern-looking structure, long and low, with walls mostly made out of glass brick, a recessed entryway sheltered by a pergola, and the whole thing half-hidden by the kind of expert landscaping that was intended to look natural, and nearly did.

It also looked like excellent shrubbery for hiding in, thick and healthy, in case, for instance, you wanted to get up close and see the house's interior. Trouble was, that glass brick might as well have been stone for all the inside views it offered, and the real windows were too high up in the walls to peer through.

"You could hop back into the driver's seat again," I told Ellie, not really expecting to need a fast getaway, but, hey, you never know. "I'll just go around back, see if anybody's home in the guesthouse," I added.

No cars but ours were in the driveway, and no lights showed in the main house. Only a dim row of solar lanterns along the curved front walk pierced the gloom.

Ellie shook her head, taking a flashlight from her bag. "Do you really think I'm going to let you go back there alone?"

She aimed the flashlight at Fairway's house, making the whorls in the glass brick seem to ripple and swirl. "Let's do this," she said.

We left the car sitting where it was. If Babs Littrell or Dory Sloan showed up, we wanted to look legit, not like we were sneaking around.

Which, of course, was just exactly what we were doing.

Bypassing the front walk curving around the landscaping, we headed down a white gravel path leading around to the side of the house. Propane tanks and a Rubbermaid shed with trash barrels in it were the only features here.

Out back, thick plank steps led up to a long deck cantilevered out over a slope. As Ellie climbed the steps, a motion-sensor light under the eaves snapped on, its glare illuminating the whole deck and the trees all around with white light.

"Ellie," I hissed, "that light. It's way too . . ."

She hurried back down to me. "Yes, it's bright. But who'll see it?" she pointed out. "Anyway, probably when it's windy, it goes on and off all the time," she added.

Also true. The place was surrounded by trees, whose branches were notorious for setting off motion sensors, and nothing makes a security system more useless than a lot of false alarms.

I relaxed a little as she went back up. "You

can see the guesthouse where Babs and Dory are staying from the deck," she reported, pointing over the edge of the precipice, below the cantilever beams. "No lights, though," she added, coming down again after another moment. "I don't think anyone's there, either."

And now that I thought about it, that made sense. The arts center put on a dinner for each night of the fair, and word had gotten around that the organizers were good cooks, so it was well attended.

But the event broke up fairly early so the dishes-and-cleanup crew could get home at a decent hour, which meant that if Babs and Dory were there, we didn't have a lot of time.

Ellie hustled back up the deck steps.

"Hey," I said quietly, "why aren't we going . . . ?" I pointed downhill.

Ellie looked back at me. "Um, because there's a sliding glass door up here, and it's unlocked."

I hadn't put trespassing on my to-do list for tonight. For one thing, I'd already committed that offense once today, and based on the outcome, once was enough. But providence left sliding glass doors open, and it was ungrateful not to walk through them.

I climbed up behind Ellie. The deck held outdoor furniture under canvas covers, a hot tub covered similarly, and a small teakwood sauna enclosure. The sliding glass door that accessed the deck stood open, and Ellie was already inside.

"Ellie?" I peered around as Ellie's flashlight beam bobbed across the wall-to-wall carpet on the floor.

"Come and look at this," she said. "But watch out for the—"

Stepping forward, I tripped over an invisible footstool, flailed but found nothing I could grab to slow my tumble, and landed on my face. Clambering up, I made out a long, low sofa in a particularly garish shade of red velour, a leather recliner so enormous you could bed an elephant down in it, and a flat-screen TV that entirely covered the wall above the fireplace.

No books. Not even a magazine.

"Jake," Ellie said insistently.

I made my way to where a clutter of bills, bank statements, and printed-out correspondence all lay in a messy jumble on a desk. Ellie held a sheet of letter-sized paper out to me.

Brad Fairway, President and CEO, the header read, and below that, *Electronics International.* The letter itself was nothing special, just a note informing somebody that somebody else would be taking delivery of a shipment after paying by wire transfer. The size of the payment, though, was impressive, well into the high six figures.

"Huh," I said, "I guess he must have parlayed those electronics stores of his into something bigger."

"Something he could run from a distance, I guess," Ellie agreed, aiming the flashlight around.

Fairway turned out to be partial to Thomas Kinkade prints, heavy gold velvet floor-to-ceiling draperies, and . . . I blinked as Ellie's flashlight reflected off a glass-fronted cabinet containing enough handguns for a militia.

Good ones, too. Among them was a beautiful Uberti top-break revolver, which I knew Wade had had his eye on for quite a while. That was how I knew it was a fifteen-hundred-dollar item. And the rest looked to be as pricey.

The cabinet itself was also a high-end item, with security glass, steel casing on the inside, and no lock at all that I could see, just a slot for a key card, like the ones in hotels, only this one was more the kind that they used at Fort Knox.

Ellie went to poke around in the kitchen, which like Choco's was a brushed-steel-appliances kind of room, just right if you needed a place to do autopsies in. I followed her.

"Here," Ellie said after pulling open kitchen drawers until she found a small flashlight. "He won't be using it."

And the batteries were fresh, too. I stuffed it into my pocket while next we went to check out the bathrooms. The first was a red-tiled monstrosity with a soaking tub, a twelve-jet, walk-in shower, surround-sound speakers, and a weird toilet-like contraption, which I didn't want to get too close to. The other one, off the master bedroom, was the same, only in black.

Standing in the master bedroom's doorway, I glanced over the slithery-looking red satin duvet on the bed and the drawn curtains over another sliding glass door. The rugs were white shaggy things, like dead animals sprawled across the floor.

In short, Brad Fairway had lived like a bachelor with plenty of money and no taste, and other than the weapons all properly locked up in their cabinet, the whole place was completely boring.

Too boring. The thought nudged me uncomfortably as Ellie urged me back out onto the deck, where she closed the sliding glass door behind us.

"Follow me," she said when we had descended the steps and were on the ground again, and then she headed away toward Babs and Dory's cottage.

"How?" I called after her. The night smelled like damp earth and chamomile, silent except for some distant bell buoys clanking and a foghorn groaning intermittently. "How are we going to get down there?"

From what I could see, the only possible way was to slide down the hill on my backside, and this hardly seemed practical. For one thing, there wasn't a whole lot of padding on my backside, and for another, with my luck, I'd get going too fast and slam into a tree.

"There are steps here," Ellie reported from below me after poking her flashlight beam into the bushes a few times.

Sure enough, when I'd scrambled partway down to her, a stairway appeared, leading crookedly down the hillside. Nice one, too, each graveled step bolstered by a big pressure-treated landscaping beam fastened into the earth with what appeared to be railroad spikes.

No handrail, though, and now the flashlight Ellie had given me, almost startlingly bright at first, was dying. Gripping her hand in the murky night, I picked my way between thickets of shiny-leaved rhododendron and holly trees with red berries gleaming like blood drops. Also, the holly's needle-tipped leaves pricked viciously, no doubt drawing real drops of blood, although I couldn't see them, and leaving me with a bunch of tiny, itchy puncture wounds.

At the bottom, my sneakers sank into a carpet of pine needles inches deep, shed no doubt by the massive old evergreens thrusting up from between granite boulders all around. Among the trees grew ferns nearly as tall as I was; beneath those, fungi the size of softballs digested the rotting trunks of fallen birches.

"Wow," I breathed. The silent woods, with the

fog drifting through it, felt primeval, as if any minute a dinosaur might loom up out of it.

Fortunately, none did.

"This way," Ellie said, her flashlight's beam picking out more low steps, which led up onto a long screened porch.

Here the air smelled like pine sap, leaf mold, cold salt water, and a saucepan with something burning at the bottom of it.

Ellie turned from trying to peer in a window. "Pitch dark," she reported. "Nobody's there. Or maybe asleep?"

I crossed the porch and opened the creaking screen door, then tried the door to the cottage and found it open, too, so I went in. The burnt-saucepan smell was much stronger in here.

"Hello? Anyone home?"

No answer.

I found a light switch and flipped it. "Hello?"

I heard the screen door creak again as Ellie entered the cottage. She came up behind me. "Wow," she remarked at the furnishings in the room. They looked like heaven and probably cost the earth: a vintage Danish modern sofa and two matching chairs, all with nubbly beige upholstery, an Eames leather lounge chair and matching ottoman, rya rugs in gleaming green, purples, and marine hues.

"Jake, if they're not here, maybe we should just . . ."

"Yeah, no." I kept looking around. A green-enameled woodstove stood on the brick hearth. Houseplants were everywhere, some small and some hulking in pots as big as lobster kettles. One end of the room was a window full of coleus, asparagus ferns, and African violets.

Parting the ferns' foliage, I peered outside but could see only mist trickling down the glass. In the kitchen, a butcher-block table, a lot of hanging copper pans, a knife holder with knives in it. Open shelves held dishware and glasses; two vintage linen tea towels hung, neatly folded, on a wooden drying rack by the sink.

The pan I'd smelled was on the gas stove's back burner. Something that might once have been soup was in it, reduced to a reeking sludge. I turned the burner off.

"Jake?" Ellie's call came from somewhere deeper in the cottage.

"I'm here." I hurried toward her. Dory and Babs could be getting home any minute.

The hallway's runner rug was woven in what looked like undyed wool: cream, tan, brown, charcoal, and black. At the hall's far end hung a large tapestry, a lush creation of silks and velvets delicately pieced together crazy quilt–style with gold thread.

I found Ellie in one of the rooms off the hall.

"This is Babs's, or it was," she said, gesturing at the yanked-open drawers, ransacked closet, and swept-clean dresser top. "Looks like a room someone's vacated," she said, "if you ask me."

That was what I thought, too. "Maybe Dory's with her?" I peered into the bedside table's lower cabinet. Nada.

"No," came a new voice from behind me. "Dory's not with her."

I looked up with a start to find Dory herself standing there in the bedroom doorway. That wasn't the biggest shock, though. The really startling part was who was with her.

"What're you doing here?" I blurted. Sam's dark, curly hair clung in damp ringlets to his forehead, and his eyes widened when he saw me.

"The arts center's supper was over, but Dory's ride wasn't around. So I gave her a lift," he explained. A sudden frown creased his forehead. "Why? What did you think I was doing?"

"What's going on?" Dory demanded of me, ignoring Sam. Her hair was wet, her clothes looked soaked, and she was shivering. "Is Babs here with you?"

Oh, brother. Apparently, it had begun pouring rain while we were in here. Also, it hadn't occurred to me before that Babs Littrell might head for the hills. Dory looked as if the same thought might just now be occurring to her, also.

"Come on, dear," Ellie told Dory kindly. *Dee-yah,* the Maine way of saying it. "Let's get you warmed up first of all, okay?"

Clasping Dory's arm, Ellie took charge of the young woman, then led her away down the hall.

"Hot shower, dry clothes. I'll make some coffee while you're in there," I heard Ellie saying, and Dory murmured obediently.

"Okay, well, I'm going," said Sam, still leaning in the doorway. "If you guys don't need me?"

I pulled open another dresser drawer, peered into it. As empty as the rest. "No, that's okay." I turned to him. "It was nice of you to drive her home. And to come down that steep, dark path with her, too."

A sheepish laugh escaped him. "Ma, if you ever found out I'd just dropped her off alone, didn't make sure she got inside okay, I'd never hear the end of it."

True enough, and what had I thought he was doing, anyway? The idea that he might have been, well, *flirting* with her . . .

My face must've said he had made a good point and was off the hook for whatever imaginary thing I might've thought he'd done.

"See you later, then," he called back over his shoulder, and once he was gone, I examined that room like there was treasure hidden in it. Rug, bedding, inside the lamps . . . I felt up and down the bed's fabric-covered headboard, ran my fingers over the tops of the door and windows, investigated the closet shelf. But with no result. Not even a scrap of an envelope showed up to suggest where Babs Littrell might've taken off to.

Fifteen minutes later, the three of us sat in the living room, where Ellie had put a fire in the green-enameled woodstove. With her hands cupped around a steaming coffee mug and her light brown hair curling damply around her face, Dory leaned forward, listening.

"We wanted to talk with Babs, but no one was around, and then Jake smelled something burning, so we came in," Ellie told the young woman. "And found . . . Well, you saw it all."

The emptied drawers, the cleared closet . . . Even Babs's toothbrush was gone from the bathroom.

Dory shook her head puzzledly. "But why would she . . . Did you search through the whole house? In her studio?" she asked.

I looked at Ellie, and she looked at me. We'd have thought of it eventually, I supposed, but then Dory had arrived.

"No," we said together, hopping up.

"She might have fallen," Dory said anxiously as she led us back down the hall. "Or she could've had a fainting spell or—"

She pushed aside the hanging tapestry and found a doorknob that I hadn't spotted. "I made that," she murmured shyly of the tapestry.

She opened the door and started down the stairs; I hung back. The wall hanging really was lovely: dark velvets and satins all melded together in a pattern that was equally random and regular, somehow.

Suddenly Dory was at the top of the steps again. "You coming?"

She'd caught me staring at her work. "It's beautiful, Dory. I'm surprised you're not teaching your own classes at the arts center."

A dark look flitted across her face and vanished, or maybe I'd imagined it. "Oh, thanks," she replied, shrugging self-deprecatingly. "I've got a lot to learn, though. Just ask Babs," she added with a laugh. "She's my teacher."

I followed her down the cellar stairs. "So Babs is pretty hard on you?"

At the bottom, Dory picked her way among folded looms, multiple yarn skeins on pegs, wooden shuttles in sizes from as long as my arm to as small as a finger, all tucked into a wicker basket. . . .

"Oh, no," she demurred. "I've learned more from Babs than in all the other classes and workshops I've taken put together."

The light down here came from long fluorescent tubes hung from cellar crossbeams. Babs's own working loom and its bench plus a worktable occupied one end of the cellar, its shuttle laid neatly to the left of the work. A stovetop, two double sinks, and an open cabinet full of color-smeared jars were at the other, along with drying

105

racks, a washing machine, and some stuff that I didn't recognize.

I crossed back to where Ellie was admiring the material on the loom, which was as beautiful as the work Babs had been doing at the art fair but very different. Lime, acid yellow, palest lavender, and red hues, which should've fought one another tooth and nail, swirled and blended like waves on a strange sea, and when I touched the fabric, it felt warm.

"Silk," Dory said, watching me. "Wrapped around a cotton core. It's spun in Japan. That's where her textile factory is, too."

My ears pricked up. "Babs has a factory? Mass production?"

Dory nodded, seemingly proud of her mentor's business acumen. "You didn't think she made a living from her art, did you?"

Until now I hadn't thought much about it, but upon reflection, I guessed not. "So this only looks like it's worth a million bucks?"

Dory smiled, neatening the yarn spools on the worktable. "Babs designs custom fabrics for drapers, upholsterers . . . for the people who finish and furnish big mansions and ultra-fancy hotels—"

"Jake," Ellie interrupted from the other end of the cellar.

I made my way past the cellar steps, the furnace, and a large collection of mysterious wooden items stacked up against both sides of the stairway's risers.

"Did you find something?" I asked.

Behind me, Dory kept puttering around Babs's loom, before pausing to straighten the stacks of stuff leaning against the stairs.

"No, and I don't think we're going to," said Ellie. "But it's crossed my mind that maybe Babs didn't go on her own." She glanced over at Dory, who, after neatening the weaving area and the stacks of stuff, was now throwing a dust sheet over the loom with Babs's unfinished work on it. Lowering her voice, Ellie went on. "Maybe someone helped her. Or forced her. You know?"

"Mmm. Possible," I agreed. "But nothing I've seen here makes me think there was a struggle. And, anyway, why force her to do anything?"

"Jake, she was in Choco's last night, all upset, and we don't know the why of that, either. But it still happened."

Good point. The truth was that we didn't know what was going on, only that Ellie would probably get blamed for it if we didn't hurry up and do something to stop such a very unhappy outcome.

"Dory, has Babs ever done this kind of thing before?" Ellie asked as the girl approached us. "Just taken off without a word to anyone?"

"Yeah," Dory sighed. "She has. She gets fed up with business or frustrated with the way her

107

own work is going. Or, you know, just mad at somebody, so she bugs out for a few days." The girl took a breath. "But not lately," she added. "And now I don't know how I'm going to handle her art fair booth alone."

"Maybe you won't have to," Ellie put in. "Maybe she just went for tonight, and she'll be back in the morning."

"Anyway, where's your studio?" I asked, realizing what I'd been missing down here. "You're a textile artist, too, after all."

The girl's pale cheeks flushed. "Well, sort of. I'm still really only a student."

"Nonsense," I said. "That hanging piece upstairs is striking, and I'm sure you've done others just as fine."

Not only will flattery get you almost anywhere, but that textile piece of hers was flat-out gorgeous.

The pink on her cheeks deepened. "Well. Thank you. That's nice to hear. But . . . what am I going to do about finding Babs?"

Ellie glanced at me. "Her car would be parked up in the driveway ordinarily? But it's not, so we can assume she's in it somewhere?"

"I guess so," said Dory, leading us back up the stairs. At the top, she turned to Ellie and me again. "She's allowed to go somewhere if she wants, of course. I mean, she's a grown woman. There's no rule that says she'd have to tell me about it. But—"

Yeah, but it was weird, especially considering the timing: Fairway dead one day, Babs gone the next.

"Anyway, thank you so much," Dory said as we all moved through the cottage, past the dozens of lush, silent houseplants, then back out onto the dark, chilly screened porch.

Rain dripped steadily off the pine boughs drooping with moisture all around the cottage. It looked like the Hound of the Baskervilles ought to be prowling out there.

"I guess I'll just have to wait to see if she shows up," said Dory. "Until tomorrow, anyway. And then I'll have to reconsider."

"Sounds like a plan," I said. There was no sense getting Bob Arnold involved if Babs was just going to show right back up on her own.

But Ellie didn't leave it at that. "Do you want to come and stay with one of us?" she offered.

I glanced gratefully at her for thinking of this. It was dark out here, isolated and remote. And the place's owner had just been murdered, which on a night like this one, with the fog creeping ghostily among the trees, seemed extra-pertinent.

"No thanks," Dory replied appreciatively. In the dim light from inside, she looked very young but not scared. "I'll be fine, really." She backed toward the porch door to the outside, still smiling but with an air of finality.

"Who does all those lovely houseplants?" I

asked as we followed her. "It must be a lot of work."

One potted geranium was about all I could manage at home, and I'm sure it didn't think it was getting top-notch treatment.

"Oh, I do that," Dory responded, pleased that I'd noticed. "I like having a lot of green things around."

She looked at the door. It was our signal to go: up the gravel-and-beam steps between wet, face-slapping birch branches and sleeve-snagging pine boughs, then across the graveled circle driveway out in front of Fairway's house.

"Well, that was unsatisfying," Ellie said as she started the car. The dashboard clock read 10:13 p.m.

"Oh, I don't know. We found out how Fairway made his money, and how Babs made hers."

I always think that stuff is important, and sometimes it really is. We started down the narrow lane leading to the main road.

"I don't like wondering where Babs is, though," I said. The more I thought about it, the stranger it seemed for her to be gone.

Ellie turned back toward town, squinting through the windshield in the drifting fog. "Is Sam okay?" she asked suddenly.

I looked at her, surprised. "Sure. Why wouldn't he be?"

She shrugged. "No reason." Across the bay, the

blurry lights on Campobello played hide-and-seek through the murk.

"What about you?" I asked Ellie when she pulled up to let me out in front of my house. Key Street gleamed wetly under the streetlamps. "How are you feeling about all this?"

It's not every day, after all, that a person becomes a murder suspect. On the other hand, I often think Ellie is made of some space-age material that's strongest under pressure.

"I'm good," she replied. "Tired, and a little nervous about when those homicide investigators might decide to pay me a visit."

"I'll call about your lawyer again," I promised, though I'd tried earlier, just before leaving the shop, and got sent to voice mail.

If I didn't get a callback soon, I'd have to think up some other strategy, a way of finding not just another lawyer, but a defense attorney with experience in this kind of . . . Well, the word I want here isn't polite, so let's just say "mess."

"And you call me if you want. Anytime," I added as I climbed out of the car. She nodded, smiling.

But watching her taillights dissolve to red gleams in the dripping gloom, I knew she wouldn't.

Inside, the house was quiet. Bella and my dad were already upstairs, and Wade was in bed, too.

"How's things?" he murmured drowsily when I crawled in beside him.

Sighing, I relaxed against him as well as I could after the day I'd had. "Okay, I guess. Murder, mayhem, a missing woman . . . you know, the usual. Oh, and Ellie's suspected of murder."

Silence from Wade.

As I might've said earlier, Ellie and I had snooped into murder before. Once we'd found the town butcher neatly dissected, wrapped, and stored in his own freezer, and we'd had to clear his widow of killing him. Another time, it was my own ex-husband who was accused; luckily for him, I am the forgiving type.

Just not the forgetting type. Anyway, Wade was fairly used to this stuff.

"Okay, well, that's bad, I guess. But you'd still better get some sleep," he said. His big arm curved around me. "Things might look terrible now, but in the morning it could be an entirely different story." His voice grew drowsy. "You don't know what might happen," he murmured.

Right, I thought as he drifted back to sleep. I didn't, and that was exactly why I was so worried about it.

Six

There was an obvious reason why Babs Littrell might go on the lam right after Brad Fairway got murdered: because she'd done it. As far as I could tell, though, nobody had even looked twice at her after the event, and now hardly anyone knew she was gone.

"You don't look so good," Bob Arnold told me the morning after we'd discovered that . . . Well, even I couldn't be sure Babs was actually missing. She could show up again.

But something told me she wouldn't as I stood with Bob out on the breakwater overlooking the boat basin. At this hour, the wide concrete expanse sticking out over the waves bustled with fishermen readying their gear, tromping up and down the metal gangs in their heavy rubber boots.

"No kidding," I replied. Last night's rain had passed, and the sun was almost up, the eastern sky's deep purple, burnt orange, and citron spreading over the brightening water like spilled paints. "Didn't get much sleep," I said.

As I was finally about to drop off, my lawyer friend in Portland had called to say she had somebody to represent Ellie. He'd call Ellie directly, my friend said. So I'd spent another few wide-eyed hours ruminating over that, and then when Bob had called, I'd walked down here in the pre-dawn silence.

"So what was so important that you had to get me down here at the crack of dawn for it?" I asked.

Bob wore a flannel-lined blue denim jacket over a gray Eastport sweatshirt, old khaki pants, and sneakers; his ball cap sported a Portland Sea Dogs logo, faded with age.

It was his day off. Still, his radio was on his belt, and I knew without needing to look that he'd secured his personal weapon in his car.

"Talked to the homicide guys who were here yesterday," he said. "They've got a couple of court cases to show up for, going to be a bit of a delay in the proceedings here."

"Yeah, I know." The sun's blazing-red edge peeked up over the watery horizon. "They called Ellie."

The phone message had been waiting when she'd gotten home the night before.

Down in the boat basin, one diesel engine after another rumbled to life as men threw coolers and duffels aboard the fishing vessels and leapt onto the decks. Bob and I walked back up to Water Street, where dawn flared in the storefronts' plate-glass windows.

"Reason I was up so early," he said as we reached the big granite post office building on the corner, "is that a young woman named Dory Sloan called me."

"Really." I hadn't told him about our visit with Dory the night before.

"She says her employer, Babs Littrell, the same woman who was so upset there in Choco's the other night—"

"I remember," I cut in. This was the reason he'd gotten me out here so early, I realized.

Water Street gleamed damply after last night's fog and rain, was still nearly deserted. We wove our way between the tents, tables, plastic-draped racks of the art fair—today was the last day—and heavy extension cords snaking from big portable generators to the food vendors' carts, still all shuttered now, too.

Bob's car was across the street. I walked him to it. "Seems she's gone missing," he was saying. "Sloan girl's worried about her."

Me too. "Ellie and I went out there last night and chatted with Dory," I said.

Bob didn't need to know what else we'd done, I decided. It would just put him in an even more awkward position to find out that Ellie had been in the dead man's house. For one thing, it would be easy to claim that she'd gone there to tamper with evidence or to destroy it. But there was another problem I hadn't thought of.

"Babs's car is gone," I went on to Bob. "Along with a lot of her things. I thought Dory might wait a day or so before she called you, though. Babs could have just gone off on her own."

Bob got into his car and settled behind the wheel. "Yeah. Maybe." He started the car. "Or maybe Babs Littrell's got connections to Fairway that we don't understand yet. Weeping over his death, living in his guesthouse . . . How'd all that happen, do you suppose?"

"Right," I began, pleased that someone besides me had at least begun wondering those things. But the "being pleased" portion of this morning's program ended fast. "There's got to be—"

"And now," he said, cutting me off, "someone suspected of killing Fairway, namely Ellie, could've reported that Babs had gone missing, only she didn't. And *you* didn't." Bob looked up at me from behind his steering wheel. "And if she turns up fine, that'll be okay. But what if she doesn't? Then do you see how it's going to look?"

I nodded slowly. "It'll look as if Babs knew or saw something that made Ellie appear even guiltier, so Ellie got rid of her somehow and made it seem as if Babs left on her own."

"Bingo," said Bob, putting the car in gear. "I told Dory to sit tight and try not to worry, that I'd put the word out to keep an eye peeled, but that Babs would come home on her own, most likely."

His pale blue eyes met mine. He didn't believe

116

that last part any more than I did, and we both knew it. "Meanwhile," he said, "people noticed Sam leaving the arts center dinner with Dory last night."

In Eastport, if you burn yourself on a hot skillet at one end of the island, ten minutes later people at the other end are breaking a piece of aloe off a plant in their windowsill for you.

Bob put a hand up. "Now, you know and I know that nothing's going on there. But you also know how people talk."

"He was driving her home. I doubt the need will arise again," I replied, although Dory was without a car now, wasn't she? So I couldn't be sure what she might need.

"And you can let Ellie know not to be expecting those homicide cops right away," Bob added. "Couple more days is what I'd probably be thinking."

He took an unhappy breath. "Thing is, Jake, think for a minute about what all has got to be true for Ellie not to have shot him." He put a finger up. "One, someone knew about the gun at all, although I don't suppose she advertised its presence. Two, they stole it without being noticed, first out of a locked car, then from a locked glove compartment, and finally, out of a locked gun box."

He paused. Then, "And one more thing. Don't go imagining those guys as villains, those state cops, okay? They've got bosses, too. Just doing their jobs, you know?"

Bob knew me pretty well; I'd already been picturing the homicide detectives with little red horns and pitchfork tails.

"Yeah, I guess," I said grudgingly. "But, Bob, why haven't they arrested her already, then? If there are so many strikes against her?"

He looked down at his hands. "First, they're in no hurry. They want their case all wrapped up with a bow on it before they present it. And Ellie's not a flight risk." He considered his next words before he spoke. "And because I told them that if they did arrest her now, they'd end up looking like the world's biggest fools, that her good character alone would give a jury reasonable doubt. And by some miracle, they believed me."

It wasn't a miracle; it was a solid argument for getting their ducks in a row before they acted. But the delay wouldn't last forever.

Bob backed out and drove off. By now it was full daylight and a few cars were moving in the street. I walked half a block to the Chocolate Moose and went in, glancing sadly at the masses of purple and yellow pansies blooming in our window box as I passed and wondering who would plant them next year if Ellie couldn't.

Inside, I went around turning on lights, the radio, the fan, our laptop computer for taking email orders, and the credit card reader. I didn't need any of them yet, but they made me feel less alone. Then I started preheating the oven for more of those chocolate chip cookies. I'd softened the butter, got out the sugar, vanilla, and eggs, and begun creaming the butter and sugar together when the little bell over the door out front jingled.

"Hello?" a voice called.

It was Sam. I hurried out, wiping my hands on a towel and thinking that maybe I would drop a quiet word about Dory Sloan and the Eastport gossip factory on him. But when I saw his face, that plan dropped to the bottom of my to-do list.

"Mom, has Ellie called you?" he wanted to know.

My heart dropped. "No. Why?"

"Because," Sam said, "I just drove by her and George's place, and there's a pair of state cop cars out front."

"What's going on?" I demanded. "I thought you said—"

Ellie and George's home at the north end of the island was an old farmhouse, built when this area supported more livestock than people: cows, pigs, the occasional mule. Now only ancient apple trees, massive old lilac bushes, and huge, overgrown daylily patches remained of the original homestead.

"I don't know," Bob fumed, standing with me out front. "This is the opposite of what they told me."

He'd swung back to tell me the same bad news that Sam had just delivered, then given me a ride out here so Sam could close up the shop for me. Now we were both in Ellie's driveway, behind a pair of state police vehicles, waiting.

The minutes ticked by. "They've done well with the old place," Bob mused, squinting up at the refurbished farmhouse's new metal roof.

"George has done a lot of work," I murmured, trying hard not to think about what might be going on inside.

Then it hit me that George's truck wasn't here. That meant Ellie was alone in there. "Isn't she supposed to be able to have a—"

"Lawyer," I'd have finished, but just then the front door opened, and Ellie came out, followed by three men in dark suits.

Bob strode toward them, and what looked like a heated conversation ensued. From a dozen yards away, I saw a flush rise up his neck until it seemed that steam might start puffing out of his ears.

Ellie's eyes widened as one of the dark-suited guys waved Bob away dismissively. From Bob's look then, I thought it was a wonder the guy's whole arm didn't get bitten off.

Instead, Bob stalked back toward me, just as Sam pulled up in his pickup truck and got out.

"What's the deal?" he wanted to know. "Are they taking her into custody? Did they let her call George?"

After hearing that Ellie's interview with the police wouldn't happen for a few days, George was probably on his way to Bangor, a hundred-plus miles away. He was working a construction job there and was likely to be doing so next week, as well, according to Ellie.

Bob spread his hands at us as he approached me, looking by now as if he'd cooled off some. "Calm down," he said, seeing my face.

I just love being told that, don't you? "But—"

"Change of plan," he said. "Ellie is going to go down to my office and talk with them," Bob explained. "She called Skip Vining, and he's agreed to meet her there."

I felt my shoulders slump. Skip Vining was a fine fellow and an excellent local attorney who'd helped plenty of Eastport folks with traffic violations and so on. But that was different from defending against a murder charge.

"Skip's already got Ellie's new attorney's phone number," Bob went on, "and with any luck, they're discussing this whole matter as we speak."

I sure hoped they were, because as far as I was concerned, this whole surprise "change of plan" thing was completely bogus, as Sam would've put it.

"When the DA got wind of the delay, he blew

his top," Bob went on. "Called it 'unacceptable' and sent down some orders from on high."

Oh, great. Now the boss was involved, just as Bob had suggested might happen. And getting the boss involved in anything didn't often result in things going better, in my experience.

Like now, for instance.

"So these guys'll do a preliminary interview, just basic background stuff. Saves time. Then the other guys'll take over again when they're done testifying," Bob continued.

My face must've shown how I felt about this.

"Look," Bob said, "we get this done now, it'll get them off her back for a day or two."

I opened my mouth. Bob cut me off before I could speak, luckily for me, probably.

"Skip can hold down the fort," he said. "He won't screw it up. He's no Clarence Darrow, but he knows he's not."

Which I had to admit was true. Skip could shepherd Ellie through basic preliminary queries as well as any other lawyer, and he wouldn't let it go any farther than that. He could even end the conversation if things got dicey; Ellie could, too, if I understood this right.

"I'll ride back to the shop with Sam," I said as the cop car with Ellie in it departed, heading back downtown. She fluttered her fingers bravely at me through the passenger-side window, and then she was gone.

"Tell her to call me when she can?" I asked Bob, and he nodded. Then he left, too, and Sam looked troubledly at me.

"You maybe want to go home first," he said.

"Uh-uh," I said firmly. No one had been up when I left, and I'd liked it that way. "Why, though? What's he up to now?"

Because whatever it was, of course, it was my dad who'd be up to it. But Sam shook his head.

"It's Bella. She's changed her mind. Now she says if Gramps goes to the nursing home, she's going with him. And he says . . ."

Oh, good grief.

"He says," Sam went on, "over his dead body."

I climbed into his truck, a bright red Ford F-250 with a leather interior, heated bucket seats, and a sound system so powerful, they could probably hear it on Campobello.

Fortunately, the music wasn't on this morning.

"Why'd you stop at our house at all?" I asked.

"Got lonesome for Bella's breakfasts," he answered casually.

Which wasn't much of an answer, but I didn't press him. Right now I had other things to worry about besides my son's personal life, which, I reminded myself yet again, was none of my business.

"Oh," I said finally as I passed the ferry dock. Next came the Chowder House restaurant, with its wide outdoor-dining deck

123

stretched out over the water, then the new red-roofed Coast Guard headquarters and the breakwater.

In the fish pier parking lot, the artists and their helpers were opening tents and pulling blue tarps off display tables. I wondered if Dory Sloan would run the weaving demonstrations today or if she would call them off.

"So when is he leaving? Your grandfather, did he say?"

We pulled up in front of the Moose. "For the nursing home? Not today, I think. He and Bella are too busy bickering."

A mild term for what was happening, I suspected. My father was a skilled, enthusiastic arguer, and when she was provoked, our dear Bella gave as good as she got.

"Good," I said, "It'll keep them occupied. Anyway, I'm not going home to play referee. I've got things to do."

Opening the shop again, first of all. But then I realized that operating the Moose would be a problem, too, if I meant to spend the day getting Ellie out of the jam she was in.

Thinking this, I muscled the truck's door open. "Sam, can you ask Mika to come down for a few hours?"

"Um. Yeah." He didn't sound eager. "Sure, I'll call her." He started to back out.

"Sam," I began, wondering again why he'd

gotten out of his own house and into mine so early this morning.

But it really was none of my business, and besides, I was in no mood for it, I realized suddenly, so instead I shut up.

It was not yet even eight o'clock, but since I was there, I opened the shop, anyway. Then the art fair people started showing up, already hungry and thirsty, and for the next hour, I alternated between baking more chocolate chip cookies and selling them almost as fast as I could pull them out of the oven.

I ate a few, too, figuring that any extra energy I took in today would be all to the good, and between customers I was hastily dipping the third one into a mug of coffee when Mika arrived.

Shiny black hair, blunt cut at her jawline, crisp white shirt, and black slacks . . . Mika always looked well put together.

Also, she took no guff. "Your son," she told me as she put on a fresh apron and took her place behind the counter, "is impossible."

I stuffed the rest of the cookie into my mouth so as to avoid commenting. If her wide, dark eyes looked faintly puffy and red, it could be allergies or perhaps a cold she'd caught from one of the children.

So I didn't remark on that, either. "Bake whatever you want to," I said instead. "Or Ellie's

125

got this chocolate marshmallow pie idea she's fiddling with. You could work on that if you felt like it."

Mika nodded agreement. Yes, she said, she could stay for however long I needed her, and no, she didn't need to collect her children from their playdate. Sam, she told me, could do that, and handle the dinner-baths-and-bedtime routine, too. He would, she informed me briskly, be staying in tonight, so he'd have plenty of time.

Unlike last night, I was pretty sure she meant. At any rate, it seemed Sam had been given his marching orders for today.

"Just in case you should happen to need me at your house this evening . . . ," she added, her eyes on the napkins and the miniature ceramic pitcher full of toothpicks that she was straightening on the counter.

Oh, brother. "Uh, yeah," I said noncommittally and got out of there so fast, you'd have thought I just robbed the place.

The trouble was, I wasn't sure where I was going. The only one I thought could help me right now was Dory Sloan, and with Sam behaving so strangely and Mika clearly miffed at him, Dory was approximately the last person I wanted to see. I couldn't help thinking she might be the cause of their domestic drama.

Still, with Ellie in the clutches of some homicide cops, who were probably not showing her a good time, I had little choice, so I headed down Water Street to the fish pier parking lot, where Dory might be.

"Did they find her?" she said anxiously when I approached her.

Babs Littrell's collection of small woven items for sale offered scarves, shawls, tapestries, and a pair of nubbly wheat-colored pillow shams that would've looked excellent in my parlor at home. Also, Bella would've loved them.

But I was in no mood to buy anything. "No," I replied, "and until the police get around to realizing that they want to talk to her and finding out they can't, I doubt they'll be looking for her."

Dory wore tan slacks, a pink-striped blouse, and a pale pink cardigan, whose hue tried and failed to enliven her pale, drawn face. Bobby pins neatly pinned back her light brown curls, as usual, but no amount of grooming could cover the look of a sleepless night.

"Or unless you give the police a reason to think she's in some kind of trouble," I added.

Bob Arnold would keep an eye out, like he'd said, but no one was going to go haring around the countryside, looking for a grown woman who already had a history of making herself scarce whenever anything bad happened, then returning on her own when the dust cleared.

Dory reached up to pull off the tarp draped over the looms still set up behind the sales table. I stepped to the far side of the looms to help.

"Look, Dory," I said as we dragged back the heavy blue plastic, "I could do a few things myself to try finding her, but you need to give me a little guidance if you can." I kept my tone light, and my smile firmly tacked on.

Around us the happy chatter of the fair's early arrivals covered our voices, along with a flute-and-fiddle combo tuning up. Finally, we finished folding the tarp, and Dory stowed it under the sales table.

"There's Richie Perrone," she said when she returned. "He's a potter. I mean a ceramics artist," she amended, putting a faint twist on the words. "Richie and Babs . . . Well, he should tell you," she went on. "He lives on River Road, the first long dirt driveway on the other side of Route One."

At my questioning glance around the parking lot, she added, "Oh, he's not here. For an event like this, a public show that just anyone could be in, Richie is way too, um . . ."

"Snooty?" I suggested. Over the years we'd had artists of all types visiting Eastport. Most were what Sam called "regular people."

Some weren't.

"I guess you could say that," Dory replied. Her small fingers busied themselves straightening the shuttles that lay across the threads on each of the student looms. "He quit the arts center, doesn't come to the events, hardly ever even shows up in town. Thinks a lot of himself, Richie does."

Five of the shuttles lay on the right side of their respective works in progress, and one on the left. "Some weavers are right handed. Some left handed," Dory told me, seeing my puzzled look. She sat down behind the sales table. "Anyway, I'm not sure what help he's going to be, but you could talk to Richie," she said. "That is, if he'll talk to you."

The vintage 1974 Fiat 124 Sport Spider, with five speeds forward, a rack-and-pinion steering, and a zippy, invigorating way of speeding down steep, twisty two-lane roads, had been my housewarming gift to myself when we first came to Eastport, and I got rid of my ex's car.

Even as old as it was, the Fiat was gorgeous—apricot paint, classic Pininfarina body, as streamlined as a flying bullet—and I had loved it at once, even though it already had plenty of miles on it.

Since then, I'd blown a head gasket while accelerating in a passing lane out on Route 9, where the 18-wheelers sniff disdainfully at you as they blow past doing seventy. The timing belt snapped on the way up Day Hill (same road, different trip), and the muffler unmuffled itself all at once in the IGA parking lot, nearly giving the lady parked next to me a heart attack.

As for seeing out the rear window when the top was up, forget it. The window was made of a thick Plasticine sheet, about as transparent as waxed paper. I didn't drive the car very often, and especially not in winter, but when I got home that day from talking to Dory Sloan at the art fair, no other cars but the Fiat were in the driveway.

My regular car, an old Toyota sedan, was at the garage, having its oil replaced, its brakes adjusted, and its snow tires at long last changed out for the summer. Bella's car wasn't there either.

"Hello?" In the house, I picked up a shoe from the row of them in the back hall and peered absently into it. "Anyone home?"

Nobody was.

"All righty, then," I said. Maybe Bella had hustled my dad into her car and driven him somewhere to read him the riot act in privacy. Or maybe they had made up after their quarrel and were off on an afternoon adventure to celebrate.

Hoping for the latter but fearing that the former was a good deal more likely, I got the Fiat keys from their hook by the back door and went out again. This Richie Perrone guy that Dory had mentioned might not want to talk to me, but I sure wanted to talk to him.

Thinking this, I got into the Fiat and turned the ignition key. Nothing. I tried it again, then several times more, and finally got the vehicle started by releasing the emergency brake and letting the car roll downhill into the yard while popping the clutch. After that, I motored sedately down Key Street and out Route 190 until I'd left the EASTPORT sign behind.

And then I hit the gas, feeling the engine surge forward like a small but scrappy animal let out of its cage while the Pirelli tires bit hungrily into the road.

Speeding across the causeway under a wide blue sky with the top down (and anchored that way with twisted coat-hanger wire, as the latches were busted), I felt like a million bucks suddenly. The cool, salt-tinctured air oxygenated my brain cells and invigorated my courage, so that by the time I reached the mainland, I actually knew what I would say to Richie Perrone.

Five minutes later I crossed Route 1 and soon found the narrow turnoff into forested land that had to be Perrone's driveway. The Fiat's underside scraped over the gravel-studded ridge between ancient tire ruts, but this time the muffler stayed on.

The mingled scents of rising pine sap, last year's rotting leaves steeping slowly in shady dampness, and the cold, fresh water trickling in the stream sparkling by the road were refreshing, but the trees all around blocked the sunlight, and suddenly the forest's chill hit me with its refrigerated breath.

But soon the driveway widened into a bright, wide dooryard with a picket fence, a broad patch of green grass, and a neat brick path to the front of the house.

I got out of the Fiat into a silence so complete, it felt like my ears had stopped working. But then I heard it.

Snork, snork!

Turning, I found the sound's source already charging at me. My assailant had small, unfriendly eyes; dainty, hooved feet, moving fast; and a long, curly tail with a jaunty little tassel of bristles at the end, black and white, like the rest of the animal's short, flat coat.

Also, it was huge, and as it galloped toward me, I was horribly aware that I was about to be devoured by the Biggest Pig in the World.

"Hey!" I shouted, hoping either to discourage the pig or to alert its owner, and preferably both.

"Jillian!" The answering shout came from the long wooden shed at the back of the property. In the shed's double-wide doorway, something big and dark colored stood on a wooden pallet.

"Jillian!" It was a man's voice.

The pig hesitated.

Directly in front of me stood a two-story white farmhouse that looked like a painting entitled *Country Home*. It had a railed front porch, two chimneys—one for the furnace and one for the woodstove, judging from the stack of split firewood at one end of the porch—and a new-looking metal roof very much like George and Ellie's, only this one was dark green to match the shutters and trim.

No one whose name might've been Jillian emerged from the house. In the clearing behind it were some apple trees gnarled with age; no Jillian-type persons were visible there, either.

The pig, now strategically positioned between me and the Fiat, took a deliberate step toward me. In response I took one backward, and the pig and I repeated the routine a few more times until finally a man came out of the shed.

"Jillian!" The pig turned as the man strode toward us, clapping his hands. "Come, pig. Come, piggy," he crooned.

The man was tall and solidly built, with a thick neck and broad shoulders above a wide, powerful-looking chest. Clean-shaven, he wore faded blue jeans and red, white, and blue suspenders over a brown plaid flannel shirt; a large brightly beaded key fob with a bunch of keys on it hung from his belt.

The pig hurtled itself toward him with what looked to me very much like joy, the tiny little legs under its big body trotting faster than any pig's legs had a right to be able to, I thought.

"Hey!" he laughed when the animal bumped him affectionately. He reached down to scratch between the pig's bristly ears with one hand while feeding it a tidbit from his pocket with the other.

"Snork! Snork!" it commented happily, and when no more treats were forthcoming, it wandered away to continue whatever piggy deeds it had been doing before I arrived.

"Sorry about that." The man strode toward me. "She thinks she's a watch pig," he said, wiping his hands on his pants. "What's up?"

After what Dory had said, I'd been steeling myself for possible unfriendliness. But this guy seemed pretty normal so far.

Well, except for owning the Biggest Pig in the World. But, hey, everybody's got quirks.

I stuck my hand out. "I'm Jake Tiptree. Are you Richie Perrone?"

His grip felt like a bunch of steel cables with calluses wrapped around them. "Yep."

Friendly, but he kept eyeing me curiously. *Your move,* his face said. Then he glanced back at the barn. An old yellow Jeep Wrangler was parked alongside it. *And I don't have all day,* his look said.

Yeah, me neither, I thought. I sucked in a deep breath. "My friend is in bad trouble. Babs Littrell might know something that could help. But right now Babs is missing, so I need to find her as soon as possible."

His thick, dark eyebrows knit at the sound of Babs's name, and his eyes grew less friendly.

Suddenly he seemed to be deciding whether to toss me out bodily or just sic the pig on me. Finally, he asked, "Want to know the difference between Jillian and Babs Littrell?"

At the sound of her name, the animal peeked at me from behind the house. Now I knew what a snack being eyed by a teenager felt like.

"If you scrub hard enough, you can get Jillian clean," Perrone said.

He glanced back at the barn again. "Look, I don't mind talking, but I've got to tend to a couple things. Go on in. There's coffee," he said, waving toward the house. "Help yourself." His face, though, barely changed from its suddenly closed-up expression. "I should've known somebody would come asking about her sooner or later," he added.

"Someone like me?" I asked, and his bark of unamused laughter was like Jillian's snork when she was thinking of devouring me.

"No," he said, "I mean like the cops."

Having caught my nervous glance at Jillian, Perrone walked along with me through the picket-fence gate and up the walk to the house. The pig seemed to know that the lawn was off-limits to porky four-leggeds.

Perrone understood my surprised glance. "Yeah, she's smart," he said, although the animal's intelligence hadn't been my concern.

More like her toothiness.

"I'd let her in the house," he said, "but if I did, she'd never go back to sleeping in the shed at night." He pulled open the screen door. "I wouldn't even mind, but she snores," he said, going ahead of me into a sunny kitchen so neat and clean that even Bella would've approved.

He set cups and saucers out, produced a china cream pitcher in the shape of a cow, and gestured at a vintage Formica-topped table with four chairs upholstered in red vinyl.

"Okay, just chill here a minute," he said when I was settled, and once he'd gone, I watched through the kitchen window as he headed out to the shed.

He returned in just a few minutes, as good as his word.

After seating himself at the table, he clasped his hands together on it. "Okay, now, what's going on?"

He was good at managing a conversation, taking control by asking a question before I did. So I made an end run around him and cut to the chase.

"Babs is missing," I told him again and went on to summarize recent events. When I'd finished, he was frowning.

"Wait here."

He got up and left, then returned moments later with a thin sheaf of official-looking papers. "This is a no-contact order that the court issued against her a few months ago. Go on. Have a look."

I did, and that was what they were, all right. Signed and sealed, State of Maine, County of Washington, yada yada.

I looked up. "She's your ex-wife?"

Bitter humor infused his smile. "Yep. Maybe not my worst mistake, but close. It lasted two years, which for Babs has got to be some kind of a relationship record."

I tipped my head inquiringly.

"She usually wears people out in a matter of weeks," he said. "Maybe months, if they're masochists and want as much emotional pain as possible." He drank some coffee. "Hang on too long, though, she'll decide to get rid of you. Long term makes her nervous."

I put the papers down. "That's what happened? You wouldn't give up on her, so she dumped you? But then why . . . ?"

Perrone sighed. "That's how it would've looked from the outside. What really happened was, she got worse and worse, until I had to bail for the sake of my own sanity, and then she panicked. Started begging me to reconcile and so on."

He gestured at the papers. His hands were thickly calloused, and his nails, trimmed to the quick, were clean but stained a sludgy-looking yellowish brown, as if they dug regularly in mud.

"Finally, I got a court order," he went on, "and surprisingly, it worked." He got up. "And that's

137

why I haven't seen her, don't want to see her, and would call the cops pronto if I did see her."

I opened my mouth but he anticipated my question. "Nor," he added before I could ask, "do I have any idea where she might be now."

Outside, Jillian had been performing an activity that I could only call talking—piggily, but also urgently—as if making good on Perrone's "watch pig" description. Perrone crossed to the window, cursed mildly at what he saw out there.

"Chickens are loose," he said exasperatedly, heading for the door.

I followed, and together we hurried outside and around the farmhouse to the back, where a dozen hens were busily picking insects from among the green grass blades.

Perrone stopped, seeing the birds. "Oh, what the hell," he said. "They're happy." He glanced over at the brushy forest edge beyond the fence. "I worry about foxes, is all. And coyotes."

"And eagles," I said, pointing up to where a large, dark-bodied bird with a telltale white head and the wingspan of a small passenger plane circled lazily overhead.

Perrone let out an amused snort, opening the side gate and waving the pig into the enclosure where the poultry was. "Yeah, eagles, too. So go on out there and watch those chickens, Jillian. Watch 'em."

Lifting her pale pink snout determinedly, the

pig marched out into the grass. "Oink," she said clearly, which I gathered meant, "You got it, boss." And I had to admit I wouldn't want to be the eagle that crossed her.

"Now, if you'll excuse me, I've got work to do," Perrone said.

Reluctantly I took the hint, but out in front of the house where I'd left the Fiat, I pressed him again. "So you can't think of anywhere that Babs might go? Even just to get away for a while?"

He eyed me sideways. "Uh, in case you hadn't noticed, I'm fairly certain that Eastport is already where you go to do that."

Yeah, if you're a city dude who thinks that makes him smart, I thought but didn't say. Perrone was okay, I guessed, well spoken and polite, but for some reason, he kept not winning me over at all, and his snide remark about Eastport didn't help.

He went on, "I'm betting she's seeing someone, though. A male someone. It would fit her pattern. There's always a guy in her life." Then a new thought seemed to strike him. "D'you know Hadley Owens?"

I indicated that I didn't.

"Nice lady, excellent painter. She lives in that big third-floor place over the variety store downtown," he said, walking over to the Fiat.

Walking me over there, actually. His manners were good, but they didn't prevent him from letting me know I was interrupting his work.

139

"She uses the first-floor rear space as a painting studio." He smoothed his hand along the Fiat's gleaming fender. The car's body was so prone to rust that if I hadn't kept it indoors during the winter, it wouldn't have had fenders at all. "Somewhere she could get away, though, huh?" he said. "So that's how you're thinking? Guy's dead, and she's gone, so therefore et cetera?"

"Just somewhere she might go to clear her head or whatever," I said. He could draw his own conclusions about what I might think or might not think, but I wasn't going to confirm them for him.

"Why? 'Cause something's stressful? Nah, she eats that stuff up. The more drama, the better. Now, as an artist, Babs is top-notch."

The eagle overhead sailed away, shrinking to a small black dot on the cloudless sky, then circled back low and slow, waiting for his moment.

Perrone turned seriously to me. "But personally, and business-wise, too, she gets into situations without thinking and then can't get out again."

"Whereupon?"

I could tell by his face that he still wanted to get rid of me and get back to his work, but he wanted to make sure I knew a few things, too, before I left. Such as that he wasn't involved in whatever trouble Babs had gotten herself into. His wanting to separate himself from it made me think *he* thought it might be something bad.

Really bad.

"Whereupon she runs out of money again," he said. "That business of hers isn't as profitable as she wants people to think. I'm not sure how she gets by at all, to tell you the truth."

It occurred to me to wonder how he did—get by, I mean. He saw the thought occur to me, and my glance over at the shed.

"Yeah," he said, "I do get by. Thirty years ago I lived on beans and ramen, but now . . ." He waved toward the shed. "That piece you can see from the yard, the tall one on the pallet? That's getting shipped out tomorrow to a collector in Palm Springs."

Whatever it was, it was indeed very big. And, Perrone seemed to think, valuable. "Let me guess. Ten thousand?" Dollars, I meant.

Perrone shook his head. "Multiply that by ten. This isn't a hobby. I'm serious, and so is what I'm doing."

Art, he meant. Not a pastime or a leisure pursuit but work, a discipline. A thing that had artistic reasons behind it.

I nodded slowly and, somewhat to my surprise, appreciatively. I hadn't thought much about it before, but now it felt good to know there were people in the world treating art almost as seriously as religion, whether or not they made money at it.

That wasn't the point. Perrone saw me getting

it and nodded minutely. He was, I realized, a perceptive guy.

"I've been lucky to be recognized, to be taken seriously. For one thing, it's why I could pay for everything when Babs and I were married. But it's when I also found out she always wants other people to help clean up her inevitable messes, and when they can't or won't, she goes ballistic."

"Huh. And the messes were in the side business she had?"

To me, she'd been an artist first and foremost, but of course, even artists had to make a living somehow.

"Yep," said Perrone. "She kept coming to me even after we were divorced, and I couldn't keep bailing her out. That's why I ended up having to get the court order finally. She wanted me to lend her some more money, and when I wouldn't, she got into my potting shed and went on a rampage. Destroyed a lot of my work."

"What did she want the money for?" I asked, thinking that there was nothing like a ceramics artist's workplace for a truly satisfying session of rage-fueled smashing and breaking. The way he must have felt seeing the aftermath, Babs was lucky he hadn't murdered her.

"An immigration lawyer," he said. "She's here in the States on a visa that she let expire, on top of all her other problems."

His gaze returned to the Fiat, gleaming prettily

in the midday sunshine. I felt conversational gears shifting.

"Nice ride you've got here. I had one of these once. You ever bust a timing belt? Bonus points if you were in the passing lane. Or blow a head gasket or three?"

I nodded as I got into the car. I'd earned the bonus points, all right, and it seemed that he had, too, once upon a time. "I used to haul jerricans full of water so I could pull over and refill the radiator anytime steam started billowing from beneath the hood," I laughed.

Well, it was funny now. Not so much back when it was happening.

Meanwhile, from where I sat, I could look into Perrone's shed. Or I could have if it weren't so bright out here and so seemingly pitch dark in there. But, hey, in for a penny and so on.

"Before I go, can I see what you make?" I hazarded.

He glanced sharply at me, seeming to realize that I was stalling, but this guy knew more about Babs than he'd said so far. I was certain of it.

"Sure," he said finally, turning toward the shed. I hopped out and trailed him, and Jillian eyed us from a distance but oinked out no piggy protests as we went in.

"Oh," I said inadequately once my sun-dazzled eyes had adjusted to the relative gloom inside. Directly before me stood an urn nearly twice as tall as I was; it was the object I'd seen from outside.

Black, glossy, with clouds of pale pewter-colored stars drifting endlessly through its layers of glaze. It looked like some alien being's enormous funeral container or maybe a portal into deep space.

"Wow," I breathed, touching the urn's cool surface hesitantly. No otherworldly spark leapt to meet my fingers, no strange views of other worlds rose in my mind's eye, even though the vessel's otherworldly appearance made it seem they should.

Perrone watched me impassively, his rough hands stuffed in his jeans pockets.

"It's beautiful. Or something," I said.

That was when he smiled, a look of pride that was clearly genuine. " 'Or something' is what I'm going for," he said. "Glad it worked on you."

"Doesn't it on everyone?" I couldn't imagine not being moved by this huge, weirdly evocative object, with its star-flocked depths and oddly familiar-feeling curves.

"No." His face turned briefly rueful, then less so. "Not sure I want everyone, though. Letting the urns pick their own people seems to work, so I just try not to get in the way."

"Is that why you left the arts center? The urns . . . didn't like it there or something?"

The space inside the high-raftered shed felt vast as a cathedral. Large and small unglazed clay vases, bowls, and platters stood on wooden pallets; the hearth of a huge brick fireplace turned out to be the mouth of a room-sized kiln.

"The arts center?" he answered eventually, sounding as if I'd just now reminded him of the place. "Oh, no, that wasn't it at all."

He strolled toward the door. After another moment in the urn's enigmatic presence, I followed.

Outside, the pig had escaped the fence. Snorking out a loud greeting, she trotted to Perrone and bumped her meaty side against him companionably. He staggered sideways, then bent to scratch between her ears.

"The arts center worked fine for me at first," he said as he let the animal nibble on one of his ears.

Personally, I'd be paging members of the surgical reattachment team at the hospital before I let that creature's pointy incisors get near any of my appendages, but I guessed Perrone felt otherwise.

"For firing big pieces like that urn, though, I had to build an oversized kiln," he went on. "And at that point it was better to make them here, also. Unfired, they're just too fragile to move, unless I have to."

From outside the shed, I couldn't see the stars in the big urn's glaze anymore, just its shape, flinging shards of reflected light away from itself, as if rejecting them.

Or repelling them. Also, I couldn't help noticing now that the urn was large enough to hide a human body inside. My body, even.

When I turned, Perrone was right next to me. "Dory Sloan doesn't seem to share your negative opinion of Babs," I said, stepping back. "She seems to feel Babs has treated her well."

He waved my comment away. "Oh, Dory. She's another whole story entirely," he said, and I was about to ask why, but just then Jillian trotted up on her tiny black cloven hooves to shove her pink-tipped snout under my hand.

"Umph," she grunted softly, rubbing her bristly cheek against my thigh. Her little piggy eyes gazed up at me affectionately. I guessed the way Perrone had accepted me made me a potential pal.

But those choppers of hers still meant business. I eased away, walked back to the driveway with Perrone trailing behind me, and got into the Fiat and slammed the door shut swiftly and efficiently.

"Anyway, sorry I couldn't help you more," Perrone said. "Ask that painter, Hadley Owens, though. They've got a family connection of some kind, I think. She might know something." He stepped back as I fired up the Fiat and shifted into reverse.

"Thanks. And thanks for the tour." I backed the car around.

"No problem." Perrone waved, then watched

me go; Jillian didn't wave, but she watched, too. Standing there, with a farmhouse and a yard full of chickens behind them, they were like some primitive painting depicting an idyllic rural scene. *Farmer with Pig*, it might be called.

And although I still wasn't sure why, as I drove off, I already knew that of the two of them, I trusted the pig more.

Seven

Ellie didn't get out of Bob Arnold's cop shop until the end of the day.

"You could have left, though. And you did have Skip Vining there with you, right?" I asked her.

"Yes. Skip was great," she said. "I really just wanted to make sure I wouldn't get called back in. And, anyway, they didn't ask me anything tricky, just went over and over the same facts. Where I was born, what George does for work, things like that."

We were in Ellie's kitchen, where she was putting dinner together for herself—George was back in Bangor, where his job was the kind that you either showed up at or got fired from, and her daughter, Lee, was away at a sleepover tonight— and I was putting off going home.

"They kept going over and over our money situation, too," she said as she cut off an onion slice so thin you could read a newspaper through it.

At her request, George had redone the kitchen in knotty pine, red Formica, dark green linoleum tiles, and new white porcelain. With its big farmhouse sink, enameled woodstove, and the butcher-block worktable all gleaming like the day they were new, the kitchen now resembled the stage set for some rustic variety of cooking show. Knives bristled from racks; above them, pots and pans hanging from hooks flashed rosy-copper bottoms.

"But what about your day?" she said, plucking a pickle from a home-canned jar. "Is that really all you got out of Richie Perrone?"

She was fixing herself a bacon cheeseburger, frozen french fries, and a salad made from the kinds of raw vegetables that no one else in her family would touch: kale, broccoli, artichoke hearts, and so on. Plus plenty of blue cheese.

It looked delicious.

"Yep," I said. "He was pretty much no help. To be fair, though, I got the strong sense that Babs was the very last person whose whereabouts he wanted to know."

Ellie got out the hamburger, looked quizzically at it and then at me. "You want one of these? There's plenty of everything. And . . ."

From the back of the refrigerator, she plucked out two bottles of Moxie, Maine's official soft drink. Invented by a Mainer in the late 1800s and originally called Moxie Nerve Food, it tasted to me like strange berries, the crushed roots of little-known herbs, and a dash of swamp water, all stewed up at midnight in a hollow tree stump, and I loved the stuff.

"Sure," I said, and fifteen minutes later, we

sat eating our burgers and drinking our Moxies, feeling that we'd earned our suppers.

"How're your dad and Bella doing?" Ellie asked, poking a french fry into a puddle of ketchup.

I groaned, chewing a baby radish she'd grown in her garden. "As bullheaded as ever," I said when I'd swallowed. "Bella wants him to stay home and behave himself," I went on. "Not go setting up extra living quarters elsewhere. Now she's trying reverse psychology, but it's not working."

She knew my dad pretty well, but it seemed that Bella had missed learning one thing about him: he never gave up.

"And your dad?" Ellie washed down a french fry with a gulp of Moxie.

I sighed past a bite of avocado. "He says to trust him, it'll all work out fine, and he's not listening to any more negative comments about him moving into assisted living."

I'd stopped at home to check in before coming to Ellie's, then departed hastily again. Now I swiped the last of my sandwich through the last of the creamy salad dressing while behind me, on the stove, the percolator burbled enthusiastically, puffing fragrant steam.

"But he does listen to the comments," I said, "because Bella keeps making them, trying to wear him down."

We took our plates to the sink, made quick work of our dishes, and moved to the parlor, with its old Persian rugs, bentwood rocker, and a thrift-store recliner, re-covered by Ellie, in tan leather George had salvaged when an upholstery-supply store went belly-up.

A low fire flickered orange on the parlor hearth. I sat down and leaned back into the deliciously soft green velvet sofa and sighed. "I've got half a mind to stay here tonight. Let them battle it out."

Ellie sank into the rocker and propped her sock-clad feet on the brick hearth. "Just say the word," she replied.

Instead, we sat in silence a while.

Finally, I remarked, "There's one thing Perrone did tell me, though."

Her eyes snapped open. "What?"

I hated to say it. I knew what she would want once she knew. But at this point we couldn't afford to be casual about anything.

"He said he thought Babs might be seeing someone. Romantically."

Her eyes widened as she sprang up. "Who? Where? Can we talk to him?" Her brow knit. "Or her, I suppose, but . . ."

I sighed inwardly. Of course she would want to go out and pursue this right now. We should go, too; there was really no time to waste.

Besides, I had nothing else to do except listen

to my elders fighting. I hauled myself up from the sofa.

"Him," I said. "But Perrone didn't know who. He suggested that I ask Hadley Owens. D'you know her? Lives upstairs in the building two doors from the Moose?"

Ellie was already pulling her shoes on. "So what are we waiting for?" she wanted to know as she grabbed her jacket and mine off their hooks in the back hall.

The breezeway led out to a small barn housing two small, tame goats and a dozen chickens. Sweet whiffs of warm, well-kept animals met my nostrils.

"I'm pretty sure she's a painter," I managed as she hustled me through it and outside.

Following a grassy path between two rows of crab apple trees, we emerged at the front of the house.

"And she might know who Babs is seeing? And then we could go and find him, and—"

The Fiat was parked in her driveway, its top still folded down over the trunk lid and fastened that way. Seeing it, I shivered in advance. Eastport summers may be balmy in the daytime, but once the sun went down, you could swear it was November. At least we didn't have far to go.

I fired the car up and backed out under a sky full of pinprick stars.

"Have you talked to Sam again?" Ellie asked

as we passed small houses so close to the street that their front doors opened directly onto the sidewalk.

"Nope."

Four deer stepped out from a vacant lot, then turned to stare at our oncoming headlights as if they'd never seen a car before.

"And I'm not looking forward to talking to him again, either," I said as the deer finally moved on.

In the quiet evening we passed Moose Island Marine on one side of lower Water Street and a sail-making and repair shop on the other.

"I don't know what's bugging him," I went on, "but I don't like the way he reacted when I mentioned Dory Sloan."

He should've made fun of me, said something sarcastic. Instead, he'd seemed defensive and even a little resentful, as if I'd touched on something he didn't like thinking about.

And Mika was mad at him, which was the strongest indication I could think of that he had been—or was still being—a complete jerk about something.

Passing the fish pier parking lot in the dark, I saw that the tents and awnings had been hauled away and the tables were stacked, waiting to be removed. Only Babs Littrell's things still stood in the chilly moonlight, the looms still with students' works in progress on them and their shuttles laid neatly to the left or right of the works.

"Seems like much ado about nothing," Ellie said, meaning the Sam-and-Dory thing. "Anyway, gossip goes away on its own here, you know."

Sure it did. When there was nothing to it. We parked on Water Street, in front of the variety store, which made me think of Sam yet again. At thirteen he had laboriously saved ten dollars, then had come down to this place and bought himself a no-kidding leather bullwhip.

I'd been horrified until after some practice he called me outside, where he proceeded to flick a marble off a fence post with the thing.

"Up there?" Ellie asked, snapping me back to the present.

I nodded and turned off the Fiat. The building was three stories high, and the lights were on only in the windows at the top.

We got out of the car and trudged uphill to the building's rear. Steep exterior stairs angled up to the top-floor apartment.

"Yikes," I panted as we reached the first stairway landing. The brisk, chilly breeze I'd endured in the car felt like ice up here. "Let's get this over with," I muttered, looking out over Water Street very briefly. The height made me feel dizzy and as if I might sail right off into it.

But when we reached the top landing at last, my legs threatened to go out from under me entirely. Black sky yawned above, solid ground lay way too far below, and the wind here was like a fire hose blasting air so cold that it might as well have had ice crystals in it.

With Ellie behind me, unfazed, of course— Ellie likes Ferris wheels, roller coasters, and those ungodly contraptions that catapult riders way too high by means of a long rubber band—I gripped the wooden railing around the third floor's small deck with one hand and knocked on the door with the other.

Inside the apartment, soft music was playing, and lamps glowed brightly in the interior rooms. I pounded on the door again and was rewarded finally by the sound of footsteps.

Not, unfortunately, human footsteps. "Grr," said something on the other side of the door.

I let a tired breath out. Apparently, a pig with fangs like a timber wolf's hadn't been enough animal trouble for me for one day.

"Anybody home?" I cupped my hands around my face to try peering through the door's small window. To my not very great surprise, eyes peered back: dark brown, intelligent eyes with gold rings around their pupils. Above and behind the eyes stood a pair of pointed ears.

The ears had fur on them, the mouth had teeth in them, and unless I was badly mistaken, they all belonged to a large German shepherd dog.

And was he ever mad. Not bothering to bark, the dog curled his lip back over his gleaming teeth. There were lots of them, all looking to be in excellent repair. A pinkish shred of what I could only assume was human flesh clung to one of his upper canines.

"Nice doggy," I whispered, meanwhile thinking about lights on and music playing but no one answering the door. When I glanced over at Ellie, it was clear from her face that she thought the same.

"Try the doorknob," she whispered, so I did, and it turned. The dog made a sound deep in its throat, not a happy sound.

"Ellie, how the heck are we going to get—"

The dog rumbled again. My only question now was, if we opened the door, would he eat me out here or drag me inside to do it? Also, have I mentioned that it was cold out on that deck?

My only hope was that the dog might not like eating frozen food. But while I stood shivering miserably and thinking this, Ellie reached past me, pushed the door open, and walked inside.

"Nice doggy," she said, repeating my hopeless attempt at greeting the canine.

I waited, trying to remember how to tie a tourniquet. But to my amazement, no mayhem ensued.

"Come on in, Jake," Ellie called back to me. "It's okay in here."

Doubting this, I complied. The dog glanced up alertly at me, then returned to gobbling kibble from Ellie's hand. She'd gotten it from a plastic bag on the kitchen counter; there was plenty more.

So the animal was pacified for the moment, but I still had a very bad feeling about all this, and as I moved deeper into the apartment, I discovered with dawning horror that I'd been right.

It wasn't okay in here.

It wasn't okay at all.

The white-haired old woman lay in the living room, near one of the big plate-glass windows that looked out over downtown Eastport and the dark water beyond. Sprawled facedown, with blood thickly pooled by her head, she was either out cold or dead.

A long red smear streaked the glass-topped coffee table nearby, made, I imagined, when she'd tried reaching the cell phone lying there but lost consciousness instead.

Ellie knelt, felt for a pulse on the side of the woman's throat, then grabbed the phone. I'd have tried helping, but the dog, although no longer actively hostile, wouldn't let me near.

"Breathing and she has a pulse," I heard Ellie telling the 911 operator as I started looking around. If an ambulance was coming, I wouldn't have much time.

The room we were in was actually a combination living and dining area. We'd come in through the kitchen, and besides that, there was a bedroom and bath. The walls were covered in paintings and prints; small, delicate art objects stood on shelves and littered the wide, flat windowsills.

In the small galley kitchen, a pair of wine-glasses stood in the sink. An elegant French press coffeemaker, still warm, held an inch of black coffee; in the sink was a plate with crackers-and-cheese crumbs on it.

Outside, the paramedics thumped up the stairs. As I'd expected, they were prompt, having come from the fire station just blocks away. The two young men in blue uniforms rushed past to crouch by the fallen woman, who, I now saw, had begun waking up.

"Oh!" she murmured faintly, clearly taken aback at the sight of the strangers hovering over her. Well-meaning ones, but still. "Where . . . ?"

She sat up, looked unsteadily around while the med techs took her blood pressure, examined her head wound, and asked her questions like "Who's the president?" and "What day is it?"

In response she shoved back her white hair with her liver-spotted hands, then blinked down at the blood on her fingers. "Is that mine? Oh, my. What . . . what happened?"

Her face was like something you'd see on an old Roman coin: high forehead, prominent nose, strong, stubborn-looking jawline. Big copper loops hung heavily from her fleshy earlobes, and a strand of flat clay disks engraved to look like sand dollars hung around her neck.

She struggled up, one hand flat on the couch behind her. The paramedics tried stopping her, but she was clearly one of those forces of nature that I've heard about but can never quite manage to be.

"I'm fine," she told them sharply. "Just let me have some more of those gauze pads for my head. I must've hit it on the coffee table."

She was obviously a resilient woman, one I already thought could probably give my dad a run for his money in the argument department. But that wasn't what I was mostly thinking of right that minute.

Instead, I stared at the couch she was pushing herself up on. I'd been so shocked by the sight of a bleeding, out-cold elderly person who might be dead, I'd failed to notice the upholstery on the low, simply designed piece of furniture: nubbly blue yarns, gold threaded and surrounded by strands of a dozen other rich hues. It was very much like the fabric Babs Littrell had on her loom at the art fair.

Finally, Hadley Owens managed to shoo the persistent medical guys away, mostly by assuring them that Ellie and I were going to drive her to the emergency room stat.

Which we were not going to do, her glance

toward us added very clearly, but she convinced the paramedics, so finally Ellie and I were alone with the bloodily head-bonked painter.

"Put some of the wine in the refrigerator into a mug," she told me. "Pour the rest of the coffee into it and heat it all up. Then mix a spoonful of honey into it."

I obeyed, noticing when I got out the wine that the fridge was stocked with all kinds of fruits and vegetables, a number of curries and chutneys, two store-bought kale smoothies, and a jug of oat milk. No wonder she looked so hale and hearty.

"Thank you," she said when I'd brought her wine toddy, smiling at the cinnamon stick I'd found and put into it. Sighing, she inhaled the vapors rising from the cup, still pressing the gauze to her forehead.

"Somebody hit me," she said after she'd had a rejuvenating gulp of the stuff. "But . . . I don't know who. I don't remember . . ."

Bottom line, though, someone had been here, someone she knew well enough to serve snacks, coffee, and wine to.

"It'll come back to you," Ellie gently assured the white-haired old woman. "Your memory of what happened, I mean."

Cautiously, Hadley Owens got to her feet. She was wearing a long-sleeved black leotard top with a short-sleeved green smock over it, the smock belted at the waist by a paisley scarf. Maroon leggings and black velvet slippers completed her outfit.

"No, no." She brushed me away impatiently as I went to lend her a hand. "I'm fine. A bump on the noggin won't stop a tough old bird like me."

It was more than a bump. She should've gone with the paramedics to get X-rays and maybe to be medicated, possibly even kept for observation. But the alcohol and caffeine she kept swigging seemed to be reviving her spirits, at least.

"Now I suppose you've come to see the paintings," she went on, pulling a bright pink shawl from the back of a chair and wrapping it around herself.

"Oh, no," I began, but she was already out the kitchen door to the stairway landing and on her way to that dizzyingly steep descent.

She started down, those velvet slippers of hers scuffing faintly on each step. Ellie rushed past me to catch up with the elderly artist.

"Be right with you," I called, stepping outside to watch them descend. When they'd reached the ground safely, I went back into the apartment, where the big German Shepherd eyed me gravely but offered no objection, for now.

Okay, now: Neither of the wineglasses in the sink had residue in them. No drugs or medications were anywhere in evidence. Hadley Owens didn't have a gun, or, anyway, I couldn't find it. The only self-defense item I found was a pepper-spray canister on a key chain, along with a small flashlight, in one of the kitchen drawers.

I looked under the bed in the neat, spartan bedroom: nothing. A flat pillow, a narrow mattress, which I thoroughly felt around under, and a plain pine dresser and bed table were all the room contained, and eventually, I gave up and followed the other two downstairs.

"Very strange," Hadley Owens was telling Ellie when I joined them at ground level. The last gleams of light were draining from the sky in the west, where dark clouds towered on the horizon.

Thunderstorms later, I noted uneasily as Hadley Owens unlocked the door to her ground-floor painting studio . . . or tried.

"Now, why is this door already open?" she inquired vexedly, with a frown down at the key, as if perhaps the problem were its fault. Then she stepped through the doorway, and the lights went on in there.

"You okay?" Ellie asked me quietly when we were inside. The large open space was filled with big, brightly colored paintings of flowers that were fanciful and bizarre, as if grown in some strange, otherworldly jungle.

"Fine," I said, figuring the less said about that open stairway, the better. The long, precarious-feeling descent was probably better than just jumping off the top step, but only because of the brief, unpleasant landing portion of the program.

In here, though, the air smelled intoxicatingly of oil paints and turpentine. No other smell makes my heart quicken just that way, as if I were still a teenager and learning for the first time that people painted pictures at all, or wrote books or played music for the sake of doing it, nothing more.

It was the smell of a life beyond the scuttling, street-dwelling little wretch I'd been back then. Now I breathed it in gratefully once more, remembering what a blessing it had seemed to me the first time I smelled it.

Then I heard the rest of what Ms. Owens was saying. "*Sure* that I'd locked it."

I caught Ellie's eye over a pile of unstretched canvases in one corner of the large, completely white-painted room. Could someone else have a key? Or had Ms. Owens forgotten she'd let someone in? Someone who'd gone with her upstairs to the apartment, perhaps.

"Anyway, here you have it." The old painter's gesture took in the whole studio. At one end, a battered old white-metal sink unit heavily spattered with paint stood by a table holding coffee cans with brush handles sticking up out of them. Beside those lay scissors and razor knives, a packet of blades, and a straightedge, plus a carpenter's tape measure.

Nearby stood an easel with a tantalizingly blank canvas on it. A drop cord with a dangling utility lamp hung over the easel. A wooden stool stood in front of the easel.

But the finished paintings were what I couldn't stop looking at, the rich, deep hues of tropical red shading to black, and azure blue to darkest purple, the sensual, almost erotic shapes, and the clear sense of danger lurking behind the loveliness.

Despite my appreciation, I'd never been an artist. Money and numbers were what I was good at, things that were cold and dead and wouldn't change on you whether you added them up once or a hundred times. But this . . .

This made me want to be. A purple-and-yellow pansy whose orange stamen emerged from a throat-like black hole drew me in swooningly.

"Jake? Come and look," Ellie called, breaking the spell.

I blinked. Hadley Owens was watching me from a little distance. A quiet smile of pride creased the parchment skin of her face. When our eyes met, she nodded, as if acknowledging what I'd felt. Then the moment was over.

"What?" I asked Ellie, crossing the scuffed paint on the studio's concrete floor to where she stood by an open door. *A storage closet?* I wondered as I approached. *Or a small bathroom?*

One of the latter would come in very handy here, I thought, especially on snow days, when those outdoor stairs would be tantamount to suicide. As if they weren't now.

Finally, I breathed, "Ohh." The door in front of me now opened onto a narrow staircase leading steeply up into deeper darkness. An *inside* staircase . . .

"So I don't need to go outdoors," Hadley Owens confirmed when I turned to her. "But I do love that sailing-into-the-sky feeling, don't you?" she added, and, of course, I didn't punch her.

More to the point, though, these stairs had been someone's escape route a little earlier; I felt sure of it. I'd simply missed seeing where they came out in the apartment above.

"Ms. Owens," I asked, figuring what the heck, I'd just go for it. "Do you know Babs Littrell? I mean, she's an artist, so I imagine you must, but . . ."

"Why, yes!" Suddenly she was all smiles. "I went to art school with her mother in Norway. Such a long time ago, but Hannah and I kept in touch until she passed away." Hadley Owens really did have the loveliest face: strong, clear eyed, full of intelligence and humor. "Babs is a dear girl, isn't she? Do you know her, too?"

"No, I'm afraid I don't. But right now she seems to be missing, and I wondered whether . . ."

Ms. Owens's eyes widened with concern. "Oh, no. Are you sure? She must've been upset about poor Brad Fairway dying so suddenly. And in such a terrible way . . . The two of them came for supper a few times, and Babs just seemed to be so much in . . ." But here Hadley Owens paused. "Well, perhaps not in love," she amended. "I'm not sure Babs has ever really been interested in that."

She reached out to touch the soft-pink petal of a painted rose nesting in painted thorns. "She's probably just gone off somewhere to be alone, grieve her loss," Hadley Owens said.

That was what Dory Sloan had thought, too. But I didn't. Too much of a coinky-dink, as Sam would've put it.

"Do you know where she might've gone?" I persisted.

Because either Babs Littrell had killed Brad Fairway herself or she knew things that might lead me to whoever had, I felt fairly sure.

Hadley Owens brushed impatiently at the dried blood in her hair. Her strong-boned wrist and forearm looked improbably muscular for a woman her age. From manipulating a paintbrush for hours, I supposed.

"I have no idea where Babs would go," she said. "Her mother and I were close, but Babs is a sort of lone ranger, doesn't confide much. I don't really know how Brad Fairway managed to win her over."

On the way out, Hadley Owens stopped next to a bowl of key chains like the one in her kitchen drawer. Each chain held a flat plastic tab with one of her rose paintings laminated on it in miniature.

A promotional item, in other words. My opinion of her went up another notch. We went out the way we'd come in, and Hadley Owens locked up with her key. We walked her back to the foot of the steep stairs, where, by the dim gleam from the streetlamps down on Water Street, I could still see the dark stains matted in her hair.

"Thank you, both of you," she said, brushing off our offers of further help. "Isn't it silly, but I still don't remember what happened up there," she said puzzledly. "There was someone, I think, but . . ."

The ambulance crew had pronounced her head wound nonserious, but she'd still bonked it pretty hard, thus their urging her to visit the emergency room, which she had refused to do.

I disliked letting her climb those three precipitous flights of steps alone, but she was firm about that, as well.

"Now, dear," she began kindly when I'd expressed my concern and offered to accompany her. "Don't worry. I really am fine." She rapped her knuckles against the side of her head lightly, but I still winced. "Hard old noggin," she said. And then in gentler tones, she added, "Those stairs used to terrify me, too, you know."

"They did? But then why did you . . . ?"

"Because I got myself up there just to see it. I'd always been curious. It would be like living in a treetop, I'd thought, and it was."

She turned to look up at the top-floor landing, which widened out into a little deck. Warm yellow light slanted down onto the deck from the kitchen window.

"And I wanted it. I could go up and down those stairs blindfolded now if I had to," she said, and I believed her. "Or even if I didn't have to," she finished. I believed that, too.

Minutes later, when we'd seen her go safely into her apartment, I turned to Ellie in the darkness behind the building just as she was turning to me.

"Doesn't make sense," Ellie said, taking the words right out of my mouth. "Why would somebody sit there eating snacks and drinking coffee or wine, then shove an old lady so hard that she fell into a coffee table?"

Somewhere out on the water, a bell buoy clanked lonesomely. In Hadley Owens's kitchen window, the light went out.

"It doesn't make sense, because that's not what happened," I said as we made our way back to the Fiat.

The top was still down, so the car's heater was even less useful than usual. But I cranked it up anyway as we pulled away from the curb; wrestling the top's stiff canvas and frame and wrangling the coat-hanger wire fasteners was too much work for such a short trip.

"Someone visited," I said. "Ate snacks, drank

wine. Or coffee. And departed, likely down those inside back stairs."

"And then?" Ellie asked as the Fiat zipped us uphill past the Coast Guard and the port authority buildings again. Beyond them, the breakwater's concrete deck stretched out bright as an airport runway over the watery darkness.

"Then someone else came," I said. "A third person, someone who wanted something. Or who wanted to stop something."

In the dashboard's dim glow, Ellie looked thoughtful. "Maybe to stop Hadley Owens from telling something she knows?"

We passed the CHOWDER HOUSE sign with the happy red lobster cavorting on it.

"But that means somebody knew we were coming?" Ellie said, continuing to theorize.

After the Chowder House, outer Water Street was lined on both sides with small houses with lit windows, their curtains drawn over what I always imagined were happy domestic scenes straight out of a Norman Rockwell painting.

Even though I knew better.

In the open car, the breeze off the water was scouringly fresh, like cold champagne.

"But why only wound her if what you want is to silence her?" Ellie went on. "I mean, you can't count on her not remembering who hit her, can you? And when she wakes up, she'll tell who . . . oh . . ." Her voice trailed off as the truth struck her.

Meanwhile, we had left the little houses behind; here at the island's thinly settled north end, the breeze dropped to chilly stillness under the ice-chip stars.

"Right," I told her, confirming what she hadn't said. "Someone wanted Hadley Owens's mouth shut permanently. We interrupted. If we hadn't . . ."

I pulled up in front of the small barn. Ellie got her phone out and pushed one of the FRONT PAGE icons. That was another of the improvements that her husband, George, had made: a really good home security system. She could turn on the lights, disarm the door alarm, even dial 911 right from the app on her phone.

"Oh!" Ellie said, peering down at the device. She'd muted the ringer while we were out. "There are calls here from an attorney in Portland, it looks like, and here's a text message, too."

Relief hit me. Without a good referral, we'd be reduced to reading through Maine newspaper archives to find lawyers who'd won big murder cases for clients reasonably recently. The attorneys around here, like Skip Vining, were fine people and excellent lawyers, but dead bodies and the defendants who'd allegedly made them that way just weren't any local attorney's wheelhouse.

Ellie looked up. "He says that he's the attorney your friend in Portland recommended. He's already spoken with the district attorney, and now he's getting all the information and paperwork together."

In case they really did decide to arrest her and charge her with murder, he meant, a prospect so hideously unattractive to me that I decided not to think about it right now.

For one thing, I had enough to think about. "Lock up again once you're inside, okay?" I said as Ellie got out of the car.

Up on the porch, the outside light went on. So did the ones in the breezeway between the barn and the house; tiny lights twinkled among the arbor's grape leaves.

"I will." A pale moon had risen, and despite Ellie's energy this evening, in its light her face looked pale and drawn.

I waited until lights had gone on in there. Then, chilled to the bone, I drove back through the quiet night to my own big old house on Key Street, where a different kind of worry awaited me.

"Dad, come on. Talk to me." I pulled off my hoodie, out of habit felt my head for my hat, and didn't find it. I'd wanted it on the way home, too, but it hadn't been in the car. Now I realized I hadn't seen it in a day or so.

"Dad?"

He sat at the big round kitchen table, which I hadn't had the heart to get rid of when Sam and

Mika and my grandchildren moved out, despite my earlier resolution.

My father remained stubbornly silent.

"All right, but I'll be back," I warned him before heading hastily upstairs and into the hottest shower I could stand.

In fuzzy slippers, flannel pajamas, quilted robe, back downstairs, I heated some coffee and confronted my father again.

"Spill it, Dad. I can't stand much more of this. So do us both a favor, why don't you, and tell me what's got you so discombobulated."

The word brought a grudging smile to his face, as deeply wrinkled as a walnut. Dressed in a black turtleneck, tan corduroy trousers, and a knitted vest, he wore thick wool socks and moccasins on his feet.

"All right," he said at last. "I don't want to go, but I guess I've got to if I want any peace."

He'd been sitting there when I came in, rocking and thinking. He wasn't angry. He wasn't sad. I knew both those moods, and they weren't this. I waited.

"I've been remembering all the dinners we've had at this table," he said. "You, Sam, his and Mika's kids. Wade and Bella and me."

Bella was already upstairs, and Wade was out with the guys, seeing the Red Sox game tonight. The port authority had a massive TV screen.

"And it's been grand," said my dad, his heavy-lidded eyes full of remembered happiness. "You've done well here, Jacobia."

"Thanks," I said, surprised. He rarely said these things. "But, Dad, what's this all really about? Because I don't get it."

"I know. Bella doesn't, either. Have you heard yet that now she's saying she wants to come along?"

"Sam told me." I drank more hot coffee. "But do you think she really does?"

He shook his head. "No, of course not. It's her try at reverse psychology, that's all."

He could summon up a very convincing stern-old-man gaze when he wanted to, and now he fixed me in it. "But look, Jacobia, the thing is this. All the children—yours, Sam's—are gone."

Well, I couldn't deny that. You could get into a bathroom around here now without taking a number, and I'd finally gotten used to not hearing the *SpongeBob SquarePants* theme all day and night.

"And with all of them gone"—he gestured with a bony hand—"the house is practically empty now."

Also true. From being so desperately over-crowded that people were practically tumbling out the upper windows, the house now had empty beds, tidy rooms, and stairway newel posts that did not occasionally have pairs of toddler-sized, cartoon character–themed underpants draped casually over them.

And I hated it. I'd known that I would, and I did. But I'd told no one this. "So, you want to make it even emptier?" I asked now.

"No," my dad replied promptly. "I think you should sell it."

"You . . . but . . . I should what?" If there'd been a feather around, you could've knocked me unconscious with it. He'd never said anything even remotely like this before. "Sell?" I repeated. "You mean, move out and live somewhere else? In some other house, while *other* people . . . ?"

I waved around wordlessly at the old-fashioned kitchen's high wooden wainscoting, the venerable old soapstone sink and beadboard cabinets, and the woodstove in the corner, clucking contentedly over its meal of sticks.

"Dad, they'd remodel." It was a way too pleasant word for what renovators would do if they ever got hold of this place. "They'd tear out all this . . . the vintage wallpaper, the wavy-glass windowpanes . . . and put in marble countertops and subway-tiled backsplashes and block letters that spell *love* on the wall. And a fake-wood floor."

My dad nodded agreement, but his lips tightened stubbornly. "You and Wade have never had a place to yourselves," he said. "And now with Bella and me here . . ."

I heard Wade's truck pull into the driveway. "Dad, I still don't get it. What've you and Bella got to do with anything?"

And then it hit me, what he was trying to tell me, and what he was trying to accomplish. He was doing it for me, and he knew that when push came to shove, Bella would go with him.

"Once we go, you can forget about all the repairs piling up around here," he said. "Find something smaller, not so much work."

Wade's boots climbed the porch steps, then turned and went back down again. He'd forgotten something in the truck probably.

"Otherwise, Bella will still be here doing your housework," my dad said.

Not on my account. I'd tried firing her, telling her she was my family now, not my employee. But Bella had never seen a dustrag she didn't like, and trying to stop her relentless mopping and sweeping was an exercise in futility. Even now I could see my face clearly in the polished-shiny side of the toaster oven.

"And she's getting older, you know," my dad added, like I didn't already feel guilty enough about allowing Bella's cleaning compulsion, and as if I could do anything to stop it, anyway.

I started to say something about this to him, not a nice thing, possibly. He knew how to get my dander up. But just then Wade came in.

"We'll talk more about this later," I told my

dad. "We'll find some compromise, I promise you."

My dad got up stiffly but without hesitation, his answering look resolute. "No," he said kindly but very firmly, indeed. "We won't."

"Huh," was all Wade said an hour later, when I'd finished describing my day. I still hadn't found my hat.

"Fiat ran all right, though, did it?" he asked, turning a page of the book he was reading. In it, a nuclear submarine was missing, and a guy had to find it before it went boom.

Just once, I'd like to read one in which the submarine does go boom, but never mind.

"It ran great," I said. Wade always expected the car to quit on me in some remote spot out in the puckerbrush without any cell phone signal.

"I've got to do something about that back window, though. With the top up, it's practically impossible to see through." My old house wasn't the only thing that needed repairs around here.

His eyes were on the page, but his eyebrows went up. "I'll talk to Jana at the sail shop," he said. "I'll bet she can put a new window in for you." He was right.

"Thanks." I let him read a while longer. Then I said, "I'm really worried about Ellie."

My uneasy mind kept returning to Richie Perrone's towering urn, big enough to hide a

176

body in, and Hadley Owens's lofty apartment, whose hidden stairs offered a stealthy entry method, possibly.

Something else was bothering me, too, but I couldn't quite put my mental finger on it.

"Ellie's lawyer in touch yet?" Wade asked.

I reported what Ellie had told me, that the attorney I'd found for her had been in touch. "Now we've got to find him some money, but there are worse problems to have."

Wade turned a page while nodding at what I'd said. "Yes, I guess there are."

Another question kept nagging at me. I didn't want to ask it. But I couldn't just walk around worrying about it alone anymore, and Ellie had too many worries already for me to bring it up again with her.

"Wade, do you think Sam could possibly have a . . . a girlfriend?"

He laid his book down, turning to me. "What? No, I don't think he's got a . . . Jake, Sam's crazy about Mika and the kids, you know that. Whatever gave you the idea he might?"

I let out a heavy sigh. "He drove a nice young woman named Dory Sloan home the other night, and that's all there was to it, I thought. But when I asked about it, he seemed uncomfortable, and something's up between him and Mika. They're just not themselves."

He leaned back onto his pillow. "Yes, well, I

177

think you might be imagining things," he said. "Sam's not canoodling with any nice young women but Mika, you can take it from me."

Here I should probably tell you that my husband, Wade, can spot canoodling a mile away. He once intuited a red-hot romance between a deckhand and a girl who sold mussels by the bushel off the dock, just by noticing a single glance between them.

So I took some comfort in what he'd said, and that was the end of talking until he snapped off his lamp. I closed my eyes and counted sheep; ten minutes later I had 632 of them.

"Wade. Are you awake?"

His warm hand covered mine. "Yep."

"Dad's moving out so we can sell this house," I said. "He told me so."

Brief silence from Wade. He was mulling this. Finally: "No, he's not moving out, and no, we're not going to," he replied sleepily.

He rolled over and wrapped his arm around me, smelling of pine soap and the lanolin-heavy salve he rubbed into his hands to keep them from cracking in harsh conditions.

"Go to sleep, Jacobia," he said quietly into my hair, and I did.

But later I woke up again, and suddenly it hit me: my hat.

I knew where I'd lost it.

Eight

The Fiat's engine was too loud for me to start it in our driveway in the middle of the night. Ditto for Ellie picking me up out front in her car: too much noise, leading to way too many questions.

So I did the sensible thing; I sneaked out, dressed in dark sweatpants, a navy blue hoodie, and running shoes. Speed walking down Key Street, under a clear black sky prickling with stars, I called Ellie on my cell, and by the time I reached the Chocolate Moose, she was there waiting for me.

"Hop in," she said through her open car window, and a few moments later we were heading out Route 190 toward Brad Fairway's house again.

"What's so urgent that we need to do it right now?" she wanted to know as the night zipped by.

Even in the car I could feel those icy stars gazing implacably down. "I left my hat out at Fairway's place."

That was the troublesome thing I hadn't been able to think of earlier. But then I'd remembered taking the hat off in Fairway's kitchen, and that was the last place I recalled having it.

Our headlights picked out the narrow driveway

opening between the trees. We took the turn and started up the grassy track between trees whose trunks seemed to march whitely into the headlights, then vanish as we went by.

"Anyone who goes in there will find it," I said, "and they'll wonder whose it is and how it got there."

And that would open a can of worms, since half the town knew I always wore a pink baseball cap.

Ellie said nothing about the cap or my carelessness in losing it, coming up instead with a new angle on Babs's possible whereabouts.

"You know, she'd be safe in Fairway's house right now. She'd see headlights if anyone drove in, so she could scram if she wanted to." She slowed for a rut that spring rains had put in the driveway. "Dory might not even know Babs is there," she added.

I hadn't thought of that, either: that Babs might not want Dory to know. Plenty of things could be true that just hadn't occurred to me until now. What, for instance, if Babs really was there, but she was dead, and Ellie and I found her body?

It wouldn't be a good look. But I needed that hat. When the long, grassy track widened, Ellie doused the headlights and shut the car off before we hit the circle driveway's noisy pea gravel.

"Okay," I exhaled. We got out of the car and began walking. The darkness all around felt as thick as tar and nearly as trap-like. On the other hand, the only way to see us in this pitch-blackness would be with a pair of night-vision goggles or maybe a trail camera. Or—

"Ellie. Stop right where you are. Then back up toward the car."

She didn't ask why, just did as I'd said. Together, we reversed ourselves away from the large, low shape that was Fairway's house. Then I nudged Ellie and pointed up. A tiny red light blinked from halfway up a power pole at the driveway's edge.

"See that?" I whispered. "It's a security camera. Probably it's recording. We'll have to go through the woods and around back."

In daylight, we hadn't noticed the red light. At least this time we'd stopped the car far enough back, and thus out of the device's range, to keep the vehicle—and probably its license plate, too—from appearing on candid camera.

We stepped off the driveway into the unkempt area alongside the house.

"Oof," I said almost immediately.

"You okay?" Ellie went ahead of me as we traipsed downhill toward the deck we'd climbed last time.

"Yeah, fine," I said quietly. But I was remembering again why my favorite location was definitely not out in the woods in the middle of the night, especially when my feet kept sinking into wet leaf slime, bumping against rocks, and tripping over exposed tree roots.

The second time I tripped, I toppled forward and bumped hard into Ellie, then sat down in a mossy puddle. When I struggled up, the seat of my pants dripped soggily.

She'd stopped short directly ahead of me. "Jake."

Stepping forward again, I nearly stumbled over a rock, but I kept my balance by pinwheeling my arms . . . and slammed one of them against a tree trunk. "What?" I snapped, then remembered to keep my voice low.

"Couldn't that security camera out front have caught us going in here the other night, when Sam brought Dory home? Us going into Fairway's house?"

"Yup." The house sat at just enough of an angle so that from the driveway, you could see most of the back deck. That meant the camera on the pole could, too.

So not only was my hat not going to retrieve itself, but now we also had to do something about that damned security camera. I just hoped it wasn't the really fancy kind that automatically uploaded to the internet at regular intervals.

Actually, I hoped it was the kind that broke, and nobody noticed, but that was too much to hope for. Ellie turned and started bushwhacking through tall weeds again, making her way . . .

Well, I couldn't tell where she was making it, because she was so quiet about it, and also in the dark I lost my bearings somehow. I stood immobilized in the chilly, pine-smelling darkness, not even able to see my foot in front of me.

If it even was in front of me, I couldn't be sure. But then, all at once, like a cartoon lightning bolt . . .

"Ellie, wait!" I dug in my pocket until my fingers found . . . *there.*

It was the key-chain flashlight that Ellie had found and given to me in Fairway's kitchen. When I snapped it on, a beam of very white light shone out of it.

Ellie's face popped from among the saplings and brambles. "What are you doing? Come on. We've got to get in there," she called.

Her face in the gloom looked grimly determined. I was happy to see this, since this errand was starting to look like that was what it would take, along with enough crazy to stuff a mattress, with plenty left over.

"Quit fooling around with that thing and come on. We're almost to the deck," she said.

This time no sliding glass doors were helpfully left open, of course, but I wasn't about to leave my hat inside on that account. There was a side door the security camera couldn't see, but the lock on that was a key-card contraption, so high tech I didn't even know how to think about defeating it.

The place had no cellar door that might somehow offer entry, just a blank steel panel, which I thought must open only from the inside. The place did have windows, but the ones around back were too high off the ground to reach without a ladder, and the front ones were that glass brick stuff and didn't open at all, that I could see.

That left just one option. We stayed away from the out-front security camera's view, and Ellie stood at the foot of the deck steps so she could alert me in case anyone showed up.

Not that I knew what the heck I would do if that happened, but at least I had made it back up onto the deck without incident.

"Now what?" Ellie said quietly from below.

I didn't reply, just took a deep breath of the chilly night air. Then, imitating something I'd seen someone do once in a movie—and yes, by then I really was that desperate—I pulled my sweatshirt's hood up, laced my fingers behind my neck, and brought both my elbows forward in front of my face.

Finally, I planted my feet and aimed my shoulder at the glass door. Secretly I'd always wondered what doing this would feel like, and now I imagined it fully, preparatory to really doing it: hurling myself at the door, feeling it bow inward, then crack and give way, sending me tumbling onto the (I hoped) soft carpeting inside. . . .

"Jake!" It was Ellie's voice, no longer coming from the foot of the steps. "Don't . . . Jake. What are you *doing?* Come down here. You've got to see—"

Drat. But I couldn't ignore the urgency in her voice. "What?" I groused, hurrying back down to where she stood waiting for me.

"Look!" She pointed up, aiming her flashlight. "A window!"

"Uh-huh," I agreed unenthusiastically. It was a window, all right, but the way that the house stood, built into the back of the hill the way it was, meant the windows at the rear of the structure were too high off the ground to climb through without a ladder.

And we didn't have a ladder. I could see, though, how doing it this way could eliminate the breaking-and-entering portion of the program.

Or the breaking part, anyway.

Ellie's lips tightened. "We're getting in there," she uttered determinedly. "Come with me."

She led me across the uneven ground, through the tangled weeds and impenetrable-feeling darkness, back to the Rubbermaid shed we'd seen earlier, and I must say she was a dab hand with that flashlight. I twisted my ankle only once.

But it was worth it. While I waited, she yanked open the shed's thick rubber door and waved the flash around inside. Rakes, a garden cart, two big trash cans, and a large red lawn tractor with a cart on a trailer hitch behind it filled the space almost entirely. But a metal ladder hung on the shed's rear wall . . . or was that another door?

No matter. Ellie squeezed her way between the tractor and the trash cans, climbed over the cart, and lifted the ladder. She managed to pass one end out to me before scrambling out with the other end in her hands.

"Now *this*," she pronounced, "is an entry method."

Right, and it was a neck-breaking method, too. But I had to admit that in the "less likely to land me in jail" department, it was probably an improvement. If we did it right, no one would ever even know we'd been there.

And if I didn't break my neck, of course. Once we'd carried the ladder to the house and positioned it under the high window, I started up before my fear of heights could talk me out of it, and at first, it was fine.

Then I put my foot on the second rung, and the third. *Yeeks.* The ladder felt solid, and Ellie stood below me, silently encouraging. But dizziness and panic swept through me, nevertheless.

Fourth rung. Fifth. *Don't stop,* I instructed myself. *Just do this and get it over with.*

Finally, I reached the window. It was a vinyl replacement window, the kind some people said that I should put into my old house to replace the two-hundred-year-old wooden ones it had now.

Not people I ever wanted to see again, by the way, but back to the ladder.

"Ellie?" I called down. "Hold the ladder. Hang on to it."

I wished somebody would hang on to me. But that wasn't going to happen, so I loosened my death grip on the ladder's top rung, then stepped up until I was standing on the second rung from the top.

Where you are not supposed to stand. But, heck, I wasn't supposed to be climbing in a dead guy's window, either. A little safety-rule breaking was nothing compared to the felonies I was about to commit.

The window was unlocked. I'd figured it would be. What I hadn't figured on was how narrow it was.

Narrower than me, I suspected. But in for a penny and all that. I raised the sash and stuck my head through into a large bathroom whose glowing night-light showed white tiles.

Not, alas, soft carpet. But I got my shoulders through, and then the upper part of my body, all the way to my . . .

"Jake?" Ellie's voice. "What's going on? Are you all right?"

No, I was not all right. I was stuck was what I was. My hips were jammed into the opening and wouldn't move forward.

Or backward. I couldn't get back out of the window opening, either. But maybe if I pushed harder, I thought, stepping up onto the ladder's top rung.

That being the one that you *really* shouldn't stand on, and in the next fraction of a second, I learned why: my feet pushed the ladder, and my body didn't move.

But the ladder did, toppling away backward and falling past Ellie downhill into the darkness thick with trees and undergrowth.

"Hey," I said quietly into the bathroom's dim silence. Half my body hung over the tiled floor; the other half out the window.

"Jake?" Ellie called up to me in alarm.

I waggled my feet to show that at least I was alive.

Then, in an effort to stay that way, I wormed, squirmed, shimmied, and squinched through that damned window opening, shoving against the inside wall with my elbows until at last I got hold of a towel rack mounted between the bathtub and the vanity cabinet.

The rack promptly pulled out of the wall when I hauled on it, but in the moments before it let go entirely, I managed to yank myself the rest of the way in. Then I hotfooted it down a dark hallway to where I thought the deck and the sliding glass door would be.

They were, and Ellie had already reached the

deck. I unlocked the door and slid it open; she stepped inside.

"Wow," she exhaled, meaning the ladder-and-window trick I'd just pulled off.

"Yeah," I said, feeling like I'd had at least an inch of flesh scraped off each hip. Also, I was pretty sure those hard bathroom tiles had loosened a front tooth.

But I didn't want to dwell on it. "Let's just get this over with," I said as we began exploring the house.

A few night-lights plugged into the baseboards showed the red velour sofa, in the gloom as dark as blood; the leather recliner, like some big animal crouching; and the big-screen TV, flanked on one side by the dark rectangle of a doorway. The air in here had a faint ozone smell, like the inside of an electronics store, but at least it smelled clean.

In the kitchen I found a pair of unused rubber gloves under the sink and another flashlight in a drawer. I tucked the gloves in my pants pocket. Maybe I wouldn't need them, but maybe I would.

The doorway by the wall-mounted TV led to the bedrooms and the guest bath, which was the one I'd fallen into. At the end of the hall, a room was set up for an office, with a desk, a laptop computer, and a security-monitor screen just like the one I'd seen at Choco's.

But this screen was black, and the whole

system was unplugged. It was where the video from the security camera out front was supposed to be viewed, but with the cables and wires all still stuffed into clear factory-wrapped packages, it looked as if none ever had been.

I straightened, with a sigh of relief, savoring the first bit of good luck we'd had for a while. Nobody was going to see Ellie or me on that security monitor, because it hadn't recorded us. Fairway had gotten the camera mounted, I guessed, then had never got around to setting up the rest of the system.

"Jake?" Ellie appeared in the doorway's gloom. "I found your hat." She held it up, a pink ball cap that everyone in town had seen me wearing.

Relief flooded me.

"But listen," she added, "the lights just went on down in Dory and Babs's house. I can see them through the trees."

I glanced around once more; now that we were in here, I didn't want to miss anything. "Don't worry. We're not going to be here very much—"

But then it hit me.

"I'm going down there," said Ellie, who'd already realized that our car was in the driveway, clearly visible. "I'll tell Dory I came out here to check on her and see if she'd heard anything from Babs. Or I'll tell both of them, if Babs is there, too."

"Okay. I'll just be a minute," I said distractedly,

and when she was gone, I made sure everything in the office was exactly the way I'd found it, then had another look through the house.

The air still smelled metallic, like the taste of an old fork. I wondered why and was about to snoop further, but then it occurred to me that when Ellie came back here, Dory Sloan might be with her.

So instead, on the theory that you never know what foolish detail is going to trip you up, I returned the rubber gloves to their place in the cabinet under the sink, and it was while I was stuffing them in that I glimpsed something else, shoved all the way to the back.

It was the corner of a manila envelope that had been wedged up behind the sink's underside but then had slid down a little. I grabbed the envelope, flattened it, and stuffed it into the front of my hoodie.

Now the right thing was for me to get back to the car, so I'd be there and ready with a plausible story in case Dory Sloan happened to show up. So I scrammed out of there, and I'd just gotten into Ellie's car when a set of headlights blazed in the rearview mirror.

Of course, my heart didn't literally leap into my throat, but it did a very impressive warm-up jump. Luckily, I was already behind the wheel, and the keys were in the ignition. I'd thought that any minute Ellie would arrive, jump in, and we'd be out of here in a jiffy.

But now not so much. I waited until the approaching headlights reached a place where the driveway curved sharply. When the lights vanished around it, I started Ellie's car and dropped it into reverse, then backed off the driveway and bumped over a low embankment into the brush alongside. In the darkness I hoped that was good enough.

Then I turned the key off and waited to find out, hoping we'd be able to get the car back up out of the thicket once our visitor had gone.

The headlights brightened again, coming out of the driveway's curve. Next came the car. A cherry beacon gleamed dimly from the car's dashboard as the Eastport Police emblem with the sunrise design on the door glided by.

It was Bob Arnold's squad car. His taillights dimmed, went out. He was right in front of Fairway's house, and any minute now, Ellie would appear. She would be wondering where I'd gotten to, probably, and would have, I hoped, the good sense not to say anything to Bob about it.

Because there was only one thing I could think of to get us out of this pickle without him finding out what we'd been up to. But I still wasn't sure I'd be able to drive Ellie's car back up out of the thicket I'd hastily plunged rearward into.

Might as well find out. I started the car, put it in gear, and eased forward. But halfway up the embankment, the tires spun.

I let the car roll back, hit the gas, and shot straight ahead. But it still wasn't enough, and the next thing I heard was the rear bumper burying itself in the thicket again.

And I was running out of time. By now up in the driveway Bob Arnold would've likely gotten out of the squad car. But unless Ellie came out at just the wrong time, he'd see nothing amiss, and probably he'd just go on around and come right back out again.

I had to get out of this ditch first, so I could appear to be just now arriving. Dropped Ellie off for a social call, came back to pick her up was going to be my story, but it wouldn't work if I also had to explain getting stuck in this ditch backward.

In desperation, I remembered a thing I'd seen Wade do once. He'd been stuck in the mud that had collected in a little valley between two small hills at the boat launch on Deep Cove. He'd had four-wheel drive then, and I didn't now, but what the heck? My goose was cooked, anyway, probably, so why not try?

Come on, come on . . . I stomped the gas pedal while in reverse, shot back fast, and hit the bushes behind me like a gymnast hits a trampoline.

Sproing! The bushes bent backward, then flew forward again while I jammed the car into drive. The instant I felt the springy saplings and branches giving me the tiniest push—because please, dear God, that was all I needed—I hit the gas pedal so hard that my head flew back and bounced off the headrest twice.

Seeing stars, I swung the wheel blindly when I felt the front tires bumping up over the embankment and onto the driveway. The car's rear end came around cooperatively. Then, once I'd gotten my heart rate a little more under control and a reasonably calm expression slapped onto my face, I drove Ellie's car back toward Fairway's house.

Bob hadn't come back out yet. That meant he'd found something that interested him, probably. And *that* meant somehow convincing him that whatever it was, we'd had nothing to do with it.

But it was likelier that Bob would get the truth out of us—that we'd been snooping, meddling, trespassing. . . . *Time to face the music.*

I just hoped it didn't end up being my swan song.

In front of the low, modern-looking structure that was Fairway's house—for one thing, that glass brick was a complete nonstarter, I'd decided—Ellie leaned on the squad car's door, talking through the open driver's-side window with Bob Arnold, who sat behind the wheel.

They looked over in surprise when I rolled in, Ellie shielding her eyes with her hand. I doused the headlights and got out.

"Sorry to get back so late," I told Ellie as I approached. "I was looking at the stars."

From me, an excuse like that would arouse less of Bob Arnold's suspicion than a sensible one, or so I hoped.

"Were you waiting very long?" I added, and Ellie, so quick on the uptake that it's a wonder her brain doesn't get whiplash, caught on at once.

"No, I'm fine," she said with an easy smile. "I was just telling Bob that I went to visit Dory, to make sure she's doing okay."

Ellie is a good and decent person, and when a situation requires it, she is also the most convincing liar I have ever met. What nails it is the simplicity of her expression, so transparent you could practically read through it.

But Bob, of course, knew this, too. "That was nice of you," Bob said approvingly, then eyed me. "You didn't go along?"

I summoned an "aw, shucks" shrug. "We didn't want to make her feel overwhelmed."

Bob nodded, looking past me. "There's some branches or something stuck under your car," he pointed out to Ellie.

I turned quickly to her. "Oh, I'm so sorry. I pulled off the road, like I said, to get out and look up at the stars, and I must've driven over some . . ."

Yeah, I'd driven over some branches, all right. And if it weren't for Wade's winter-driving trick,

I'd still be stuck in them. Meanwhile, I kept thinking about Bob going by, looking neither to the right nor the left.

Bob always looked to the right and the left, scanning for things that pinged his experienced-cop alarms. Also, his peripheral vision was so good, he could practically see the thinning hair on the back of his own head.

And yet he hadn't spotted me.

Ellie grabbed my arm. "Never mind, we'll pull the branches out when we get where we can see better. Come on, though. Dory's upset, and just talking with her took the starch out of me. I want to go home and put my feet up."

"But . . ." I tried to think of a way to stall. Leaving Bob here alone could be a recipe for disaster if he talked to Dory and her report didn't match Ellie's.

Luckily, he was parked so that he had to drive out before we could. I watched him go while Ellie dragged a birch sapling from under the car and flung it away.

Then we drove home, exhausted.

"Dory say anything?" I managed.

Ellie shook her head. "No word from Babs. Dory's packing up the art fair stuff, but she doesn't know what she'll do after that."

In downtown Eastport, the sidewalks were pretty well all rolled up, not a car in a parking space or a pedestrian on the street, and nothing moved in the boat basin but small waves slopping the seaweed on the granite riprap.

"Meanwhile, Dory's not very happy with us," Ellie said suddenly.

It was one of Eastport's charms, that a person could be alone in it. Bella said that was why some people liked it here so much, that not feeling crowded let their real personalities bloom.

Like I said, Bella was no fool. But seeing the town now, still and silent under a sliver of moon, made me feel very lonely indeed.

"Why not?" I asked finally. "Why is Dory not happy?"

Ellie pulled up in front of my house and turned to me. "Because I let her know I thought that Babs might have killed Fairway herself, that, in general, that's why people run, because they've done something they can't face, so they're letting someone else take the blame."

I blinked at her. "Whoa. Not that you're wrong. I've thought it, too. But . . ."

But how would Babs have gotten the gun? For that matter, how had anyone gotten it? I couldn't figure that part out however hard I puzzled over it.

"There are a lot of problems with the idea," I said finally, "and they start with motive. But they don't end there."

Ellie nodded, looking down at her hands on the steering wheel. "I know," she said disconsolately.

Then she looked up at that sliver of moon, hanging over us like a thin, curved blade. "I'm just tired. Tomorrow at the Moose, okay?"

To talk about all that had happened, she meant, and about what we'd do next. Probably her new lawyer would have called by then, too.

"Be there or be square," I responded lightly, and she managed a smile, but as she pulled away, I saw it fade to a line of worry.

Inside, the house was quiet except for the hollow tick of the old grandfather clock in the hall. I pulled out the manila envelope from beneath Fairway's kitchen sink, but when I opened it and looked at the pages inside the lines and columns of numbers swam blurrily before my eyes.

Oh, great, I thought, so exhausted by now that the idea of cataracts, glaucoma, or some other, even worse vision trouble that was (a) incurable, (b) undiagnosable, and (c) probably fatal suddenly seemed entirely reasonable to me.

Speaking of undiagnosable, I didn't like recalling Bob Arnold's unexpected arrival out at Fairway's place, either, or that odd metallic twang in the air inside Fairway's house.

Most of all, though, I didn't like knowing that Bob had seen me on his way in, and if he hadn't, he'd certainly seen muddy tire tracks in the embankment where I'd gone over it.

But he hadn't said anything about it, and that

made me nervous. The whole episode, in fact, felt worrisomely unfinished, as if the other shoe hadn't dropped.

It wasn't until later, after I'd gone to bed and lain awake for a few hours, that I sat up wide eyed, wondering suddenly what it was that had brought Bob Arnold out to Brad Fairway's house so late at night in the first place.

Dawn was breaking when I made my way downstairs, pearl-pink light brightening the windows and the house so silent that it seemed to be holding its breath. In the kitchen I started the coffeemaker and got the woodstove going. Outside, tangled forsythia branches formed a thin screen through which the back lawn showed emerald green.

I took my coffee to the dining room and set it beside the manila envelope from Fairway's place on the dining room table. My dad's canvas duffel bag was there, too, full to overflowing. I moved it aside.

Then, after only a few moments, familiar footsteps came padding down the stairs, and the *swish-swish* of Bella's quilted robe whispered down the hall.

Finally, with her own mug cupped in her hands, she joined me.

"Morning," she uttered, not sitting down.

"Mmm," I replied, looking up from the columns

of numbers. Then: "Bella, I'm really sorry," I said, gesturing sideways at the overstuffed duffel bag, "but I'm just not sure I'm going to be able to persuade Dad not to move to—"

"Never mind," she said quietly, stopping me. "It'll be all right."

She began poking around in my dad's bag. "You'd think he never packed for himself before. I suppose I'll have to find some bags for myself, too. And a few cardboard boxes."

I'd known Bella for years, and I could tell from her voice that this was no reverse psychology maneuver. She meant it this time.

"He told you why?" I asked, knowing he must have. It was the only thing that could've convinced her, the idea that their going to live somewhere else would make life better for us, cheaper, easier.

That I would no more sell my beloved old house than I would eat my own foot was an idea that hadn't occurred to him, apparently. But saying that to Bella now would only make her feel more confused.

"You just let me know how I can help," I told Bella, getting up and putting my arm around her skinny, robe-clad shoulders.

"Thank you," she sighed. Then, leaning against me, she said, "We've been together a long time, you and I."

She smelled like witch hazel. "That we have,"

I agreed. She'd been my housekeeper, then my stepmother. And now, in addition to both those things, we were friends.

She pulled away suddenly. "Well. I can't be standing here staring out the window all day, can I?" she asked a little too briskly.

Then she bustled back out to the kitchen. I heard the woodstove's door get clankingly opened, then a crackle and pop as she shoved in a stick of the firewood that Ellie's husband, George, had brought us the previous winter.

So much for a quiet place to resume my examination of that envelope's contents. Carrying my now-cooled mug of coffee, I tried the living room, where, to my not entirely complete surprise, I found Sam asleep on the couch.

I thought about waking him, but now my dad was coming downstairs, too, so unless I wanted to reread those pages in the bathroom, my opportunity had vanished for now.

Meanwhile, Sam hadn't spent a night in this house for a couple of years, not since he and his own young family had moved into the place they'd rented on the other side of town.

But now here he was, which to me meant that something was going on over there at the cute little cottage with my daughter-in-law and grandchildren in it. And perhaps recent events had put me in a too-pessimistic mood, but I doubted it was anything good.

Nine

"Bob Arnold is onto us," I told Ellie later that morning, when I got down to the Chocolate Moose.

It was just eight o'clock, too early to open, but I knew she'd be there, probably working on the chocolate marshmallow pie. And sure enough, the worktable in the kitchen was already littered with a lot of ingredients that I recognized: cocoa powder, chocolate chips, some chocolate syrup, et cetera.

There was even a bottle of chocolate liqueur; I gathered that the obstacle now was getting the pie filling to taste chocolaty enough. Marshmallows do tend to taste overwhelmingly like themselves, after all, no matter what.

"Ellie, did you hear what I just said?"

Even a truly generous topping of chocolate curls, followed by a quick run under the broiler, hadn't done the trick, I saw by the way she looked up from the taste test she was doing.

Grimacing, she dumped the pie into the trash, which meant it was too awful even to give away. Then she turned to me.

"I heard you. And I wondered about it myself, that he'd swallow a story about paying a social call so late at night. But if Bob wanted to jump all over us about something, don't you think he'd have done it on the spot?"

She rinsed her hands, then took a sip of coffee to do the same for the inside of her mouth. "Instead, he seemed as meek as a lamb."

When she pulled off her apron smock, I saw that she was dressed for a normal day, in light khaki pants and a pink three-quarter-sleeved leotard top with a loose black T-shirt over it. The shirt's front read BOOK CLUB in pink capital letters; the club's rules were listed on the back, but of course she never talked about those.

"So why do you think he knows what we were doing?" she queried, pouring coffee for herself.

"I'm not sure," I said, "but for one thing, he didn't give us an ounce of side-eye, did he? No suspicious 'What are you doing here?' questions, and not a bit of skepticism about our story." I took a breath. "Now, does that sound like Bob?"

It didn't, and Ellie knew it.

"He's just different lately," I said.

He missed his ex-wife and his daughter, I knew that much. And he didn't at all like Ellie being in the crosshairs of the law. That went without saying. But Bob didn't talk a whole lot about his feelings, so I knew little more.

"Well, I guess we'll find out why sooner or later," said Ellie, sitting down at a café table with her coffee, a pencil, and a sheet of lined notebook paper. "Okay, now," she said. "Buttery shortbread crust, check."

And that in a nutshell was Ellie: maybe the cops would be coming for her later, but she'd done what she could about it, and now she had a different task to complete. I swear, if the angel Gabriel showed up with a big horn, she'd say, "Wait a minute, please," then ask if I could stay back with her, too, because we had baking to finish.

Following her example, I got a block of semisweet chocolate out of the cooler and began shaving more curls from it with a vegetable peeler. Except for marshmallow pie, there's hardly any baking disaster that can't be repaired by piling on enough chocolate curls.

"What about a dark chocolate mousse?" I said idly a few minutes later. The idea had just popped into my head. "For pie filling."

She looked up. "That's perfect. Why didn't I think of that?" She scrawled on the notebook paper. "Okay, we've got the crust, the filling, and the marshmallows nailed down. Now something on top."

"A pair of tweezers to pick off the marsh-mallows?" I suggested, earning myself a look of exasperation from Ellie.

Then I put down the vegetable peeler. "Ellie, do you remember the guy Babs was talking to at the art fair? She seemed kind of happy to see him, and he was . . ."

"Not so happy," she finished for me. "But he was showing her something on his phone, right? Something animated, like a cartoon? Or at least the colors were moving."

He'd been colorful, as well: the corn-silk-pale hair, that black felt hat with the ribbon of silver medallions, the pipestem necklace.

"I'd really like to know who that was," I said, and it turned out to be "your wish is my command" day. Ellie dug her phone out of her bag immediately and punched in a number.

"Harriet? Hi. I was hoping you'd be the one who answered. This is Ellie White down at the Moose."

Pleasantries followed.

Then: "So, listen, the tall, slender guy . . . ? He wears a black hat, silver medallions. Comes to town occasionally?"

She listened.

"That's right, with the long blond hair. Looks like he irons it. Do you happen to know who that is?"

More listening.

Then: "Leo Montaine? That's his name? Thanks, Harriet. I was sure you'd know."

But of course she'd known. Harriet Stone had been Eastport's city clerk for going on twenty-five years and knew everything. Ellie had been on the school board with her.

"You have a nice day, too, dear," said Ellie. *Dee-yah*, the Maine way of saying it.

205

She put the phone away. "He's an electronic installation artist, whatever that is. Lives at the end of Toll Bridge Road."

Nodding, I put the chocolate block and the pile of shavings I'd made into a plastic container and put the container back into the cooler.

"I don't suppose it would hurt to take a ride out there, see if he's home," I said, because for one thing, if we didn't come up with something soon, Ellie was screwed. You should excuse the expression.

"Bob Arnold did call me this morning," she said when we'd gotten outside and locked the door. "But not about last night."

My heart sank. She hadn't wanted to tell me this, or she'd have said it sooner, and there was only one other topic that he'd have called to discuss so early in the day.

We got into her car. "Today's the day," she said, closing the driver's-side door. "He said they're coming for me this afternoon."

The homicide detectives, she meant, possibly even with an arrest warrant. We started up Washington Street, past the arts center and the Full Gospel church.

"Have you talked to George?" I asked. If she hadn't, all this was going to come as an awful surprise.

She nodded, negotiating the turn onto Route 190. "Yes, and the lawyer from Portland who's handling my case got in touch with him late last night, too. I asked him to."

So now George was up to speed, and most likely hopping mad. The idea that anyone had accused Ellie of anything, much less of bloody murder, must have infuriated him.

"We will," Ellie added calmly, "discuss it again when George gets home from Bangor."

No kidding. I could imagine George trying to come to grips with the whole situation. He was a complete prince, but he was not by any means an analytical sort of a person. In defense of his family, he was apt to punch first and ask questions later.

We passed the airport on one side of Route 190 and Seaview Campground on the other. Then beyond Carrying Place Cove, Ellie slowed for the turn onto Toll Bridge Road and went on past the DEAD END sign.

The road went by a rail-fenced pasture with llamas in it. Chewing their cud, the long-necked, doe-eyed creatures watched us go by. After that the road narrowed, birches and maples creeping nearer on each side, until we reached a paved driveway that led in among the trees.

No power line running in, though. No mailbox, either. The only evidence of human habitation here at all was that beautifully paved blacktop. I imagined the power line must be buried.

Sitting there in the silence, we took deep

breaths in unison. Then Ellie pulled into the driveway and kept on going.

"Do you really think Bob Arnold knows what we were doing last night?" she asked. "That instead of visiting Dory, we were in Fairway's house, snooping around?"

The blacktop curved among spindly young evergreens growing between old tree stumps and scattered wood-chip heaps, evidence of a lumber harvest that must have happened decades ago. Then the vegetation thickened again.

"Why else would he be out there that late?" I asked. "He knows us, so he knew we wouldn't give up and do nothing." Two quail flew up startledly as we came upon them. "He'd been cruising around town, keeping an eye out for us, I'll bet," I said.

Outside my open car window, a woodpecker slammed his long beak into the bark of a dead tree. The bird's red head blurred as he pecked for an insect, imagining, I supposed, that if he just punched himself in the nose hard enough, he would find it.

Yeah, I know the feeling, I thought at the woodpecker as we went by, passing between a pair of garden plots full of vegetables: peas, beans, tomatoes, salad greens, and so on.

At last, Ellie pulled over and parked in front of a new-looking two-car garage. Parked outside it was a lawn tractor hitched to a small open trailer, with garden tools on the trailer.

She turned the car off. It was a beautiful summer morning, with a light breeze moving the smell of salt water and flowers gently around.

"You wanted to know about George's reaction," Ellie said into the silence. Obviously, she'd been thinking about this. "To what the lawyer said, what's going to happen, and so on."

I did want to know, but I was almost afraid to hear. What if he was furious at Ellie and nobody else? What if . . .

She drew in another deep breath. "He said he was on my side and not to forget that no matter what happened, we'd do whatever we had to *together* to get this all straightened out and get past it."

Like I said, no analysis, just a prince among men. I opened the car door and swung my legs out into the sunshine.

The blacktop narrowed to a path leading past newly planted apple saplings. Next came half barrels full of black loam with purple and yellow pansies in them. Beyond a bed of old-fashioned blue irises gave off fruity perfume.

"Somebody's a gardener," Ellie commented as we ducked under a trellis, and maybe it was the sunshine slanting between the woven strips that penetrated my brain, suddenly lighting up brain cells.

"Ellie." The footpath now wound between perennial beds: poppies, hostas, echinacea.

Bees hummed among the blooms. "Ellie, there's something I forgot to tell you," I said, and then I filled her in on the manila envelope I'd taken from Fairway's.

"I haven't fully examined what's in it yet, but I know there's a lot of numbers. Pages and pages of them, handwritten, that look like purchase and sales records."

"So?" At last, the outlines of a house showed between thick stands of raspberry bushes studded with baby berries.

"It means maybe he didn't want the numbers in his computer," I went on. "Because you never know where a computer file might end up, but in case of an investigation, you can always burn paper, you know?"

The handwritten records were still going to need studying. Unlabeled columns of numbers don't clarify themselves, but the patterns in them can. The thought made me want to go home and examine them immediately, but now we were past the raspberries, and the house we'd been seeking showed clearly and in all its lofty—very lofty—glory.

Ellie's mouth fell open at the sight of it. Mine too. The house seemed to be built of sticks, the kind that broke off dry branches that had fallen from trees.

"Jake?" she said softly, staring up.

"Yeah," I replied. There must have been

thousands and thousands of rough wooden pieces, ranging from tiny to forearm sized: horizontal ones for siding, fat upright tree trunks on either side of the door, long, dark gray bark strips framing the windows. Around the roof's eaves, slender willow whips looped in tight spiral patterns.

Also, it was a tree house. Trees, rather. The structure's bottom edges, which ordinarily would've sat on a foundation, hovered at least twenty feet up. Under it bulked huge steel beams, which were bolted to the trunks of four massive, sturdy-looking, and very much alive old oak trees.

"How . . . creative," Ellie said. On the ground to the left of the treehouse stood a large metal Quonset building, with its bay doors slid open. From inside stared the blank gray screens of televisions, dozens of them, ranging from wall-sized behemoths to tiny desktop displays.

I left Ellie still gazing and went around the support trees to where a flagstone patio held a bentwood rocker with floral cushions, a low wicker table with a glass jug of purple coneflowers on it, and a trio of Adirondack chairs painted green.

Blue canvas chair pads were on the Adirondack chairs. No people, though, or no sign of them, and when I returned to where Ellie still stood, I realized what else I hadn't seen. The house had no front stairs, only a completely ridiculous rope ladder dangling uninvitingly from two stout posts.

"Oh, no," I murmured, backing away. But Ellie did no such thing. Monkeys in the jungle had nothing on her when it came to agility, and she was good in the fearlessness department, too.

"Here goes," she uttered, then scampered straight up the rope ladder to the door up there and knocked on it.

Nothing. From a nearby tree came the woodpecker's answering rat-a-tat, as if in imitation. Then the door opened, and a man came out.

"Yes?" he asked pleasantly, his glance flicking from Ellie down to me and back up again.

He was the fellow we'd seen with Babs Littrell at the art fair, all right: tall, wiry thin, with pale blue eyes whose piercing color I could see even from down here. His straight whiteish-blond hair hung down past the short sleeves of the black Grateful Dead T-shirt he wore over faded jeans.

"Can I help you?" he asked, trying again, his expression now quizzical.

Still on the ground, I considered the rope ladder again. Then, because I certainly wasn't going to stay down here, and there didn't seem to be any other choice, I started up it.

Everything went fine until I got to the fourth rung. Then the whole thing started to swing, twist, turn, and perform other maneuvers sure to terrify my wits out, and have I mentioned that I dislike heights?

And ladders. But *never mind that, Jake. Just*

reach up and grab. Pull. And . . . here comes the hard part . . . Take a step.

And then another one, whereupon somehow the next rung wasn't there when I put my foot down on it. Fright bloomed in my brain and radiated outward. A feeling of actually leaving my body and being out of control, perhaps permanently, made me believe I would grab for thin air, then step into it.

From above, I heard Ellie introducing us both. I supposed that the frantic shifting of the rope loops collared around the top posts communicated where I still was fairly clearly. But . . .

"Being brave," I'd once heard Ellie say, "doesn't mean not doing it. It means doing it, anyway."

And drat her commonsense pronouncements, anyway, I thought, but also, *Step. Pull. Step. Repeat.*

The key to the whole process was ignoring my brain's input. Keeping it physical let me stick to the important thing: not falling. When at last my head rose above porch level, Leo Montaine's blue eyes widened bemusedly.

Yeah, bemuse this, I thought grouchily as I hauled myself up the rest of the way onto the narrow porch. What was this place, anyway, a home for retired circus performers?

"We're here about Babs Littrell," Ellie said while I composed myself as best I could. "She's missing. We hope you can help."

A worried look passed across his face as he

stepped back. The tall black hat with the silver-medallion hatband hung in the hall behind him.

"You'd better come in," he said.

The tree house was all cool, dim rooms in the front part, where the oak trees' leaves shaded it, and all bright sunshine in the back half. Looking around as Montaine led us in, I thought those steel beams had their work cut out for them. The large room he brought us to, almost entirely walled with glass, must've weighed tons all by itself.

But it was lovely, a lush green hideaway in the sky. Big glossy-leafed plants in enormous clay pots, enough to revegetate a jungle, stood around looking healthy on the red-tiled floor. Bloom-heavy vines as thick as my wrist twined in crossbeams under the high ceiling.

"Have a seat," Montaine said, still looking troubled. "Can I offer you anything? Tea, sparkling water?"

The furniture was cushioned wicker, pleasantly comfy; the floor coverings were rattan; plus here and there was one of those worn-looking East Asian rugs that look like castoffs but cost a mint.

"Thank you," said Ellie. "I'd love a cup of tea." And I asked for some, too. Montaine pressed the palms of his slim hands together, then went off to make it.

When he was gone, I wandered to the windows, which offered a bird's-eye view of the backyard.

214

Ellie bent to examine the books on the bamboo-and-glass coffee table and in the adjacent bookcases.

"Ellie, come look at this."

Behind the metal Quonset building, not visible from the patio, was a large open tent of the kind that outdoor wedding ceremonies got held under. This one was screened on all sides by fabric netting in either black or dark blue. Through a folded-back section of it at the front of the tent, I glimpsed . . .

"More TVs," said Ellie.

"Lots more," I agreed. They were set up in a circle, with their screens all slightly angled, facing inward toward some kind of chair contraption at the circle's center.

"What is that? Some kind of torture device?" I said. I could never find anything worth watching on one TV; the idea of looking at so many at a time was mind numbing.

"That chair thing on the raised platform in the middle looks like it got salvaged from a carnival ride," Ellie observed.

A Siamese cat with crossed blue eyes, a sharply kinked tail, and a yowl like an ice pick jammed straight into my eardrum sprang out from behind a potted lemon tree, where he'd been lurking.

I'd have had a heart attack, but just then Montaine returned with the tea. "Here we are."

He set the tray down, did the necessaries, and

when we all had our steaming cups, he got down to business. "Now, tell me what's going on."

So I went through the whole thing for him, starting with Fairway's murder and ending with our inability to locate Babs Littrell, plus what our interest in it all was: Ellie's current position as prime suspect and her imminent peril.

"So you need to find 'who dun it,'" Montaine commented acutely when I was done, "and you think Babs might know something that could help."

The cat had returned; now it leapt up to settle in his lap, where he petted it absently.

"Babs is an old friend of mine." He frowned into his cup. "I worked with her on a collaborative art installation in Boston a few years ago. We've kept in touch."

The cat jumped down again.

"We toured the Northeast, put the whole show up and took it down in a different small museum every week. It was a good time. We got along well. I already knew she was one hell of an artist, and she turned out to be a real worker bee, too."

He finished off his tea. "Would you like to see it? The piece we toured? The whole thing's set up right down there."

He went to the windows, waved in the direction of the large screened tent with the TVs in it. "Babs had a fabric-in-motion part of the installation, but that's not here right now." Turning back to us, he added, "That's just my section of it in the tent. I'm making a few improvements."

All I wanted was to hear about Babs, with special emphasis on where she was right this minute. But I sensed an unspoken quid pro quo in the air: that for all his concern, he might be more forthcoming if we appreciated his art first.

Ellie thought so, too. I could tell by the look she shot me. And, anyway, I was curious about what this guy was up to. We followed him back through the shady part of the house and out the front door.

The porch, which I hadn't noticed much earlier, was perhaps three feet wide: narrow, in other words. The awful sucking sensation I always feel when I'm somewhere up high . . . well, it sucked.

At me. Which reminded me. *That ladder.* Trying to look casual, I glanced down at it, and it didn't quite smirk evilly back up at me.

Not quite. And while that ordinarily would've frightened me even more, now it made me mad. Ellie was in trouble, we were running out of time, and it was getting in the way, dammit.

Grimly I stalked to the edge of the porch and stood between the posts that the ladder hung from. Next, I did a quick one-eighty, turning my back on thin air, and grabbed the posts, one in each hand.

Then, ignoring the fright pulsing through me—*Hey, if she dies, she dies,* I thought a little wildly—I took a step backward and down with my right foot. The thin air I felt tested my faith very strenuously until at last my sneaker's sole touched the thick braided rope of the second-from-the-top ladder rung.

But there I froze, looking up, because I didn't dare look down, hanging on, because I couldn't think of anything else to do. Or at all, actually. The Siamese walked over and looked over the porch's edge at me.

"Hi, cat," I croaked. "Got any tips on how to—"

The animal leapt abruptly from the porch to my head, ran down my back, and ended with his front claws sunk deeply into the seat of my pants. After that I'm not sure what he did, but when I dared to look down again, he was sitting below me in the grass, licking his paw.

Then a hornet and a couple of his friends drifted by ominously. After dive-bombing me warningly a few times, two of them lit, whisper light, on the backs of my hands.

Which, as you may remember, were what I was using to hang on to the ladder. I tried blowing them away, but they clung on stubbornly, until one of them stung me, and I began flailing while dropping like a stone.

Luckily, one of my wildly flapping hands hit a ladder rung and grabbed it. I don't remember the next part, but I'm sure it involved cursing plus rope burns. Then I was on the ground, mad, hornet stung, and embarrassed beyond belief at my clumsy performance.

But when the other two came down behind me, Ellie graceful and Montaine clumsy but efficient, neither of them seemed to have noticed anything amiss. Ellie even gave me an eyebrows-raised, silent *Way to go* look. It just goes to show, I guess, that things really can look very different on the outside from the way they feel on the inside.

The interior of the tent with the TVs in it was dim, like a movie theater. The space was much bigger than I'd guessed from outside, and the round, raised center platform wasn't as high as I'd thought when I'd glimpsed it from above.

"There you go," said Montaine. "Now, each of you take a seat up there."

The pair of seats centered on the platform were velveteen-covered movie-theater seats, mounted back-to-back, each seat facing outward, on a solid round metal disk. It moved slightly when I stepped onto it.

"So if Babs wanted to lie low for a while, where would she go?" I asked.

The chair's maroon velveteen was luxurious-feeling, and it was clean, smelling of recent upholstery shampooing. Ellie took the seat behind me.

Montaine looked up from a stack of computer components that he was fiddling with, all ranged out on a long folding table near where we'd come in. Heavy black wires snaked from the table to somewhere beneath us. Now the disk that our chairs were secured to thrummed, as if a small engine had begun running down there.

"She likes camping, oddly enough," Montaine answered a little distractedly. He poked at a keyboard a few more times. "Doesn't seem the type, but I know she likes going out camping alone when she's brainstorming a new project and needs to concentrate."

He eyed the keyboard, tapped a final few keys. "There, good to go."

As he spoke, the tent's drop cord–hung interior lights dimmed even further; somehow the fabric screening enclosing the whole structure stopped letting daylight in, as well.

So, pitch darkness. A hushed, expectant feeling. Then a dozen blank gray eyes opened, forming a large circle around us. They were the televisions, I realized, their screens full of fine gray static.

"I promise you that nothing bad will happen," Montaine said from the darkness beyond the screens.

And I promise you that if it does, something worse will happen right after that, I assured him silently.

The platform began turning, rotating me slowly past one blank gray TV screen after another. Only now they weren't gray and blank anymore. Uncertain shapes flashing colors as iridescent as birds' wings writhed, smokelike, on the screens. Next came patterns forming and dissolving, fantastic creatures, bizarre landscapes with unearthly skies boiling above them.

They couldn't be real, I knew, those fish—but were they fish?—swimming in an alien sea. It was just my brain trying to make sense of what my eyes were delivering to it.

But it felt real while it was happening. I'm not sure how much time passed until my chair slowed and glided smoothly to a stop.

At once Montaine was beside me, helping me to get up.

"Whoa," Ellie murmured from behind us. "That was . . . different."

Montaine's long, thin face opened in a delighted grin, and all at once he was no longer merely a tall, pale man with corn-silk hair and the fragile-looking build of a malnourished angel. He was an artist. I'd been skeptical, but now I could feel it. What I'd just experienced was . . . really something.

"Precisely the reaction I was hoping for," he pronounced, seeing my no doubt dazed expression and looking triumphant.

I blinked away static patterns dancing on my retinas. "How . . . how did you do that?"

Leo looked wise but still pleased as punch, like a kid whose remote-control lawn-mowing contraption has worked yet again.

"Some of it's proprietary," he informed me. "But without going into detail, it supplies random images, and the viewer's mind makes of them whatever it likes."

He waved at the table by the door. "I use the computer to control the displays on the screens, what they show and when. To some degree, I can predict the effects viewers get. If the chairs turn too fast, say, or if I've forgotten to turn the ambient light all the way down, then what you see can get . . . not nice."

He frowned briefly, perhaps remembering an experience of his own. Then, brightening again, he added, "But you're the real creator here. You're the artist, working with the materials you've been given. I'm the mechanic. A glorified computer nerd, really."

"Leo," I said, still dazed by the memory of those alien fish with their intelligent eyes and benevolent expressions, "you're a lot more than that. I just don't know quite what yet."

But now that I'd seen for myself where his head and his heart were at, I wanted even more to know what he thought of Babs Littrell.

So when we got back to the front of the house, where the gardens bloomed profusely and the bees just wanted pollen, not a stinging party—also we were not, I realized with relief, going back up that damned ladder—I asked him.

He frowned thoughtfully before replying. "Babs is smart," he said at last. "And like I said before, a hard worker. She makes her design business run like Swiss clockwork, and it's a good thing she does, too, because her art's not very commercial."

From behind me, where she crouched in the grass by the cross-eyed Siamese, Ellie piped up. "You mean it doesn't make money."

The cat allowed Ellie to pet it.

Leo's eyebrows rose. "But her commercial designs do," he replied. "The trouble is . . ." He paused, as if wondering whether to say the next thing. "She's got immigration problems," he finished finally. "She's been here lots longer than her visa allows. Now if she leaves the country, they won't let her in again."

Richie Perrone had said so, too. We walked between the gardens and under the arched trellis thickly covered with scarlet runner beans to Ellie's car, the cat trailing us, with its kinked tail switching.

"Why doesn't she renew it?" Ellie asked as she got behind the wheel. "Her visa."

"She tried. Got turned down. She'd stayed too long already. She would've had to leave the country and apply again."

I got into the passenger seat. That hornet had stung me hard, and the red, puffy welt on the back of my hand felt like World War III was being conducted inside it, but I was damned if I was going to say anything about it.

"And," Montaine went on, "it's not at all sure she'd be let in again, anyway. Seems the immigration folks think design meetings with American clients can be done online. But that's not how the high-end textile business works."

Not how any business worked, really, or at least not without a lot of technical help, which I gathered Babs Littrell also couldn't afford. "She doesn't have enough European business to stay afloat?"

"She did," said Leo. "It dropped off some when she came over here, though. Again, not enough personal attention." He shook his head ruefully. "Sometimes I think business types like dragging artists in for meetings just to show that they can, you know?"

He backed away from the car a few steps. "You get there, travel and so on, the expenses, or you go to a lot of trouble for a Zoom meeting, God help us."

The cat leapt up into his arms, nuzzled its blocky head against his chest.

"And then all they want to do," he went on, "is meddle with whatever you've given your life to, let you know they could do it much better than you." He took a breath. "If they only had time," he finished.

I thought about Montaine trying to demonstrate

his art to a bunch of suit-clad corporate board members and felt glad I wasn't an artist myself. But we were getting off track.

"So getting deported . . . ," I began as Ellie waited behind the wheel.

"Would just about ruin her," he finished. "She worried about it a lot. I went to the art fair to show her my plans for a new setup, but only because I'd promised to. I knew she'd ask me for another loan, and she did."

"What about Brad Fairway, the guy whose cottage she lives in? How'd she get hooked up with him?"

Montaine looked troubled. "I don't know. Met him briefly once at a gallery opening in Eastport. I didn't stick around. He's the guy who got killed?"

He rubbed the cat's head. "She'd mentioned a business deal she was thinking about doing with him, right around the time she moved into his place. But I never heard much else about him. Don't know how they met."

A new thought hit him. "I doubt she had any reason to harm him, though. And even if she did have, I really don't think she would. She has a temper, Babs does, but she's not a violent person."

He thought a moment. "I'll give you an example. When we were in Chicago, we ended up staying a few months so Babs could give classes and work on another big project she had going. But she still took the time to volunteer for an organization that helped troubled women."

Sunshine through his almost-white hair made a halo around his head. I didn't take it as a sign, but he sounded sincere.

"Very good of her," I agreed, trying to hide my disappointment. Maybe the risk of getting sent out of the country worried Babs, but I didn't see how that would make her want to murder Brad Fairway, or how past volunteering would stop her if she did want to.

And we didn't know any more about how to find her than we had when we'd arrived. Now we departed, after thanking Leo for his hospitality and getting his promise to call us if he might hear from Babs.

"Damn," I uttered as we backed out. "All that talk and exertion and we learned almost nothing."

I hadn't even found out why the guy lived in a tree. Then . . .

"Listen, we could still get you into Canada," I said as we passed the fenced llama pasture once again. The llamas had gathered around a feed trough and were chewing what was in it.

"Wade could take you," I said. "Or somebody from the boatyard could." I was only half-serious, but all I could hear in the back of my mind was time passing: *ticktock, ticktock.*

"No," she declared flatly. She'd thought about

this, it seemed. "I'm not going to run. I've talked about it with George, and we agree that if I did, I might as well just say I killed Fairway. That taking off would be tantamount to a confession."

Back in town, we drove past the fire station and the Little League baseball field. Volunteers were painting the dugouts, tidying the baselines, and touching up the advertising on the fences.

"Besides, what would I do once I got there?" she asked, but the answer was nothing, and we both knew it. Her whole life was here.

She pulled up in front of the Chocolate Moose and left the car running. "George and I are sitting down with Lee in a little while, to try to prepare her. As soon as he gets home."

For the sight of her mother being taken away by the police, Ellie meant. And for what might come after.

She bit her lower lip, then spoke again. "The lawyer told George and me that we should be prepared. If this all ever does get as far as a trial, we might need to appeal. The verdict, I mean."

Right, if it was "guilty." The very thought made Leo Montaine's nice herb tea do a couple of flip-flops in my midsection.

Then Bob Arnold drove by, lifting an index finger from the wheel as he passed and reminding me unhappily of his strange behavior out at Fairway's place the night before.

But right now, he was the least of my problems.

"Listen," I said, "if the state cops show up, you call your lawyer and then me, in that order. All right? Promise?"

Because I really couldn't bear the idea of not seeing her again before they took her.

"He said they'd call him first," Ellie replied, "before they show up. But I'll call you both if anything happens." She sighed. "If I can," she added, squaring her shoulders and lifting her chin.

She could face this, her posture proclaimed. She absolutely could face this and get through it. And, of course, going in for questioning wasn't a disaster by itself; there wasn't even any guarantee that she would be charged.

But there was also no way either of us could pretend any of this was a good thing. I hugged her hard for a moment across the car's center console, then got out swiftly and without tears. If she could do it, so could I, I thought miserably.

Once she was gone, I hadn't even finished unlocking the shop's front door when my cell phone rang. Inside, I dug around in my bag but didn't find it, even though I could still hear it. Finally, I fished it out of the bag's phone pocket, of all places, and pressed ANSWER with one hand while flipping on the light switches and the ceiling fan with the other.

Missing even part of a day of sales was most definitely not in our business plan, but maybe I could salvage the last hour, I thought as I put the phone to my ear.

"Hello? Darn." I squinted at the phone. I didn't recognize the caller's number, and by the time I got to it, the call had already gone to voice mail. Snapping on the credit card reader with my right thumb, I pressed CALLBACK on the phone with the left.

"Come on, come on . . ." Waiting, I poured cold coffee from the carafe and swallowed some. At last, the ringing stopped, but whoever answered said nothing.

"Hello? Can I help you?" I said.

The wordless reply was a raspy, hitching sound and then a *clunk* as, I thought, the phone on the other end got dropped.

"Who is this?" I demanded, ready to hang up. Now was *not* a fine time for a prank, I thought grumpily.

Then another sound came from the phone. *Meeowwrr.*

It was a cat. An *unhappy* cat.

And I was pretty sure I recognized its voice.

Ten

Well, I lit out of the Moose like my hat was on fire and my back end was catching, as Bella would've put it. Went up Water Street, past the WaCo Diner and the Old Sow, past the fountain in front of the redbrick Tides Institute building, finally past the War of 1812 cannon on the library's front lawn, and at last made a right turn onto Key Street.

On my way I passed Bob Arnold in the middle of a discussion with a fellow who seemed to think offering Bob his open beer was a good way out of a traffic stop. As I went by, I watched Bob smiling pleasantly at the fellow while unhitching his handcuffs from his duty belt. Bob was death on drinking and driving.

Next, because Ellie had dropped me off, so I was walking, I found out yet again that the Key Street hill never got less steep. Finally, I forced my quivering legs to sprint the last half block to my house, where I grabbed my own car keys from the hook by the back door and dashed back out the door again.

No other vehicles but mine were in the driveway, so I couldn't borrow one from Bella or Wade. That left only the Fiat, which had been behaving pretty well lately, but with the Fiat, that was no guarantee of anything.

Do not, I instructed the sports car silently as I got in, *screw this up.* In response, the little convertible snarled eagerly to life, as if it, too, were feeling urgent about something. Five minutes later I was rolling up Leo Montaine's driveway. I hopped out of the Fiat and scrambled under the lattice archway.

"Leo?" The tree house still loomed from its perch on the steel crossbeams, but the rope ladder was no problem this time. I still feared heights, but right then, I was more concerned about something else: why had a cat called me on the phone?

Or at least that was how I felt until I got about three-quarters of the way up, and that last quarter was a three-way tie between passing out, throwing up, and getting stung to death by those damned hornets, who apparently remembered me.

But I made it, and when I got there, I found the door unlocked. "Leo?"

No answer. The tall black hat with the silver-medallion hatband still hung in the hall.

"Hello?" I called, hurrying past rooms I hadn't looked into earlier, some filled with books in tall bookcases, others with cables, wires, and laptop computers in heaps on long folding tables. Beside them lay complex schematics neatly drawn on white architectural paper. "Leo? You here?"

At the back of the house, in the greenhouse

231

room, the cross-eyed Siamese cat peeked down from the rafters, surrounded by a tangle of tropical-looking vines thick enough for a Tarzan movie.

A phone lay on the tiled floor. I crossed to it and bent, meaning to pick it up. "Hey, cat," I said. "Where's—"

A low groan stopped me. From behind a wicker planter overflowing with ferns, the back of Leo Montaine's blond head rose and wavered.

Only now it wasn't so blond; bright blood soaked the pale hair. I grabbed his phone up off the floor, called 911, and babbled out the information.

"It's a tree house," I told the dispatcher. "They'll need the ladder truck to get up into—"

"Right, we've got notes to that effect at that address," the dispatcher said. Somewhere in the background a siren howled. "Building inspector made a note when permits got issued to build the place, and the note got passed to us."

And that in a nutshell is Eastport, not every time, but often enough.

"Was that for us? The siren I just heard pull out?"

"Nope. 'Nother call. Don't worry. They're on their way," said the dispatcher, then told me I could hang up.

Once I had, I knelt beside Leo and watched his eyes move jerkily back and forth underneath his bluish eyelids. He was out cold, but he was breathing, and his pulse was steady.

"Leo," I told him, "it's Jake Tiptree. There's been an accident. I've called for help."

Although *accident* wasn't the right word for what had happened, I already realized. Obviously, someone had clobbered Leo with a big clay pot that had held a dwarf lemon tree. Dark, rich-looking soil and broken plant material lay among the pot's shards.

"Ugh," he uttered, his eyelids fluttering, as he tried unsuccessfully to sit up. I pushed his chest very gently with my fingertips, and he lay down again, but now his eyes were all the way open, and he was looking around semi-alertly.

"Leo, who did this to you?" I asked.

He frowned painfully. "I don't remember. Someone else came after you and Ellie White were here, but . . ." He moved his head, winced. "Christ, did a truck hit me, or what?"

Engine sounds and voices outside said that the paramedics were already here. I got up as they trooped in, and they quickly ascertained that Leo had suffered a serious blunt-trauma head injury.

Then Bob Arnold showed up. Along with the ladder truck, the first responders had brought a bucket lift to get up and down from here in. He'd come up in that.

"Thought you'd be with Ellie," he said when he saw me.

"She's home with George and Lee, getting ready to be apprehended," I said. "Bob, couldn't you get the state cops to hold off for just one more day?"

A scowl creased his face. "Jake, I did everything but promise them my firstborn. Believe me, if Ellie didn't have a clean record and that sterling reputation of hers, a lot worse would've happened by now."

She'd have been arrested and charged, he meant, instead of just imminently being taken in for questioning.

"It's not the end of the world, you know," he said. "They want to talk to her, that's all."

"And if they don't like the answers, *then* they'll place her under arrest," I shot back. "And you just tell me, if what they *do* have fits their theory and what they *don't* have is another suspect—"

He held up a hand. "Yeah, no. I get it, Jake, okay? It's not good, and I'm not saying it is."

He looked around, taking in the shattered pottery and soil and Leo's blood on the tile floor. "This is a fine mess. Any idea what happened here?"

"Somebody hit him. He doesn't remember who. And before you ask, I have zero ideas about why I'm the one he called."

Or why the cat had, but I figured Bob didn't need to know about that.

Bob went to the windows and looked down. "What's that out there?"

I explained Montaine's art installation as best I could. Probably I made it sound like an amusement park ride for adults, which, come to think of it, wasn't a bad comparison.

"So you've been on that contraption? Or in it, or whatever?" he asked.

"Yes. Ellie and I came to see Leo out here earlier today. We hoped he might know where Babs Littrell would go to hide out, so we can find her and talk with her. But he didn't know."

"Mmph." He walked around the greenhouse room, glancing at the plants, the books, the furniture, and out the big windows again. When he was finished, he stopped and faced me.

"Look," he said. "I'm on your side, yours and Ellie's. Don't go thinking I'm not. But there are limits to what I can do." He gave me a hard stare. "Or," he added significantly, "what I can ignore."

And then he just stood there letting me draw my own conclusions. Almost certainly he was talking about running into us the night before at Brad Fairway's place; of course we'd been snooping, not visiting Dory like we'd said, and he knew it because he knew us. Also, he knew no one pays social calls at that hour of the night. But he still wasn't saying anything about it.

Finally, I said, "I should get back to the shop."

The paramedics had already put Leo on a stretcher and hustled him out. I heard the electric motor on the fire department's ladder truck whine as they lowered him to the ground.

"Bob?" I gestured toward the door. "I've got to—"

"Yeah, yeah," Bob said as the Siamese cat marched boldly up to him, its voice like a jab to the eardrum. Then it was in his arms and looking over his shoulder triumphantly at me.

"You going to take it?" I asked hopefully. Bob was a sucker for other people's animals, and I hoped he'd shelter this one temporarily, as he'd done for other local crime victims over the years.

Otherwise, I'd get stuck with it, and now wasn't a good time for a new pet. But . . .

"Nah," said Bob, putting the animal down. "Leo's got household help. Whoever it is comes every day, waters plants and so on."

So that was who took care of all these houseplants; probably Leo had help with the big gardens outside, too.

I glanced curiously at Bob. "And you know that how?"

"I overheard him talking about it in the post office the other morning," he explained, "saying that his gardening helper quit, so he was looking for someone new. Wanted to find someone before he left on a trip to visit his sister, but I don't know if he did."

The cat circled his ankles insistently, meowing hoarsely and twitching its kinked tail. "Don't worry. I'll make sure someone's coming so you get fed," he was telling it as I reached the hall.

But then I went back, pricked by a sudden suspicion and by my own complete, utter disbelief in what Sam would've called a coinky-dink.

"Bob?"

He looked up from petting the cat. He'd have had one of his own, but his daughter was allergic to them. Even though she was in Arizona with her mother, and Bob was here . . . Well, hope springs eternal, I guessed, was Bob's stance on the whole matter.

"Bob, what was the other siren? That pulled out around the time I'd have been on with the dispatcher?"

He looked blank momentarily. Then: "Oh. Yeah, lady fell and hit her head the other night. Today she fell over, unconscious, in the IGA."

I sighed inwardly, already sure that I knew who the lady must be. "Hadley Owens? Is she all right?"

He looked at me oddly, shrugging. "Gone to the hospital. I guess we'll find out."

"Yeah. Thanks," I said, and then before he could ask me how I'd known and why I cared, I left again, this time for good.

The afternoon was bright and calm; the emergency vehicles were all gone. Bob must've told them he'd deal with the rope ladder on the way down, because the bucket truck was gone, too.

Unfortunately, I looked down at the ladder and then at the ground far below. I could see the exact spot where I would land if I lost my grip on the braided hemp or my foot missed a rung. The spot looked hard, as if I might bounce a few times before I settled and spread out into a puddle.

The hornets were still there, too, cruising lazily in the warm afternoon air, casting sideways glances at me while planning their attack, and wouldn't you know it, I'd forgotten my purse-sized can of Raid.

On the other hand, "No risk it, no biscuit," as Ellie often said about new recipes. Thinking this, I gripped the ladder's wooden top posts and swung my foot onto its second from the top rung, hoping I didn't wind up smashed flatter than a failed chocolate souffle.

Which I didn't, and the hornets didn't attack, either; probably they'd decided it wouldn't be sporting, with me just hanging there and shaking like I was. But eventually I did reach solid ground and got back into the Fiat again.

Headed back toward Eastport with the top down and the radio on, I thought about Hadley Owens getting attacked *before* talking with Ellie and me, and Leo getting bonked *after* doing the same thing. And unless it really was a coincidence, it didn't make sense.

On the other hand, right now it didn't have to. I didn't care why, or what sense it all made. I only cared *who*.

"Dunnit," that is. And that meant just one task remained to me on this fine downeast Maine summer afternoon: Finding Babs Littrell and getting whatever she knew out of her, whatever it took.

Back at my house, I found Bella sitting in the kitchen, drinking tea and reading a magazine.

Breakfast dishes were heaped in the sink, the trash needed emptying, and a fat housefly buzzed lazily over an empty tuna-fish can left sitting on the kitchen counter.

Also, there was a large cross-eyed cat curled up in Bella's lap, looking like it belonged there.

"Hi," Bella said, taking a chocolate-covered cherry from the box of them open on the table.

"Hi, yourself." I crossed to the coffeemaker, emptied the dregs, put in a new filter, filled it, and turned it on.

"Nice-looking cat." It was Leo Montaine's Siamese, obviously. So much for it not ending up with me.

Bella nodded, turning a page. "Bob Arnold just dropped it by a few minutes ago. He said something about how the person who he thought would be taking care of it won't be."

Of course they wouldn't. That was the kind of

day I was having, and I should probably get used to it.

"You feeling okay?" I asked, peering into the refrigerator. No leftover tuna fish was in evidence, or much of anything else, either, even though this had been Bella's usual grocery-shopping morning.

"Fine, fine," she replied, then sipped more tea.

Her frizzy red hair was rolled onto pink curlers, her long, bony feet were in fuzzy blue slippers, and the radio on the mantel over the old kitchen fireplace was playing show tunes from the 1940s.

"Never better," she said. "Would you like a chocolate?"

I shook my head. "Thanks."

The bathrobe she wore matched the music: an ancient pink chenille number whose glory days were gone.

"Your father and I visited the assisted living place earlier," she said as the cross-eyed cat jumped to the floor and stalked from the room as haughtily as if it owned the joint. "So now I'm trying out the lifestyle he thinks we should have," Bella went on serenely. "Leisure, you know. Lovely, not having to be up and doing all the time."

There were two eggs in the refrigerator, plus some cheese that I thought I could probably peel the mold from, and some blueberry jam that Ellie had made the previous autumn.

"You can say that, but I'm guessing you didn't

much care for the place," I said as I turned with my lunch fixings.

Her answering look wasn't quite one of those gag-me-with-a-spoon grimaces, but it was close. Still . . .

"I like it fine," she said. "Who wouldn't enjoy sitting around all day with nothing to do?"

I dropped a slice of bread into the toaster, scrambled the eggs, and reminded myself yet again that glaring at the coffeemaker didn't make it work any faster.

"And since at the assisted living you don't have to be ready for company at any moment, or really do very much of anything for anyone at all," Bella went on, "you needn't dress, either, if you don't feel like it."

I lifted the omelet's edge with a spatula, then flipped the whole thing over, put the cheese onto it, and folded it up to brown a little while I dealt with the toast.

"I see," I told her as I sat down to eat. "A rehearsal, sort of. And are you planning to go on this way until—"

She slapped the magazine shut. "Until we leave," she said, biting off the words, "or until your father comes to his senses, whichever's first."

"Ah." I applied myself to my lunch. Finding Babs Littrell was a task better pursued while not dizzy from hunger, I'd decided.

"Maybe you'll make new friends over there," I ventured when I'd surrounded the food.

The coffeemaker signaled "ready" with a last strangled-sounding burble and a huge burst of steam. After pouring my own cup of coffee, I poured another for Bella and set it before her.

"That," I pronounced, gesturing at the pale liquid in the teacup, "looks insipid."

A cup of properly brewed tea is indeed a thing of beauty, et cetera, but this stuff was from the sale counter at the dollar store. I knew it from the box she'd left open by the tuna-fish can.

Bella scowled. "It is insipid. Boring, dull, banal, monotonous, and every other tiresome thing you can name."

Some people think Bella must be stupid because she truly enjoys housework. These people would be mistaken. She took a swig of black coffee, made just the way she liked it: nothing in it, and so strong you could revive dead people with it.

I sipped mine judiciously and added more milk, thinking that I might take those papers of Fairway's upstairs. But just then Sam burst in. Seeing us, he caught himself in the act of slamming the porch door and turned to close it carefully instead. If he hadn't seen us, he'd have slammed that door right off its hinges.

"I need," he pronounced evenly when he'd faced us once more, "to stay here again tonight."

"Fine, Sam," I said calmly. "You can take your old room."

For his running-home-to-Mom trip today, he wore tan Levi's, an old Maine Maritime Academy sweatshirt, and what had been sneakers but were now a few tatters held together by fraying laces.

"Everything all right?" I asked, knowing it wasn't. He was still trying to hold his temper and, I thought, not quite succeeding.

Meanwhile, I was thinking about all the places I could go to where nobody could find me and I could have poolside snacks and drinks with little paper umbrellas in them, and maybe a massage.

"No, not really, but thanks for asking," Sam replied, nixing my implied offer of a sympathetic ear, then eyed Bella, who was still sitting there like a stone statue.

"Hi, Bella," he offered finally, and after receiving her curt nod of greeting, he went on upstairs.

I took my dishes to the sink and rinsed them, then put them on the dish heap with the rest. Thinking about where I could go had reminded me again of needing to find Babs Littrell; for all I knew, she could be having a drink with an umbrella in it right this minute.

But I was guessing not.

"I hate seeing you like this, you know," I told Bella. "Is there anything at all that I can do for you?"

In answer, she shook her pink-roller-covered head and flipped to the next page of *People* magazine.

Oh-kay, I thought. "Well, then, do you know where Dad is?"

Those big grape-green eyes of hers fixed me in a calm, steadfast look. "I have no idea," she pronounced. "Nor do I care."

Upstairs, Sam's duffel bag hit the floor of his old room with a loud thud.

Half an hour later, having already had more than enough of other people's bad moods—I was in a pretty lousy one myself, actually, and with much better reasons—I went back out into the warm afternoon and started the Fiat.

The engine fired up at once with a throaty growl, then settled into an amiable rumble, leading me to think that its recent good behavior in the not-leaving-me-stranded department might be more than a fluke.

Driving down Water Street, with the Moose on my left and the now-defunct Choco's on my right, I found myself wishing I'd gotten hold of a rocket launcher the moment Brad Fairway arrived in Eastport. I could have prevented all this just by aiming it and pressing the red button.

Too late now, though, even if I had a rocket launcher. Passing the fish pier, with the glittering blue bay spread beyond it, reminded me of sitting there with Ellie, basking in the sunshine while selling baked chocolate treats and enjoying good sandwiches.

And that reminded me of Dory Sloan, who I hoped very much was not connected somehow to Sam's wanting his old bedroom back.

On impulse, I swung out onto the wide concrete breakwater past Rosie's Hot Dog Stand. Fishermen's pickup trucks stood angle parked above the boat basin. At the end of the wide deck, I pulled over by the big electric winch that hauled the catch up from the boats at the end of the day.

Hard-eyed seagulls flapped low over the Fiat, cocking their heads to spy whether anything I had was edible. I turned the car off, then took the envelope full of Fairway's papers from the passenger seat and opened it.

Quickly I learned that Fairway was getting paid—and paid really well, too—for selling something whose exact nature wasn't specified in the paperwork. Also, it was a lot of something, first imported, then resold here in the United States.

I'd done this sort of thing myself back in the bad old days, and the stickers, permit numbers, and tariff information on Fairway's documents looked right. Line after line of laboriously inked, militarily neat handwriting added up to a lot of sales, deliveries, and payments, all recorded in the pages I'd pilfered. And it all looked legit.

But if Fairway had been running an import-export business of some kind, why couldn't I find any mention at all of what the product was or precisely where it came from, why were its financial records in ink instead of in a computer file and, most curious of all, why had these records been hidden, stuffed up behind Fairway's kitchen sink?

I still had uncomfortable suspicions about all of the above—organized crime guys are good at disguising dark schemes as legitimate businesses—and was mulling them over when a squawk from above made me look up.

The seagulls had mostly gone, but a single determined-looking one still circled purposefully, reminding me that with the Fiat's top pulled back all the way and fastened there, there was no roof over my own head.

The gull squawked again, circling lower. Taking the hint, I started the car and got out from under him as fast as I could, then hit the brakes hard.

Bob Arnold stood across the street, waving me over. I pulled up next to him.

"Heads-up," he said. "News about Ellie. They're not taking her tonight, after all. Her lawyer wants to be here, DA agreed, and so now it's tomorrow morning."

Several choice swear words escaped me. This had to be torture for Ellie. "Can they do that?

Just . . . yank her around like that? Criminy, Bob, they're going to give us all whiplash."

"Yeah. I know. And yes, they can." He sighed. Being jerked around wasn't his favorite thing, either.

"I'm on my way out to their place right now, to check in with her and George," Bob said. "See if there's anything I can do." As he spoke, he was already hurrying toward his squad car, parked nearby. "Want to follow me out there?" he called back.

I did, but Bob's news meant I had perhaps fifteen more hours in which to somehow keep the hammer of justice from slamming down onto my best friend's head.

"Thanks. Tell her I'll catch her later," I said, easing the Fiat away from the curb.

I started uphill on Sullivan Street, past the marine store, where boats on trailers stood waiting to be put into the water. Right then I wished I was on one of them, skipping over the waves. I wouldn't even care if the tropical breeze blew the little umbrella out of my drink.

But instead, at the top of the hill I turned right onto Washington Street, headed out of town toward Brad Fairway's place yet again.

Maybe there were details Dory Sloan hadn't mentioned the other night that might help me find Babs. Maybe the handwritten financial notes I'd found were the key to this whole thing, and possibly if I prowled around out there a little more, I might figure out how.

All I really knew, though, was that if Babs had any ideas about who might've killed Brad Fairway and why, I needed to hear them, that is, if she hadn't done it herself.

So I had to leave aside, I told myself firmly, any thoughts I might be having about Dory and my son, Sam. Maybe what Dory needed right now was someone to talk to, someone who could lend her a friendly ear in a time of trouble.

Hey, I could do that.

Ten minutes later, the narrow driveway into Fairway's property appeared between the trees, and I turned onto it.

In daylight, the place seemed idyllic; apple trees' gnarled branches, studded with green apples now starting to be tinged with red, arched over the grassy road. On either side, pale blue forget-me-nots spread beneath the trees in the dappled sunshine.

Then the larger trees, hemlock and spruce, crowded in darkly. I passed the ruts from when I'd backed Ellie's car into the undergrowth, marveling that I'd gotten out, then rolled into the circle driveway.

Fairway's aggressively modern glass-and-steel house stood silent amidst its professionally arranged greenery. A warm, salty breeze laden with pine and the smell of seaweed wafted up from the bay.

"Anyone here?" I whispered into the silence.

A chipmunk's angry chittering from somewhere above was the only reply. I headed for the path downhill to Babs and Dory's cottage.

But then I thought that maybe I didn't want to march right up to the front door. Just on general principles, I like to see what I'm walking into before I walk into it.

Also, there was no car but mine in the driveway, but that didn't mean no one other than Dory was here. And if there was someone here, I might like to know that, right? Before they knew I was, I mean.

So I took a route running roughly alongside the steps leading to the cottage, then tripped over an exposed tree root and landed nose first in a colony of beetles who'd been happily munching on a clump of tree mold. Waving their pincered foreparts, the insects surged fast toward the source of their difficulty, which was me.

"Eeyagghh," I remarked as I recoiled, noticing meanwhile that my hands had slapped down into some rotting mushrooms. Next, a snake slithered off hastily into some poison ivy, identified, of course, right after I'd blundered into it, too.

But finally I reached a vantage point, helpfully furnished, of course, with plenty of centipedes and even more of those impressively pincered beetles. Brushing them away with a shudder, I peered between the trees.

No cottage. Also, no path, or anything else that looked at all familiar. I was (insert lots more bad words here) lost.

Which turned out to be . . . inconvenient. *Stumble, flail, face-plant, repeat* was apparently the procedure for getting back to the path. This time I met a garden snake (harmless, frightened), a huge mass of some other variety of beetles (bigger pincers, but also harmless and frightened), and a squadron of ground wasps, whose nest I'd disturbed by stepping directly into it (not harmless, not frightened at all).

But at last I made it, sweating and breathless, back to familiar territory. Maybe the path was a more prudent route, after all, I'd decided after the fifth wasp sting. Just before I finally reached the cottage, though, a sound came from behind me.

I froze. *Police,* I thought. Or whoever had killed Fairway.

Or . . . maybe a bear. It was rare but not unheard of to run into one around here. And in summer they had cubs to feed and care for, so they were hungry and grouchy.

"Don't move," someone said.

So it wasn't a bear. *Oh, hell, just shoot me,* I thought tiredly as I turned to face Dory Sloan.

She was wearing tan slacks and a pretty white blouse in a gauzy fabric—it was cotton lawn—

sprigged with flowers embroidered in pink and pale green on the collar.

Who but a textile artist even remembered cotton lawn anymore? I wondered, mostly to distract myself from the sight of the gun she was pointing at me.

"Hi," I said into the silence between us. The gun was an ugly little .22 pistol with a short, stubby barrel. Nothing elegant, but at this range it would be effective.

Then it sank into her, finally, who I was. Once the realization had crossed her face, her shoulders sagged and she lowered the weapon.

"You scared the life out of me," she exhaled.

"Likewise, I'm sure. Dory, what're you doing?"

She slipped the gun into the pocket of her slacks. "I was coming up from the cottage when I heard you thrashing around out there. But I didn't know it was you, so . . ."

"Okay. No harm, no foul," I said, willing my blood pressure to drop down out of "impending stroke" range. She was, after all, alone out here; I'd probably have done the same.

"So you're nervous being in the cottage alone?" I asked as we went down the path toward the cottage together.

She bit her lip. "It takes some getting used to," she admitted. "I was going to try to come into town to see you, actually."

We reached the cottage porch. From the steps

I could see through the trees downhill to the water's edge, where small waves sparkled and shore birds hopped among the shining stones.

The screen door creaked as we entered.

"Come on in and I'll tell you," she said, using a key to open the cottage's inside door. "It's about Babs," she added.

The cottage's interior was as pleasant and low-key luxurious as I remembered, and the houseplants thriving in the windows and on tables all looked as lushly green and vigorous as before.

"So, Dory," I began when she'd led me to the kitchen and poured coffee for both of us. Dory looked pale, and thinner than I recalled. "How'd Babs ever find this place, anyway? Or did she know Brad Fairway before she came here?"

As a rental, it was a real find: pleasant, in good repair, and in a setting to die for. You should excuse the expression.

Dory frowned, getting out the cream and sugar. "I'm not sure."

A massive old Boston fern hung beneath a skylight; cacti in pots grew on the kitchen windowsill.

"I think they kind of knew each other already, her and Fairway," Dory said, joining me at the table. "I don't know from where."

I put cream into the coffee and sipped. "That

makes sense. Listen, do you think she might also have known about some sideline he might've been running? Some business besides Choco's? D'you think he'd have told her about it if he was?"

Dory hadn't made fresh coffee; mine was like crankcase oil simmered over a low flame for a couple of hours. I sipped more of it, anyway, as she looked up alertly.

"What kind of sideline? You mean like drugs or something?" Her eyes widened worriedly.

"I don't know. I just heard somewhere that he had something else going," I lied. Another thought occurred to me. "There's a strange smell inside his house, too. Have you ever noticed? Like an electrical smell?"

The cream I'd used floated in clots on the coffee's surface. Too late I saw the congealed ring on the inside of the cream pitcher.

Dory tipped her head. "Huh. I have smelled that, actually." She made a small face. "Not that he'd invited me in very often. Babs was his friend, not me."

"I see." I got up. "Well, he can't keep you out now, can he? So if you're curious, and I'm curious . . ."

"Well," she began doubtfully. "When the police left, they said they were done in there."

By now we were crossing the porch, on our way outside. Of course the police hadn't concentrated on Fairway's house; they weren't in the business of investigating victims, only villains.

"That's why I was feeling a little paranoid about hearing someone out here just now. There's no real reason for anyone to be here. So I went back and grabbed one of the guns, just to be safe."

Well, there was a bit of news. "One of them?" I queried. "There are more?"

From the top of the path, we made our way to the deck steps at the rear of Fairway's house.

"Babs had two," Dory replied, starting up the steps. "Hidden under a loose brick in the stove hearth. But when I looked just now, there was only one."

I confronted the sliding glass doors. "You think she took the other gun with her?"

Jostling one door and then the other, with no result, I thought about what needed to be done here for about a second, then turned to Dory. "But why did she take it? Was she afraid? Has she said so?"

Dory took a startled step back.

"Sorry," I told her. "It's just . . . I'm running out of time. Listen, can you drive a stick?"

Her look grew confused. "Standard transmission? No. Why?"

"Because . . . never mind."

Soon after I bought the Key Street house, I began buying tools: a hammer, a screwdriver, a pair of pliers. Soon I needed a toolbox and an electric drill. Once Sam and his family moved in, I put the tools in the Fiat's trunk, out of the kids' hands, but when they moved out again, I moved the tools to the hall closet under the front stairs.

And there was no way I was going home for them, nor could Dory go to get them.

"Are there any tools around here?" I asked.

A tiny frown creased her forehead. "In the toolshed?" she suggested. "At the far end of the house?"

Wonderful, I thought. *Another slog through hornet city, followed by a traipse across fabulous centipede-land.* But I went, anyway. The shed wasn't locked, and at the very back, I found something that would work just as well as a power screwdriver: a large crowbar.

With it, I hurried way back through biting-insect territory with only a half dozen more red, itchy welts than before. As for getting the sliding glass door open, it might've been harder if I hadn't once torn up all the floorboards in the laundry room to reach a leak.

Which had turned out to be under the kitchen instead, but that's another story. The point is, crowbars didn't scare me. The narrow deck railing that I had to stand on to reach the doorframe's top screws did scare me, but not enough to stop me, and falling off the railing headfirst onto the deck turned out to be a good move.

It happened when I was pulling on the doorframe's metal edge with the crowbar, and not only did the edge come free easily, but instants later the whole heavy doorframe, with both the doors still in it, began falling rapidly toward me.

After which I fell, and what happened after that was like in one of those old cartoons where the character gets mashed flat, then hops up and springs back into shape again.

Although not quite. My poor nose had taken a clobbering. But once we'd moved the doors aside, leaning them against the deck railing one after another, we went in, and after turning on a light Dory led me to the cellar steps.

Because that electronic smell was even strong in here now, and it had to be coming from somewhere.

"Could someone else have taken the gun?" I asked Dory as we went down.

"I don't see how. Or why," she replied. "It's one of the reasons I'm so worried about her."

The smell prickled my nose hairs, an ozone aroma that reminded me again of big-box electronics stores, with acres of boxed laptops and printers and scanners and who knows what all stacked on pallets.

"You think she might hurt herself?" I kept my voice light, but the notion set my alarms jangling. Call me coldhearted, but at this point I was getting desperate, and a dead Babs was not a helpful Babs.

"I don't know what she might do," said Dory, snapping on another set of lights as she stepped off the stairs. "At first, I thought maybe she'd just gone off somewhere to get some privacy. You know, think things over and get her head straight."

"See, that's another thing I don't understand . . ."

The cellar was clean and modern: laminate floor, whitewashed walls, a dropped tile ceiling with fluorescent lighting recessed into it. Nothing was in the cellar but a furnace, the fuse box, and a water heater.

But there was a door in the concrete-block wall at the far end of it.

"Why was she so upset about Fairway's death?" I asked. "I understand grieving for a friend, but—"

The door was unlocked. I hauled it open and flipped a switch just inside, and suddenly a very large number of cardboard boxes appeared, rows and rows of them on pallets.

I strode to the nearest stack and tore the top carton open. Packed in bubble wrap, the thing inside was rectangular, about a foot wide and six inches tall. A couple of heat vents pierced its metal top, and an electrical cord coiled neatly behind it.

Dory peered past me as I lifted the thing. "What is that? Some kind of a computer?"

The markings on the dial were familiar; half the houses in town had one of these. "It's a scanner," I told her. "For monitoring radio transmissions." I replaced the item in its carton. "You know, like people use to hear police and fire calls and emergency dispatches?" In Eastport, people kept track of this stuff just the way they did with sports.

She looked around. Seriously, it was a lot of cartons. "But why would he have so many . . . ?"

I shrugged. "Don't know." Row after row of cartons . . . "But I've seen enough."

Combined with his secret sales records, this all looked illegal as hell, even if I didn't know exactly how, and now I had to wonder if somehow Babs had been in on it. But as we went back up the stairs, I was no closer to finding her.

Outside, the two of us muscled the doorframe back into the window hole, and Dory held it there. I pushed the screws, luckily unbent, back into their holes, then hammered them in with the end of the crowbar.

By the time we finished, it was mid-afternoon.

"Now what are you going to do?" Dory wanted to know, walking back with me to the Fiat.

"It's not what I'm going to do. It's what we're going to," I told her.

What this was precisely, I had no idea. But I did know that right now Dory Sloan was my only link to Babs Littrell. And Babs, as far as I could tell, was the only one I knew who'd been close enough with Brad Fairway to say who might've killed him.

Other, I mean, than Ellie, who, of course, still hadn't done it. I pulled the Fiat's passenger door open and gestured sweepingly.

"Your carriage awaits," I intoned. She looked doubtful. "Come on, Dory. Let's get you a change of scenery. It'll do you good," I told her, meanwhile, of course, harboring no ulterior motives whatsoever.

Well, hardly any.

Eleven

"Did Babs know about all that stuff in Fairway's cellar?" I asked as we pulled out onto Route 190, this time headed not for Eastport but instead toward the mainland.

Dory didn't seem to notice. "I don't know," she said. "I didn't, but they hung out a lot without me. No idea what they might've talked about."

"They didn't include you? Wasn't that kind of rude?" I glanced at her. Eyes closed, she let the wind tousle her light brown hair.

"Didn't want them to. I'm her assistant, not her wingman."

I turned left onto Route 1. "Ever hear them arguing?"

I looked over at her again. She might look like she'd blow away in a stiff breeze, but she'd been rock solid while holding that heavy doorframe while I bashed those screws back in.

She'd grabbed that gun before coming out to investigate strange sounds in the forest, too. Now, reassessing my earlier opinion of her, I thought that Dory Sloan might just possibly have seen a few things in her young life. That maybe she was more like me than I'd thought.

"I never heard them argue," she said. She

thought a moment. "But after they'd been talking, I did hear her crying sometimes."

Now we were getting somewhere. I kept my eyes on the road. "Is that so? What about? Do you know that?"

Ahead on the right, the Polar Treat ice cream stand sported the OPEN FOR THE SEASON sign, which locals waited all winter for. Now the patch of asphalt around the small building was packed with cars. I turned in and parked.

Dory looked over miserably at me. "I do know. But . . . I'm not supposed to tell anyone."

At the take-out counter, a kid in an apron and a white paper cap took my order and then gave me two soft-serve cones.

"Here," I told Dory, handing her one of them. "It's good for what ails you."

The other thing I wanted badly to ask her about, of course, was the relationship—or, even better, the absolute, utter, and complete absence of one—between her and my son.

But at the moment I needed her to be feeling friendly toward me, and besides, I didn't have time to talk about Sam. I left the "I'm not supposed to tell" question alone for the moment, too.

"Dory, do you have any idea at all where Babs might be now? Leo Montaine said she liked camping alone, but he didn't know where."

Dory stopped licking the ice cream. "Don't you

think I've been trying to figure that out myself?"

I threw the rest of my cone into the trash barrel. I've tried to like soft serve, I really have.

Then I got back into the Fiat and turned the ignition key and was rewarded by the *click-click-click* sound of a starter motor not getting enough juice to start the engine.

I should have expected this. The Fiat was a wonderful car to drive with the top down in summer, but it was also a vicious little imp. This was a game it enjoyed playing, one I'd seen before.

That battery was no more dead than I was, I knew from experience. So instead of going around the parking lot, asking people if they had jumper cables, and if so, whether I could borrow them and also use their car's engine to get mine going again . . . Instead of all that, I cursed loudly, jumped out, opened the hood, and slammed it down again so hard, people in the parking lot looked over to see if everything was all right.

"There, dammit," I grated at it, annoyed, and when I got back in that car, it started up like a charm, just as if nothing had happened.

Dory got into the car. She had finished her cone. "The other thing is, Babs owes me a paycheck," she said as we pulled back out onto the highway, "and this might sound selfish, I know, but if she doesn't come back and pay me, I kind of don't know what I'm going to do."

We turned onto Granite Hill Road, the Fiat growling contentedly now that it had decided to run at all. Wide blue water sparkled in the distance, with the Canadian island of Grand Manan rising hazily from it.

"So, believe me, I'm as eager to find her as you are," Dory said, "even aside from how worried I am about her."

The blacktop curved sharply uphill, then turned to graded earth. "Even though it's Fairway's murder I want to talk to her about, with all that might imply?" I asked.

Dory looked troubled. "Even though. Because here's the thing." She paused again as we drove past a cluster of mobile homes with tarp-roofed carports and woodstove soot–blackened siding.

"Babs and I didn't always get along," she went on. "After all she's done for me, I have to help her if I can. But I'm not going to turn my life upside down for her, you know? Does that make sense?"

I wasn't sure what Dory meant by "all she's done for me." But I didn't want to derail whatever train of thought she was following.

"Perfect sense," I said. "But . . . what if it turns out she killed Fairway? What would you do then?"

She bit her lower lip. "I don't think she did. But if she killed him, I'd have no reason to protect her. Loyalty's one thing, but . . ."

Saying this, she turned earnestly to me, her wide gray eyes troubled and sad, and the thought sprang to mind most unwelcomely that this was exactly the type of young woman that Sam would want to help if he could.

Not in a romantic way at first. The romance would come later. I pushed the thought from my mind.

"Why do you think Babs took a gun with her?" I returned to my main worry right now: that before I could learn what was in her head, Babs Littrell would put a bullet through it.

Or somebody else would; there was still that possibility, too. Meanwhile, we'd reached road's end where, ever since the toll bridge fell down a hundred years ago, the tide rushed through unimpeded. Beyond, through the trees edging the water, I spotted the tar-black end of Leo Montaine's paved driveway.

"Do you think she meant to hurt someone? Or herself?" I asked, pressing.

"I don't know," said Dory quietly. "That's the thing I haven't wanted to say even to myself, that maybe she . . ." She looked at me, her face as sorrowful as a child's. "All I want is for this to be over," she said. "I just wish she'd come back."

Me too. Babs knew something, I was almost certain, and whatever it was, I thought she'd gotten the hell out of town on account of it.

"Yeah," I said, leaning back against the Fiat's

leather seat. "That would be great, all right, if she showed up on her own. I just don't think she's going to."

A cool breeze kicked up, blowing the tide into whitecaps, which flew foamily off the wave tops. I turned the car around on the gravel, and we drove in silence back toward town, with me feeling all the way like I was missing something obvious.

On the causeway the breeze whipped into gusts; by the time we reached the arts center in Eastport, where Dory had asked to be let out, the bright banners outside were flapping energetically.

She slid out and shut the car door. "Thanks for the ice cream. And the ride." She patted the Fiat's fender. "What a great car."

"It is when it starts," I agreed, feeling sorry for her again all at once. She looked so defenselessly young and helpless, caught up in something bad that she hadn't asked for and didn't understand.

And running out of money.

"Listen," I said suddenly as she was turning away, "do you need any cash? I could lend you . . ."

I still wasn't sure about her possible Sam-attracting tendencies, deliberate or not. But the frustrating afternoon had taught me again that I could be wrong about a lot of things, perhaps Dory included. Anyway, I felt bad for her.

She looked back gratefully. "That's so nice of

you. But no, I'm okay for now. Thanks, though."

A troop of little kids wearing bright-colored backpacks stomped up the arts center's steps, led by a young woman lugging shopping bags brimming with what looked like craft supplies. Dory followed them, then turned again on the top step.

"Say hi to Sam for me!" she called, whereupon what little bit of sympathy I'd felt for her evaporated. I loved Sam, and I trusted him.

But she was a very pretty girl. Mulling this, I drove on past the police station. Bob Arnold's black squad car, with the orange Eastport Police sunrise emblem on the door, sat in the lot. As I passed his window, I glimpsed him at his desk, talking to someone I couldn't see. I went on to Water Street and parked in front of the Chocolate Moose.

Inside, it was cool and still, smelling faintly of coffee, melted chocolate, and vanilla beans. The shop hadn't been open at all today. Ellie and I couldn't be here, obviously, and I hadn't had the heart to ask Mika to fill in again so soon.

So I left the CLOSED sign up and pulled the shade down and sat at one of our wrought-iron café tables to think. But all I could come up with was the certainty that tomorrow they'd take Ellie away to the state police headquarters in Augusta, and she might not come back.

Ten minutes later, she called. I dug my phone out of my bag.

"Listen, don't panic," she said quietly. "But there's been another change of plans, and they're here. The detectives, they just arrived."

Alarm pierced me as what little time I had left to put an end to this evaporated instantly. "Don't panic? Are you serious? Give me just one single, solitary reason why I shouldn't—"

"Jake, it'll be okay. The lawyer's coming. He's meeting us there. I just talked to him."

"So you're okay? George is okay?"

She laughed weakly. "I wouldn't say he's thrilled, but he's all right, and he's telling me and Lee that it'll be all right. You know George."

I did know George, and for all his flaws, if he'd been any more of a stand-up guy, you could've used him for a flagpole.

"Lee's upset, anyway, of course," Ellie said, and with that, her voice broke. But she recovered. "She knows I'll be home soon."

She stopped to give her nose a good blow. Fury seized me at the thought of her in tears, and even more that there was nothing I could do about it.

"Listen," she went on, "try to get that chocolate marshmallow pie done, will you? Because Lee's birthday is tomorrow, of all things, and there's a chance I'll still be . . ."

Yeah. More than a chance, in my opinion, and Bob Arnold thought so, too: that once she'd been questioned, they'd arrest her for the murder of Brad Fairway, and after that all bets were off.

"Oh," she said distractedly, "Bob Arnold's here, too, so I guess I'd better . . . Jake, I need to go. I'll see you before you know it."

I bit my lip hard enough to taste blood. "Okay, I can do the pie. Don't worry about it. But promise me now that you'll . . ."

Be careful. Be strong.

Come back.

"Okay," I whispered again into the phone. "Okay."

But she was already gone.

An hour later, Wade called the Moose to see how I was doing.

"I heard from George," he said, "that she's being taken in. Do you want time to yourself about it, or should I come get you?"

He knew me well, this husband of mine, and the best thing about it was that he really meant it, that he'd do whichever I asked.

"I don't know. This all just seems so unfair. They're not even looking for anyone else."

I heard him sigh. "Yeah. Well, but it's not over, though."

"I guess," I said.

Maybe it was, though. Ellie and I had gotten nowhere trying to find out what had really happened. Meanwhile, they had a lot of what they thought was evidence against her: a motive, the opportunity, and, oh, dear heaven, a gun with her name on it. And only hers.

"What's the level of hostilities there?" I asked. "Between Bella and my dad, that is."

I'd been deep into shortbread making when Wade called. Now, as I spoke, I pressed chilled lumps of buttery pastry into a pie dish with my free hand.

He chuckled. "No heavy artillery yet." Then his tone changed. "I really hate seeing them like this, though. Bella and your dad are . . ."

Peas in a pod. Joined at the hip. And any other phrase you want to use to describe folks whose hearts are as one.

Until now. I changed the subject. "Sam still there?"

"Oh, yeah." Wade didn't chuckle this time. "He looks like he's trying to decide whether or not to invade France."

Oh, goody, another war reference, which I guessed pretty much described the situation on my personal home front just at present.

And that settled that. "Okay, listen, I'll be here for a while. I'm baking a pie for Lee's birthday tomorrow."

"Wow, bad timing," Wade said. "But are you okay?"

I tried and failed to find words that would say how not okay I was. Finally told him that I was fine and that I'd tell him all about it when I got home, and he accepted this without comment, even though I could clearly hear him not believing that first part for an instant.

After that I wept briefly into the shortbread, hoping that the pie wouldn't end up too salty as a result, and at last I set the crust-filled pie plate in the oven, which was cold because in my distress, I'd forgotten to turn it on.

By this time, I was ready to hurl that dratted piecrust right out through the front window, dish and all. But instead, I put the crust back into the refrigerator, set the oven and let it preheat, and *then* started baking the crust.

Luckily, Ellie had put the oven timer right out on top of the stove, where I could see it easily (she knew me well, too), so I remembered to set that, and just as I'd done so, the little bell over the shop door jingled.

Because naturally I'd forgotten to lock the door, too. So I ran back out there, thinking that I had eighteen minutes, and not a second more, to spare for whatever nonsense *this* turned out to be, or the piecrust would burn.

Besides, it was after hours. "I'm sorry, but the shop is—"

Bob Arnold stood there. "Closed. But I saw the Fiat outside. Thought I'd let you know that Ellie's not going tonight, after all."

"Oh, for . . . This is ridiculous, Bob. Why not?"

Still, hope leapt in me. For a foolish moment, I thought maybe the state cops had come to their senses and arrested someone else.

But the truth was less exciting. "Car trouble," Bob said. "Dale out at Bay City Mobil says he'll have the part they need first thing in the morning." He eyed me. "Don't go getting excited, though. If he doesn't have the part by then, the state cops'll be sending another car."

"Fine." I tried to think fast, which, as you may have gathered by now, is not one of my strong points.

"Fine. At least she'll be able to sleep in her own bed for one more night," I said at last. "Maybe we'll even get together one more time before she goes."

"Yeah," Bob said, unfooled.

As he should've been. I didn't know what Ellie and I could do in only a few hours to make this reprieve permanent, but I knew we'd be trying something.

He knew it, too. But he wasn't saying anything. Outside the front window, the day was fading, and the first wispy tendrils of evening fog were slipping over the seawall.

Good, I thought. A damp, murky evening with poor visibility and not a lot of people around was just what I needed. I just wasn't quite sure for what yet.

Bob moved toward the door, not pausing to tell

me to stay home and out of trouble this evening. He stopped with his hand on the doorknob. "By the way, those cops are sitting outside Ellie's tonight. I lent them a car to get around in while theirs is at Bay City."

I felt my eyebrows go up.

"Compromise," he explained. "She can stay at home for tonight, but they've gotta watch her."

"Right, 'cause she's such a likely fugitive from justice," I said sarcastically, and his look said he agreed. "And you'll what? Bring them dinner?" I added.

He must have offered them something to get this favor for Ellie. Otherwise, they'd have rented motel rooms and taken turns babysitting her, I guessed, since apparently they'd been told to keep the suspect under surveillance.

Bob nodded. "And I'll spell them from midnight to four a.m.," he said. "So they can sleep."

I didn't bother asking when he planned to sleep. He had been mostly a cat napper ever since his wife and daughter left.

"Anyway. Just so you know," he said, and went out, with the little silver bell over the door jingling.

Outside, the purples and pinks of evening faded to marine blue, and the fog took on heft, thickening until the lights twinkling across the bay blurred and vanished.

A few cars went by, their wipers flapping, though it wasn't quite raining. Then a freighter came gliding through the foggy darkness on the water, looking like a city of lights veiled by billows of steam.

Finally, the oven timer emitted its cheerful *brrr-ing!*

Two hours later I had a nicely baked shortbread crust sitting on the cooling rack, but still nothing to put into it. Ellie had left me some premade plain piecrusts for trying out fillings, so once I had the shortbread version finished, I did just that.

First, I put the marshmallows at the bottom of one of the piecrusts and poured chocolate cream filling on top. This produced the gluiest, nastiest mess I'd ever seen, much less perpetrated.

Next, I tried the marshmallows on top. I ran the pie under the broiler this time to melt and brown them, and the result was . . . Oh, good heavens, it was awful, inedible *and* ugly.

So for the third try, I put marshmallows in the chocolate filling, and the result wasn't bad if you enjoy the sensation of a too-sweet Pillsbury Doughboy trying to battle his way out of your mouth while you're busy trying to swallow him.

By now fog had filled the street outside and had turned the dock lights on the breakwater to ghostly yellow orbs. Beginning to feel lonesome and hungry, besides, I grabbed a dream bar, devoured it, and went back to work.

And I like to think the brainstorm that hit me about ten seconds after I'd eaten the dream bar had something to do with what happened next.

I knew how to make a chocolate marshmallow pie. I mean *exactly* how. All I needed was a package of vanilla pudding.

Which I didn't have, so I would need to drive to the IGA. In the fog, and in the Fiat, of course, and never mind that the car's top was still fastened immovably *down,* when I would've preferred it *up.*

Also, the seats were wet with fog, as I discovered when I went out there. After grabbing some towels from inside the shop, I wiped the seats down, covered the seat behind the steering with more dry ones, and headed out.

Hardly anyone was on the streets, which was lucky for them and for me since the fog thickened fast. By the time I got back to the Moose, about all I could see were my fingers wrapped whitely around the steering wheel.

Finally, I hunted up the big tarp from the shop's utility closet and draped it over the car, then returned to my task. Somehow, it had gotten to be nearly eight o'clock.

Pudding mix, condensed milk, sugar, vanilla— it was all there, and the marshmallows, too, and the crust was already chilled. Taking a deep breath, I poured the milk into one of the saucepans I had ready.

And that was when my phone rang. From inside my bag, which was stuffed under the counter out front. Then, to make the whole thing even more fun, the bell over the shop door chose that moment to jingle insistently just as a breeze blew through the kitchen and put out the stove's right front burner.

I turned off the gas. Then I went out and found my phone and answered, raising a "Just a moment" finger at Bob Arnold, who'd come back in again for some reason.

"Hi," Ellie said quietly into the phone.

"Hi, yourself." In the background, I could hear a baseball game on the TV. I imagined that George must be watching it, or trying.

Bob waited patiently.

"And?" I asked into the phone, not wanting to talk a lot in front of him.

"And it seems to me that whatever happens, they'll take me in the morning."

"Right," I said, knowing what she was getting at. It was what I'd thought myself.

"Like, if I should happen to sneak out later," she said.

"Oh," I said brightly, even more conscious now of Bob standing there. "Okay, why don't I do that, then? At ten o'clock? I should be home by then."

275

"Make it eleven, will you?" she said. "By the way, we're still a couple of hours from low tide, just so you know."

"Okay, that's helpful." Now I understood where to meet her. "I'm here at the Moose now," I added, "and Bob Arnold just walked in."

"Ask him about Leo Montaine. Is he okay?"

Criminy, I'd forgotten all about him, and Hadley Owens, too. I asked Bob.

"Montaine'll live," Bob replied to my query. "They tested and scanned him up one side and down the other, to make sure he didn't have bleeding inside his head. But he didn't, so they sent him home."

I relayed this to Ellie, who approved.

"But Hadley Owens is a different story," he added. "They took her to the hospital in Bangor, and she might need surgery."

I relayed this much less welcome news to Ellie, too, and after that we hung up. "Now," I said, turning to Bob, "was there something else?"

"Saw your light on. Don't you two go trying anything harebrained tonight, okay?" He looked me in the eye. "Because I happen to know," he went on, "that the detectives sitting outside Ellie's place came equipped. They were showing off some of their gear to me earlier."

"Gear? What gear do they need besides phones and notebooks? Or whatever they use to take notes with nowadays?"

Still looking straight at me: "Guns. Night-vision glasses. It's a whole kit of stuff."

At his words, the truth washed over me with the shocking clarity of an ice-cold shower.

"Oh, really?" I said casually. "Anything else interesting?"

"Tasers," he said. "For apprehending people who don't exactly want to be apprehended."

He turned toward the shop door, with me still staring at him in stunned comprehension.

"Give Ellie my best when you talk later," he said, then looked back over his shoulder at me. "Take care of yourself, too," he added and went on out the door without waiting for a reply.

I watched his fog-blurred shape pass the window while I thought about what he'd said. *Tasers, night-vision goggles, guns . . .*

Then I went back to the kitchen, where all the pie-making materials and equipment still stood waiting for me on the counter, just like before.

But nothing was like before. Absolutely nothing.

Twelve

A miserably cold drizzle was falling as I drove home an hour later. In the driveway I hauled the tarp back up over the Fiat and anchored it with rocks from Bella's garden edging. This turned out to be a fussy task, and when I got indoors, I was soaked and shivering.

In the kitchen, Wade took one look at me. "Hot. Shower. Now."

And I didn't have much choice, unless I wanted my heart pumping icy red pellets instead of nice warm liquid blood, so I obeyed, and when I came out, he had an Irish coffee waiting for me.

Clutching it, I half fell into the big overstuffed chair in the living room. Everyone else was in bed, or at least upstairs.

"Maybe you should just let this next part play out," Wade said gently, perched on the sofa's edge. "See how things look afterward."

"I can't," I said. The coffee sent warmth flowing out through my body.

"Why not?" he asked reasonably, so finally I told him. Not about my own thoroughly checkered past. He knew all that. But about Fairway, that I'd recognized him, and from where.

"If he wasn't a mob guy, then he was a

wannabe," I said. "I didn't see how that could be linked to his death all this time later. But now that we've run out of answers everywhere else . . ." Another sip. I'd drained the mug. "And yesterday I learned he might've been laundering money."

Wade took my mug to the kitchen, refilled it, and returned.

"Dirty money," I explained when he handed me the freshly spiked hot drink. "Like from illegal gambling or some other racket."

I drank and blinked as the stuff hit me; you could've powered a rocket ship with what was in that mug.

"Then you run the money through a legitimate business, and presto, the money's got a new, spanking-clean history," I finished when I could speak again.

"But how do you get the money into the legitimate business?" Wade asked sensibly.

"Phony invoices. If I'm right, that's why Fairway's got a lot of computer equipment in his cellar. Anyone comes looking, that stuff is evidence he's really buying and selling something."

"What about Choco's? Couldn't he use that as his legit business?"

I shook my head. "I don't know. I guess he could have, but you'd want something where you could plausibly show a biggish cash flow, and cakes and cookies aren't going to give you that."

Probably that was what Fairway's tear-down-and-rebuild plans for Eastport's downtown were about, too; there were all kinds of ways to siphon funds out of a building project.

"Must've been a pretty small operation," Wade pointed out. "You can't move much volume out of a basement in Eastport, Maine. Heck, you couldn't even get a decent-sized truck down that driveway of his."

"Right, but he got here just a few months ago, so he was just getting started. Next thing, he'd have rented a storage unit. Or, if he got big enough, a warehouse."

If you knew how to doctor your business records properly, you'd be able to pass just about any kind of inspection without problems. The exception was US customs. The stuff in Fairway's cellar was almost certainly from overseas, and those import-export cops were tough.

But if I was right, then Fairway had figured out a way to handle that, too.

"Why don't the cops already know about this . . . this contraband?" Wade asked.

From upstairs, I heard Sam's old boom box radio blare on, then get turned down quickly. "I don't know that, either," I said. "Maybe they do."

I doubted they'd skipped checking out Fairway's basement while they were there. "But why should they care, with a suspect, a motive, and even the weapon already in hand?"

Wade nodded ruefully. "Good point."

Just then Leo Montaine's Siamese cat wandered in. I'd forgotten it was here. Seeing me, it let out a yowl so harsh you could've used it to strip paint. Then it leapt up into my lap and settled, purring.

Wade got up. "You want another one of those?" He pointed at my mug. "I'm going up. I've got to go out tomorrow morning at four," he added.

Out on the pilot boat to meet up with a freighter, he meant, at the time when the tide was just right for bringing the big boat into the terminal.

The cat leapt down as I rose, and I followed Wade to the kitchen.

"So I'd better hit the hay," he added, "but will you be all right?"

He'd set up the coffeemaker, his lunch pail was filled and ready in the refrigerator, and his slicker waited on a hook in the hall.

"Because believe me," he said, "nobody has come all this way, from all those years ago, to kill some guy who probably doesn't even remember you, all on account of you," Wade said.

He was right, but it was the part about believing it that was giving me trouble. What still lay ahead of me tonight felt desperately unwise, and as it turned out, talking about Fairway's possible mob links hadn't helped.

"I'll be fine," I assured Wade. "You go on to bed." Once he was asleep, you could set a bomb off under him and he wouldn't stir. "I have some things I want to say to Sam," I said.

Wade wiped his hands on a dish towel and clicked off the light over the sink. "You sure that's a good idea?" he asked mildly.

Nope, I wasn't. But that blare of music I'd heard from my son's room a little while ago said he was still awake.

So I turned and marched upstairs before I could lose my nerve.

"Hey." I knocked quietly on Sam's door, then opened it a crack. "Can I come in?"

"Sure." He'd pulled on pajamas and thick white socks after his shower. His shaving kit was open on the dresser he'd used as a boy for displaying found objects: a clay pipestem, a clear glass marble.

I still had the marble.

"So," I said, lowering myself into the chair by his bed, where he was sitting propped up against the headboard with a can of Sprite in his hand. "You know I love you, right? Like always, like forever?"

It was the phrase we'd repeated to each other when one or the other of us felt low back in the days when we first got to Eastport and things were so strange.

"Yeah," he conceded. "Like always. Like forever. But—"

"But nothing. I'll keep this short. I just want to say that you can still talk to me about anything. At any time. Whatever."

From the start, I'd made it clear to myself that I was not going to interfere in his marriage. And I didn't intend to do so now.

Still, there are things that a mother must say, so I did. "You can talk to me about why you're here, for instance." Instead of at home, I didn't add.

But he heard it, and his face stiffened. "Mom, I—"

I put my hands up, warding-off–style. "Not now," I said. "If you want to, when you want to. You decide."

I got up and put my arms around him, and he let me. Then, after a moment, he relaxed and reciprocated. Sort of. He was very unhappy.

"Thanks," he said quietly as I stepped back. Then: "I thought I'd take Gramps and Bella to Jasper Beach tomorrow. Get there at half tide. Going to be a nice day. What do you think?"

Once in a while it's revealed to me that I might not have been at all times and in every way a disaster of a mother. This was one of those times.

So we agreed on his plan for a day trip, and I went downstairs, where I put another couple of sticks on the fire still flickering in the kitchen woodstove and made some fresh coffee.

When I'd settled down with a cup, boozeless this time, in the old wooden rocker by the stove,

283

the cat came silently in and leapt back up into my lap. The stove made faint crinkling noises, radiating pleasant warmth. Only the thought of Ellie waiting just the way I was kept me from dozing.

So I was wide awake when my phone rang. It was too early for this to be Ellie. I didn't recognize the number on the caller ID, and by the time I'd decided to answer, the call had gone to voice mail.

No message, but I definitely heard breathing sounds before the hang-up. Shaky ones. I dialed the number back immediately.

A girl answered, fighting tears. "Jake? It's Dory Sloan. I can't . . . I've been trying to . . . Please, you've got to help her!"

I didn't have time to untarp the Fiat, and besides, it would wake up the household. Instead, ten minutes later I was in Sam's new, high-powered, smooth-running pickup truck—he called it the Silent Beast—headed for Ellie's house.

By the way, if you're wondering what Wade would have thought of all this, I can only say that in his view, you either put yourself out there or you didn't. You kept on trying until the bitter end, or you didn't. It was simple to him, and gender had not a thing to do with it.

He hadn't married me by accident, is what I'm saying. Anyway . . .

The truck's cab had the plushest interior this side of a luxury sedan. Every time I touched the brakes, I thought I might slide off the cushy leather seat into the large, thickly carpeted footwell.

But what I found most useful as soon as I pulled the truck out onto Key Street (besides the windshield wipers, that is, as mist still fell heavily, and in the truck's headlights, the fog stood like a wall) was the CB scanner, built right into the vehicle's dashboard.

The *silent* scanner. It was turned on, but right now no police or other emergency communications sputtered from it. That meant nothing much was going on in the area at present.

Water Street was quiet, too, not a car downtown and the storefronts all dark, and for once, Bob Arnold's squad car wasn't in the parking lot outside his office. And there were no lights on inside the office, either. By now even he was probably at home.

Driving past Ellie's on the north end of the island, I saw only a single light burning upstairs in her house. A late-model green Subaru with custom tinted windows sat at the driveway's end; it was Bob Arnold's personal car. That was what he'd lent them, I realized.

I drove on to the turnaround, where the road ended and started back. The officers at the end of Ellie's driveway wouldn't leave their post as long as they were confident she was still inside her house, I felt pretty sure.

That meant I could approach the house from the rear unseen, unless something unexpected happened. Of course, "something unexpected happening" had been my life's theme lately, but never mind.

I pulled Sam's truck into a driveway that I knew belonged to some summer people who hadn't come to Maine this year. I switched off the cab's interior lights so they stayed dark when I opened the door.

Then I got out into the damp, chilly darkness. In our cryptic phone talk earlier, Ellie and I had arranged as best we could to meet at eleven. It was ten thirty now, and half an hour was a little tight for what I was planning.

It involved first making my way down a steepish slope to the bay's edge—oh, hell, it was precipitous is what it was—then back up again. Between the two climbs—okay, they'd be scrambles, with sharp rocks and seawater below— lay a short, stony shoreline, which I meant to follow until I was directly behind Ellie's house. That was when the climb back up would happen.

Next, I'd find Ellie, and we'd rush out to Dory's as fast as we could. Something bad had gone on out there. I knew that much. But even when I'd finally managed to reach her, the girl had been too upset to say exactly what.

First things first, though. Shouldering a small backpack that had been left in the truck by, I guessed, one of Sam's kids, I eased my way around behind the truck and from there along a row of shrubberies.

Next came the reason why outer Water Street terminated here in a circle drive: it was land's end, the north edge of the island, where one more step meant a quick drop to the rocks and water below.

Gathering my nerve, I stood there in the streaming darkness, with foghorns moaning, bell buoys clanking, and waves crashing below; it was like being at the edge of the world. Then two pale, solid bars of light showed in the fog, coming from behind me: headlights.

I ducked down fast. The car entered the turnaround slowly. In the murk I couldn't see much about the vehicle, until I caught a deep-red glint from its dashboard: a cherry beacon.

It was Bob Arnold's squad car. I backed up hastily into a thicket of blackberry brambles, and while they were scratching me to death, my right sneaker slipped. Grabbing some brambles and a handful of weeds, I landed flat on my stomach, one leg dangling over the cliff's edge, and when I tried scrambling up again, a chunk of the cliff broke off.

Not a big chunk, but an important one. I'd been clinging to it at the time. "Glurp," I said quietly.

The cop car was just sitting there.

Meanwhile, my other foot suddenly joined the first one, and they did a little duet, waving around out there in thin air. This time I found a whole clump of the blackberry vines and grabbed them. Luckily, my desire to survive exceeded my pain threshold, but not by much. And then the vines broke.

"Ack," I said as what was left of the vegetation slipped greasily through my hands. Somehow at the last instant I latched onto a rock with my fingertips, then wrapped my arms around it.

Meanwhile, the cop car's headlights had finally swung away. Its red taillights diminished as the car departed into the fog.

So there I was, hanging on for dear life to a rock in the dark, with big waves crashing below. Which was fine while it lasted—well, not fine, exactly, but it beat the alternative—only pretty soon my fingers began to get tired.

Clearly, I couldn't hang on forever. The trouble was, there didn't seem to be anything else I could do instead.

Hauling myself bodily back up over the cliff's edge wasn't an option. I don't care what they do in the movies; I just didn't have the upper-body strength. My only other movable parts were my legs, but after trying every possible leg-lifting maneuver and a few that were impossible, I had to admit failure there, too.

Finally, after about twenty minutes, I put my head down on the rock to rest. A trickle of panic leaked down my spine; there had to be something left to try, but . . .

"Hey," a voice out of the darkness said suddenly.

Hands gripped my wrists, startling me, so I nearly let go of the rock.

"Just let me get a good grip," the voice said. It was Ellie.

"Good plan," I gasped as her fingers tightened painfully. By then I didn't care if my hands both turned blue and fell off, if only the rest of me got hauled up over that cliff edge.

At last, she got me to where I could find a toehold; after that, I gradually wiggled and wormed my way onto solid ground.

But no rest for the weary. She grabbed my arm. "No time to talk," she said. "Come on. Let's go."

"What's happening?" I panted, hustling along with her between clusters of birch saplings and stands of small evergreens. The land at this end of the island still had a few wild patches like this where, except for Ellie's place, no houses were visible in any direction.

"I saw Sam's truck go by," Ellie said into the darkness, parting tall weeds with both hands. "So I assume they saw it, too," she said, meaning the police detectives parked outside her house.

We were nearly to where I'd left the truck parked. Around us, the fog writhed and billowed into pale, indistinct shapes, dissolving and re-forming like genies swirling out of lamps.

Ellie pushed blackberry brambles away. Then it was my turn. The brambles tore skin off my hands, then snapped back for a try at my face. A stinging welt sizzled across my cheek.

"Did they get out?" I asked. "Of the car?" There'd been a picnic spot out here long ago, I recalled as my foot plunged without warning into an old firepit.

"They're out here now," Ellie replied. Her voice came from ahead of me, but the fog was suddenly too thick to see her in. "With flashlights," she added, briefly amused. "Much good those will do them."

In the fog, she meant, and she was right. It was, as Sam would say, as thick as sea poop. Maybe, I thought with sudden, completely unwarranted optimism, the homicide cops would get lost.

"The first thing they did after Sam's truck went by was come to the house to make sure I was there," she said. "Luckily, I still was."

Something big materialized in front of us, like a wall.

"Ellie?" I ventured, not sure what I was seeing.

No answer. Whatever it was, she'd vanished into it.

Then her hand reached back *out* of the wall to grab mine.

And yank me in.

• • •

Fog as thick as clotted cream surrounded me. Gripping Ellie's hand, I hurtled along behind her, going who knew where, but I sure hoped she did. Next, we fought our way through the thickest, stickiest cedar hedge I'd ever run into.

"Bleagh!" I sputtered, brushing at the gluey evergreen-sap stuff stuck to my lips and eyebrows. Fragrant green cedar tips clung to my hair and clothes, and my fingers were drenched with the sap.

"Never mind," Ellie muttered. "We need to go right now."

I peered past her as a cold breeze thinned the fog briefly. Big objects of some kind studded the bare-looking ground ahead.

Gravestones, I saw finally. We were in Bayside Cemetery. Our route had been roundabout in order not to be seen by those two pesky state cops, but from here it was a short, straight shot back to the truck.

Moments after we'd stepped into the graveyard, though, Ellie dropped fast into a crouch behind a tall granite obelisk. She'd seen the flashlight beams appear just as I had. They didn't find us—we'd backed ourselves into that awful cedar hedge again—but ten minutes later, when the flashlights departed, I was ten degrees colder and ten times less happy than before.

For one thing, I'd had time to think. "Ellie. Right now, they're looking for me."

"Or for whoever left Sam's truck near the turnaround," she agreed.

"A truck whose plates they've no doubt already run, so they know who owns it."

"But sooner or later, they'll check my house again, too."

And then she'd be screwed: directly to jail, do not pass Go, et cetera. I got up from where I'd been hunkering in the sticky shrubs, feeling my knees protesting. Ellie was already moving toward the road that led downhill out of the cemetery.

"Sam's going to be upset, isn't he?" Ellie said quietly when I'd caught up to her. "Good thing you didn't take the truck very far."

Correctamundo, as he'd have put it. I'd done it once before, needing to get somewhere and with the Fiat out of commission, and the ruckus he'd raised nearly started World War III.

But that wasn't what I was worried about right this minute, and it got even less important when, without any warning, a man stepped out of the fog-thick darkness right in front of us.

I froze. Ellie too. A flashlight beam blinded me briefly. Then . . .

"Mom?" the figure said. A tall, bony figure appeared from behind him. "Mom, what the hell are you doing?"

It was Sam, and he had Bella with him. Also, he had the Fiat; its apricot paint showed blurrily in the murk a few yards away. It was how they'd gotten here, I guessed. He'd simply used the extra key from the hook in the hall.

"Just what we needed," I said, stomping up to them. "The peanut gallery."

I yanked the Fiat's passenger-side door open. Sam had gotten the top up and the latches latched somehow, so if it rained, the way it suddenly looked as if it was going to, at least we wouldn't drown.

"Ellie, get in," I ordered. "You two," I told Sam and Bella, "are going home in Sam's truck. I'm sorry, but you'll have to walk to it." I told them where it was, which was not far. "And, Sam, I'm sorry also that I took it without asking."

I wasn't sorry, and he knew it; the look in his eye said we'd deal with it later. Meanwhile, though . . .

"Once you get home, you'll keep quiet about all this," I finished sternly.

Whereupon Sam looked at Bella, and Bella looked back at Sam. A real look of mutual understanding, I thought it was, and then, as if on signal, they ignored every word that I'd just said and instead climbed silently into what the Fiat called a backseat.

"We're going along," Sam declared, "wherever you're going, like it or not. You're not doing this alone, whatever it is."

With which Bella seemed to agree, and it was while I was standing there with my fists clenched, glaring helplessly at them, that Ellie tapped my shoulder.

"They're back," she said, and sure enough, here came those two cops' flashlights again. Fast too.

"Go," I told Ellie. I jumped in behind the wheel, she hit the passenger seat with her backside, and I closed the car door.

Moments later: "Nicely done," I told Sam, who crouched tortuously behind me, with his head between Ellie's shoulder and mine.

The spot he'd so cleverly chosen to park in was hidden from the road by a line of bushes along the cemetery's edge. The way out was a short, sharp downhill slope leading back to the pavement.

And Sam had backed in. Good instincts, though he didn't get them from me. Now I depressed the clutch, disengaged the parking brake, and turned the ignition key. Once the brake was let off, we began to roll out toward the road. When we were on it, I popped the clutch, and the engine caught.

And, *vroom,* off we went. "To Dory's," I said, answering Sam's question before he could ask. "She's in some kind of trouble."

No answering comment came from Sam, and so far, Bella had been about as communicative as a stone statue. At the top of the next hill, I squinted both ways into the murk, saw only more wet gray stuff drifting, then hit the gas onto Clark Street, headed out of town.

No headlights showed behind us. That didn't mean they wouldn't.

"Ma," said Sam finally, "I put the tarp in the trunk, so—"

"Sam," I interrupted, "I appreciate your getting the Fiat's top raised, I really do. And you were very helpful the way you parked back there. But the way I'm feeling right now about you and Bella hijacking this situation . . ."

In the rearview mirror, I looked him in the eye. The absolute nerve of that kid, to just show up and elbow his way right into . . .

"It's probably not appropriate for me to say where you can stick that damned tarp," I told him.

He looked taken aback. Then he chuckled. "Probably," he admitted. "But what if you need backup for what you're doing now?" He frowned. "Whatever that is," he added, sounding skeptical that it was anything sensible.

So I told him what Ellie and I were doing: responding to Dory's half-hysterical-sounding call for help.

"Which I got nearly an hour or so ago," I said as we pulled out onto Route 190. "Her call, that is."

The fog seemed to press right up against the Fiat's windshield. Only the car's low-to-the-road design put me near enough to the yellow line that I could see it through the solid-looking billows.

"I'd have told her to call Bob Arnold, but she hung up."

The road's center line vanished in the murk; I gripped the wheel.

The line reappeared.

"And when I tried calling her back, I got sent to voice mail. I don't know what's happened since," I said.

The fog thinned suddenly in front of us, like curtains being drawn back.

Ellie spoke up from beside me. "Quiet out here."

"Sure is." I glanced over at her. "I guess those homicide cops must not've called Bob, either. Embarrassed about losing you, maybe."

She nodded, her eyes still on the road. "Or they're not sharing any information with him anymore."

I thought about that a second. "Huh. Because they've tumbled to the fact that he's a friend of yours. And mine."

They'd seen me go by them, down to where I'd hidden Sam's truck. Then Bob had followed me in to where the road dead-ended, and they'd have asked him on his way out if he'd seen me.

I wondered what he'd said. I glanced up at Sam again. "How'd you find me, anyway?"

He shrugged. "Truck's got a tracker. I can

locate it on my phone. Got an alarm if the engine starts."

Beside him, Bella hunched on the bench seat, her skinny shoulders scrunched together, and her ropy arms wrapped around her knees. The car's top allowed just enough headroom for front-seat occupants, but hardly any for any unlucky passengers crammed in back there.

But, hey, it was their idea to come.

"And this tracker, you put it on when?" I inquired.

"After I found out my mother was a truck thief," he replied. "And now it turns out she's a *serial* truck thief, so . . ." He stopped, peering past me. "Is this it?" he asked as a maybe familiar break in the trees appeared in the fog-choked windshield.

I looked behind us; no headlights showed back there. Aiming the Fiat's tires gradually to the right, I waited for the break in the white line at the road's edge before making the turn.

"Dory was worried that Babs might kill herself," said Sam. "She told me so right after Babs disappeared."

"I see," I replied. "Not that same night, though. After you brought her home from the arts center dinner, you left the cottage before Ellie and I did, right?" I met his gaze in the rearview mirror.

"Right," he said slowly, a new light of comprehension dawning in his eyes. Not one that he enjoyed. "Right. I ran into her the next day on the street. That's when she said it."

I might've asked more, but just then a pair of headlights appeared behind us, their glow diffused by the clouded plastic of the Fiat's aging rear window.

"Jake," Ellie uttered quietly.

"Don't worry," I replied. We were coming up fast on the unpaved entrance to Brad Fairway's driveway. I doused our lights, yanked us hard over onto the gravel shoulder, and swung in sharply, stomping the gas pedal to get us out of sight as quickly as possible.

The car that was behind us sped past the end of the driveway, not slowing to see which way we might have gone. Not caring, either. Just a false alarm, someone out here on some errand, likely wishing they were home. Like me . . .

I snapped the headlights back on, slammed on the brakes an instant later. A person stood directly in front of us; I'd stopped just in time.

"Stay here." Leaving the car running, I got out and hurried to meet Dory Sloan as she ran sobbing toward me.

"I couldn't help it. I couldn't help it," she kept saying through her tears. "He wouldn't stop. I was so scared . . ."

I grabbed her by the shoulders, looked straight into her face. "Dory. It's okay. Calm down. What happened? Who wouldn't stop?"

She stumbled alongside me to the car, still sobbing.

"Sam, can you come out here?" I asked.

I'd have preferred not leaving them together, but I needed Ellie to come with me, and I couldn't fit all of them in the car. Sam struggled out of the cramped space behind the Fiat's bucket seats.

"Bella, you stay with us, okay?" I said. "And, Sam, here's a flashlight. You walk Dory back to her place. We'll meet you there."

"What did she mean, she couldn't help it?" Ellie wondered aloud as we drove on. The car's headlights picked out fog wisps drifting like ghosts between the trees.

"I don't know."

We pulled into Brad Fairway's circle drive and parked near an old yellow Jeep Wrangler. It looked familiar, but I couldn't think of why.

"You stay here," I told Bella, and once again, she agreed without argument. It wasn't like her, and I got the strong sense that she'd come along with Sam mostly just to get out of the house.

Which meant my father must have riled her up again somehow, but I would deal with that later, I thought as Ellie and I got out into a dark, pine-scented world of mist and silence.

The fog seemed to muffle the car door's slam. Wet moss squished underfoot like a sponge being squeezed. Everything was so quiet, it didn't even feel as if time could be passing, until a shivery breeze sent chilly droplets showering down from the fog-soaked evergreens all around us.

At Dory and Babs's cottage we didn't bother knocking, mostly due to the big black boot outline imprinted on the screen door. Also, the door itself hung half off its hinges, as if someone had kicked it in.

Inside, the dozens of large and small potted plants perched on shelves or lined up in stone-filled trays still looked as lushly healthy as the last time I'd seen them. Their glossy leaves, brilliant blooms, and thick, juicy-looking stems said that even now Dory must be caring for them.

Cautiously, we peeked into the kitchen and into Dory's room, discovering nothing beyond the normal light clutter of daily living: a cup in the sink, a stray sock on the bathroom floor.

"I can imagine George's reaction if he knew we were out here," I said to Ellie as we made our way down the hall.

"He probably does know by now."

I glanced at her in surprise.

"He sleeps like a baby, awake every two hours," she explained. "But if he gets up and finds I'm not there, he'll understand."

I turned to her. "Really. And he'll be okay with it?"

Small laugh from Ellie. "I wouldn't go that far. George grew up thinking all women were dainty little things, so it's hard for him."

Babs's room looked untouched since the last time we'd been in it.

"Anyway, he thinks you've got guts," Ellie went on.

I turned to her. "George does?"

I stepped into the room, where the dresser drawers still looked caught in the act of exploding.

Ellie nodded. "More than anyone but me, he told me."

"Oh," I said, pleased. I'd thought that George still believed I had no guts at all, owing to the one time when I'd called him to trap a skunk that was under the front porch instead of doing it myself.

I peered into an empty closet; Ellie looked under the bed. "I guess whoever Dory was talking about isn't here anymore," she said.

"There's a car in the driveway," I pointed out. The yellow Jeep, I meant.

Whoever had been driving it could've taken off on foot, I supposed. Or they were waiting around outside for the coast to be clear, which I thought was likelier.

Also, I had a few ideas about the kicked-loose cottage door. But right now, the door to the cellar beckoned; if whoever had sent Dory Sloan into hysterics was still here, they were probably downstairs.

But again, we found no one. Ellie inspected the yarn-dyeing part of the cellar; I rummaged among cardboard cartons. Babs's loom, still strung with the project she'd been working on, stood where we'd seen it last, with her shuttle laid neatly across the left side of the work.

I gazed at the fabric. Its limes and acid yellows still blended with vibrant reds and pale lavender as perfectly and impossibly as before . . .

And then I sniffed puzzledly at a whiff of sweetness mixed with something else.

"Ellie?" I peered around, trying to figure out where that really quite unpleasant smell was coming from, and then . . . *yeeks*.

Then I spotted the end of an index finger peeping out from behind the steps that Ellie and I had just descended.

"I think we've discovered what Dory was so upset about," I said, dropping to a crouch.

The hand was muscular, scarred, and leathery skinned. The face was jammed too far in under the steps to recognize, but the red, white, and blue suspenders on the body said this was Richie Perrone, the quirky ceramics artist who produced the enormous pieces of pottery and kept a pig.

"Help me haul him out, will you?" I asked Ellie, and once we'd done it and seen his face, I thought nobody was going to be identifying him from that anytime soon.

Or ever, actually.

"It's like he walked into a freight train," said Ellie.

Poor Jillian, I thought, hoping the pig would find a new home with people who didn't like pork chops. Then sounds came from above.

"They're here. Dory and Sam." Ellie pointed upward.

"Oh, terrific."

By the washtubs I found an old bedsheet. I threw it over the lifeless body. Then Ellie started upstairs, and I followed. I flipped the light switch at the top. Over my shoulder I saw the cellar go pitch dark; it seemed a more fitting setting, somehow, for a newly dead person.

Meanwhile, Dory and Sam had gone back out onto the porch. Their voices were civil, but they didn't sound at all friendly, and my heart leapt a little at the prospect of those two not getting along well.

"I mean it. He broke in," she was telling Sam urgently when I went out there, "and he *chased* me. He wanted me to tell him where—"

"The door was locked? The screen door, too?" I interrupted.

"The inside door was open, but the screen door was locked," Dory clarified, turning to me. "To get some air in the house."

"I see. And he kicked in anyway, the screen door? The heavier one? He just kicked it off its hinges?" I asked. Or halfway off, anyway. "That's how the boot mark got there?"

Dory nodded energetically. "Yes, and he was

yelling that I must know where Babs is, and when he found her, he was going to kill her."

I must've looked startled.

"Because," Dory explained, "he said she was out there again last night. That Babs was, I mean. At his place. And that she broke more pottery of his."

"Okay. Go on." I knew about Babs's previous pottery-smashing escapade. But I didn't understand this at all.

Dory continued. "When I said I hadn't heard from her, that she was missing and no one had, he thought I was lying. I got scared, he started chasing me, and—"

"Okay, look," I broke in. "Richie Perrone is down in the cellar, dead, and Ellie and I don't have time to report it to Bob Arnold right this minute."

"You're sure he's dead?" Dory asked shakily. "Really sure?"

By then I was on my last nerve. "He is," I intoned solemnly, "really, most sincerely dead."

She just stared at me. Meanwhile, it was already past midnight, and those cops would still be looking for us.

"So you two do it," I went on. "Take Bella home and call Bob Arnold. Tell him there's a body in Babs's basement."

Ellie glanced questioningly at me.

"Then sit tight until I call you, both of you," I finished.

Preferably not together, but there wasn't much I could do about that. Besides, from the look of unease on Sam's face right now, I thought he might be starting to regret his friendship with this girl.

But Sam had other ideas about what he would be doing. "Nope. We take Bella home first. After that, I'm sticking with you."

"And I'm not going home at all," Bella declared flatly. "So forget that part, too."

Which is how, a little later, we found out how many adults you can stuff into a Fiat 124 Sport Spider two-seater convertible with the top up: not as many of them as we had, as it turned out.

But we did it, anyway.

"Don't talk," I instructed them all. "Just keep still and breathe as best you can."

Not that they had room for much else. Dory sat in front, hunched on Ellie's lap, so that every time I shifted gears, I poked her in the leg. On the bench seat in back, Sam scrunched over to one side, giving himself a tiny space between his ribs and Bella's elbows.

At the end of Fairway's driveway, I stopped just before we pulled out onto the highway. "Dory. You said Babs called."

She nodded, swallowing hard. "Uh-huh. And she sounded awful, like she was desperate. I'm starting to think . . ." She turned to me, her pale eyes sparkling with tears. "I think she might have done something to Mr. Fairway. Now she wishes she hadn't but . . ."

Yeah. Too late. "Did she give you any idea at all where she might be? Somewhere nearby or . . . ?"

Heck, she could be in Timbuktu for all we knew. But . . .

Dory straightened as best she could in the cramped space. "She didn't mean to. But in the background, I heard . . . a sound. And I'm not sure, but I think I remember hearing that same thing when—"

"Island or mainland?" I broke in. "Come on, Dory. Do I turn left or right here?"

She took a deep breath. "Mainland," she said decisively. "I know where I heard it. And I think I can take you there. Oh, I hope . . ."

Me, too, so I cranked the steering wheel toward the mainland and hit the gas.

Thirteen

"Somebody's behind us again," said Dory after a few minutes.

Ellie turned, then craned her neck to squint through the Fiat's age-clouded back window. "She's right. Those are headlights."

I pressed the gas pedal harder, peering ahead. The fog was even thicker than before. "Turn the heat and the defroster on, will you?"

The inside of the windshield was clouding up, too. I could see the road's center line, but not much more.

"Are they getting closer?" I said.

"No." Dory turned frontways. "They're staying back. Can't you drive any faster?"

"Not in this." On the causeway, fog billowed up the embankments and over the pavement. I could see to the end of the headlights' beams but no farther.

"Tell me again about Richie Perrone now," I said. "Basically, you're saying he showed up, broke in, and attacked you?"

"Yes," she declared. "And he was already raging mad about the pottery he said Babs broke. He was sure it was her because she'd done something like that before, he said."

Right. He'd told me so, too. "Why did he think

you might know where to find her?" I asked. "I mean, he had to have a reason to—"

In Pleasant Point the fog was so thick, I could barely glimpse the streetlamps along the dark, winding lanes. The only one awake in the whole town seemed to be the Pleasant Point cop parked in his squad car beside the municipal building, watching for speeders.

"But then something changed Richie's mind," I said when we'd gone by. "Once he didn't find her, he decided you'd be able to. But why?"

Her voice thickened with tears. "I was on the phone with her when he broke in and started yelling, that's why. I dropped the phone, he'd scared me so badly, and he grabbed it."

I passed her a tissue; she gave it a good blow. Then . . .

"He must've heard her voice, and if I was on the phone with her, that meant I knew where she was, I guess he thought." By now she was weeping. "He chased me down the hall and grabbed me. I got the cellar door open while we were struggling, and . . . and I pushed him."

She sucked in a shuddering breath. "I don't know what happened then. I heard a thump, and then it was all quiet down there, and I was afraid to go look. Then finally you showed up."

Sam handed her more tissues.

"Babs sounded awful. She wouldn't say where she was. But like I said, I heard a sound in the background, and I think it was loons. That noise they make, like scary laughing?"

I knew. The eerie call of a loon on a lake in the dark could make you think you were in a horror movie, lined up to be the next victim.

In the rearview mirror, two hazy yellow orbs reappeared, still hanging back, still not doing anything worrisome. But I didn't like it. Quickly I turned in at the high school and doused the Fiat's headlights. After a moment the other car went by, just like the first one had. I waited briefly, then pulled out again.

"No matter what Babs has done, we have to look for her," Dory said. "We have to, before she does something . . . something *terrible*."

Fresh tears overwhelmed her, but she was able to guide us from Route 1 to Shore Road, uphill through stands of enormous ancient evergreens toward a wide ocean view.

"There's no lake out this way," Sam objected.

Towering spruces lined the curving two-lane, their low-hanging boughs like big, shadowy hands trying to grab us.

"Yes, there is," said Dory, sounding more sure of herself than before. That was when I knew at last where we must be going.

Ellie too. "There's nothing there," she said quietly from beside me, "but a sort of oversized pond. Years ago, there was a boat launch and picnic area. But even then, there was barely a road."

I shrugged, keeping my eyes on what little I could see through the Fiat's windshield. "Dory's pretty certain, though."

Dory nodded. "She's come here before. I don't know why I didn't think of it."

Ellie leaned forward to glance past Dory. "Jake, I don't suppose you have any weapons with you?" she asked, sounding hopeful.

"Only my wits, unfortunately," I said, still looking for a way to get off the road. Then as we crested the top of a hill and the fog began thinning, a break in the roadside greenery appeared.

The narrow track looked weed choked and overgrown with saplings, and likely also with poison ivy. But I turned onto it, anyway, and quickly found that what had once been a road now was barely passable, deeply rutted and cut through in places by running streams. Easing us across them in first gear, I heard sizzling; then steam gushed up from beneath us as the car's hot exhaust manifold grazed the cold water.

"This is it. I recognize that fence post," said Dory.

I saw it, too. Someone had gated this road once. Now the gate was gone, but the cedar post had survived, jutting up bone white out of a thicket in the drifting fog.

Finally, a bramble patch too thick for the Fiat to push through stopped us entirely, and Ellie and I got out, while Dory stayed in the front passenger seat.

"You really think Babs is back there?" Ellie murmured, aiming her flashlight at the dark, tangled undergrowth crowding the decayed road.

"That, or our little friend Dory is about to put bullets in our heads," I replied.

I was only half joking. What with the darkness, the fog, and the desperateness of our entire situation, anything seemed possible, and the sudden wild laughter of a loon somewhere nearby didn't help my nerves.

On the other hand, where there were loons, there were lakes, and if Babs really was here, we needed to find her, ideally before she put a bullet into her own head.

"Come on," I called back to Dory and Sam. "We're walking in from here. Bella, you stay in the car, please, all right?"

The last thing I needed was for her to get hurt scrambling around out here, and when I'd heard her agree in that rusty-hinge voice of hers, I relaxed a little.

But only a little, as we all shoved and elbowed our way around what turned out to be a tangle of ancient wild roses with thorns the size of boat hooks.

Minutes later we broke through into a dim clearing, where a lone bulb at the top of an old utility pole lit the scene like a stage set. Small waves lapped a long, narrow beach; an old wooden picnic table stood by what had been a firepit made of rocks.

Trees encircled the clearing. Under one of the trees stood a low tent, with its entrance flap closed, glowing from within.

Nothing moved inside the tent. Nothing moved at all, in fact, but the fog drifting lazily across a lake we could barely see. But then a breeze kicked up, rushing in the treetops, releasing showers of droplets, and the fog thinned, revealing a figure at the water's edge.

"Babs!" Dory cried, stepping forward, but I caught her. The woman by the water held something in her hand.

Not a flashlight. The woman's cap of white-blond hair told me that this was indeed Babs Littrell. As I thought this, she sank down into a sitting position, facing the water.

Still with something in her hand. I was pretty sure I knew what.

"Jake?" Ellie whispered. She knew, too.

I took one slow step and then another. Sam moved up behind me.

"Ma," he murmured, "be careful."

No kidding. The fog had nearly dissipated now, the way it will when the wind blows. So I could see the dull, gunmetal gleam of the pistol Babs held.

I took a few more steps. Her head lifted alertly. "Babs?" I said.

She started to get up, the gun still in her hand, and that was when the whole thing went sideways.

"Babs, no!" Dory cried, rushing toward her.

At the sound, Babs whirled, now gripping the little pistol in both hands. Dory hurled herself and knocked Babs off-balance, and then they were on the ground, struggling.

"Don't," Sam said sharply, stepping in front of me as I moved to intervene. "Which one's got the gun? Can you see?"

He was right; I couldn't see it. Dory seemed to be searching for it with one scrabbling hand while she held Babs down with the other, but then Babs broke away, thrust her own hand down after the weapon.

A sudden report like a thunderclap split the night. Then came silence. Babs and Dory lay motionless on the sand.

Ellie rushed toward them. Sam and I followed.

Dory shifted and sat up. "Ohh," she moaned, then spied Babs, who still hadn't moved.

She never would again, I saw as I crouched by her. A small, dark hole pierced her forehead just above her left eye. I put my ear down close to her slightly parted lips.

She wasn't breathing, and she wouldn't be doing that anymore, either.

I got up shakily, my heart thudding so hard I could feel my pulse bounding inside my skull. The gun lay in the sand, where it had fallen.

"Okay," I exhaled, knowing that nothing was or would be. "Go wait in the car with Bella," I told Dory, who took off obediently, her face a mask of shock and grief.

When she was gone, we approached the tent. Inside, a sleeping bag lay on a mat beside a backpack, a small supply of foodstuffs—coffee, bread, canned things, a tin box that held cheese and a few eggs—and a propane stove.

Next to the battery lantern on a milk crate now functioning as a bedside table stood several books: Babette Deutsch's *Poetry Handbook*, pocket dictionaries in German and French, and an old green hardcover gardening book, much thumbed, by someone named Nan Fairbrother.

There was also a leather-bound Moleskine notebook; I pocketed it as Ellie spoke.

"Nice hideout." It was. Leo Montaine had suggested that Babs was a somewhat experienced camper, and this snug little setup proved it.

"But from what?" I wondered aloud.

There was a good bottle of wine inside a cooler, along with some ice melt. Packets of trail mix, chocolate, and dried fruit said she knew how to eat for energy.

"Is it as simple as her killing Fairway and then herself out of guilt? Or even grief?" I asked.

But never mind. The upshot was that if Babs had known anything that would've cleared Ellie of murder—such as, for instance, that Babs had done it herself—the only way we'd find out about it now was with a Ouija board.

I pulled the wine bottle out of the cooler. It was even better than I'd thought, a Beaulieu '67. "I'd have finished it first," I commented, feeling tempted to do just that. It had been a long night.

Outside the tent we found Sam waiting for us, still looking shocked. "Why'd she do that?" he asked, not sounding as if he expected an answer.

I didn't think he'd ever seen anything like it before, and I wished he hadn't now. We started back to the car.

"Well," I began as we shoved our way between weeds and thick brush clumps, "maybe the pressure just got too . . ."

"Or maybe she didn't do it," said Ellie quietly.

Sam stopped. "What do you mean?" he asked her.

But I'd been thinking it, too, that I hadn't seen what happened, exactly. Babs and Dory were struggling; then the gun went off.

But whose finger had been on the trigger?

"Oh, we are in so much trouble," said Ellie an hour later.

We sat at the kitchen table in my big, old-fashioned kitchen.

Bella had gone straight to bed. In the corner of the kitchen, the woodstove made soft crinkling sounds as it cooled.

"Yeah, we are," I agreed glumly.

Upstairs, the shower went off. I heard Sam pad into his room and close the door. He'd called Mika when he got home, but they hadn't talked for long.

"What are we going to do with her?" Ellie angled her head toward the parlor, where we'd hastily made a place for Dory on the daybed. We couldn't very well just drop her off at the cottage and leave her after all that had happened.

"For right now, nothing," I said. "All of it's going to be Bob Arnold's problem in a little while. Until then, might as well let her sleep."

On the way home, Dory had burst out half hysterically with the notion that maybe Babs wasn't really dead, that maybe we should go back and try to help her somehow.

I'd told her no and explained why, in graphic terms. I'd seen Babs right after the gun went off, and I could guarantee that she'd been gone the very instant the bullet struck her.

Whereupon Dory had shut up and, back at Key Street, had done what I told her to: bath, Benadryl, bed. She was in shock, I thought.

"You really think she might've shot Babs?" I asked Ellie now.

I'd given Dory a jelly glass full of Bella's

316

homemade blackberry cordial, too, and that stuff will knock the socks right off your feet.

Ellie shrugged tiredly. "I'm just not sure what happened."

Leo Montaine's cross-eyed cat sidled into the room and leapt up onto my lap, then began working its claws into my thigh.

I made it stop, and it glared up resentfully at me. "We have to tell Bob soon," I said.

I meant about Babs Littrell, who was still lying dead on that lonely, cold beach in the dark. And about Richie Perrone and all the rest of it, too, I supposed miserably.

"Let me just go home and get cleaned up first and talk with George." Ellie picked up her jacket. "Then we'll tell Bob together."

I walked her to the door. "But don't you want a ride?" Outside, the fog had cleared out entirely at last, leaving a sky full of stars.

Ellie shook her head. "I'm probably going to have to sneak in, or those homicide cops will scoop me up. Before they do, I at least want the chance to take a shower."

The small, brave smile on her face when she said it just about broke my heart. Then the hall light snapped on, and Bella's voice came suddenly from behind me.

"What're you two up to, heads together like a pair of criminals?"

We jumped guiltily; her choice of words cut

a little too close to the bone. Pretty soon other people would think we were criminals, too, and some of them would be cops with arrest warrants and handcuffs.

"Gotta go." Ellie hotfooted it out the door, across the porch, and away down the sidewalk into the darkness between the streetlamps.

"Be careful," I called after her, then turned to face Bella and yawned expressively.

"All right, it's been a long night for all of us. I think I'll go on upstairs and try to get some—"

"Oh, no, you will not," she uttered indignantly, seizing me by the shoulder and ushering me firmly back into the kitchen. "You left me in the car out there," she went on, "and now I want to know just exactly what happened. Step by step." She emphasized her last three words.

So I sat her down at the table and poured her a generous dose of that blackberry cordial, so powerful you could use it for rocket fuel, and then I told her the whole thing.

By the time I finished, those big grape-green eyes of hers were as round as dinner plates. Partly, though, that was on account of the stuff she'd been sipping.

"Sakes alive," she commented wonderingly on my story, then began telling an unrelated tale about a school friend who'd fried all the inhabitants of a fish tank by dropping an electric hair dryer into it.

"Fascinating," I said appreciatively every so often. And have I mentioned that the cordial had a kick like a half-broke mule, as she herself would've put it? And by the time she'd drunk enough of it to be persuaded to go back to bed, Bob Arnold was outside, knocking.

"Hey," I said, peering through the screen door at him. From his look, I thought at first that he was angry, but once he got inside, I saw that wasn't it at all.

Not that he didn't have plenty of reasons to be. He just didn't know about most of them yet. And what he really looked was scared.

"Did Ellie come back here?" he asked, glancing hopefully past me into the kitchen. "I've been all over town," he said, "and I can't find her."

The temperature had dropped sharply since we'd gone inside, the way it can on a Maine summer night when the sky is clear.

"Maybe she took a ride," I told Bob as we crossed the street to where he'd parked the squad car. "Maybe someone offered her a lift."

We got in, and Bob pulled the car away from the curb. Around us the big old houses on Key Street stood dark and silent.

"So she started to walk home from your place, is that right?" Bob said, ignoring my suggestions as to why she might be just fine. "And she left when?"

319

As we walked out to his car, Bob had explained that Ellie had called George to say she was on her way home, but she'd never got there.

"Right," I agreed. "Maybe forty minutes ago."

"And before that?" At the foot of Key Street, he turned left and drove slowly downtown. On the fish pier, a single streetlamp shed yellow light down onto a stack of lobster traps.

"Before that," I answered, "Ellie and I took Dory Sloan out Shore Road to where Dory thought Babs Littrell might be hiding out. A little lake. Looks like it might've been a picnic spot?"

It was too late now to do anything but just come right out with it all, I realized.

Eyebrows raised, Bob turned slowly to me, his look icily inquisitive.

"Because Babs called Dory," I explained. "She made Dory think she might harm herself, and Dory called me for help."

He kept driving, still gazing straight ahead. "But you didn't call me."

Yeah, I figured we'd get to that part pretty quick. "Bob, if I'd called you, you'd have had to alert the state cops, right?"

I waited for him to say, "Sure" or "Absolutely." Or something like that.

He didn't.

"Bob," I said, "accessory after the fact wouldn't look good on you."

Or whatever they'd charge him with. He

ignored that remark, too, but before I could press him, he began asking questions.

"And when you got to the lake? Then what happened?" he wanted to know as he drove us out Water Street, scanning left and right.

"Then Babs shot herself. I mean, I didn't exactly see her do it. Not much light there, and things got a little confused when Dory tried to stop her."

Bob blew a breath out through pursed lips. "Yeah," he said wryly, perhaps recalling fraught situations he'd been involved with himself. "That can happen," he said. "So she's still out there? Babs, her body? And Dory's where now?"

"The body's still there," I admitted. "Bob," I went on before he could give me a side-eye about it, "we'd have had to stash it in the Fiat's trunk, for one thing, assuming we were able to haul it out of there in the dark."

He nodded grudgingly. Respect for the deceased, whether victim or villain, was a thing of his.

"And Dory's at my house. Asleep. She's pretty devastated," I said as we passed the big old granite-block post office building and the break-water entrance, both deserted. "I didn't want to make her stay at her place all alone after what happened," I added just as Bob took the left turn onto Sullivan Street so abruptly that my jaws snapped shut.

"Thought I saw something," he said, his narrowed eyes fixed on a spot about halfway up the tree-lined hill. "Something different."

Passing Moose Island Marine, with its high shingled storefront looming on one side of the street and its yard full of trailered boats across the way, he frowned. *Suspicions confirmed.*

"Yeah, Gene Wilson's work truck isn't here," he said, backing up a few feet to swing around in reverse and back into the boat lot.

He grabbed a flashlight off the car's center console and switched on a beam so bright that you could have used it to signal aliens on Mars. Instantly, the light picked out something red backed in among the trees lining the road: a taillight. And now I could see that the car it was attached to was . . .

The Fiat. *My* Fiat, with the black ragtop, cloudy rear window, and apricot paint job. Dashing out of the house with Bob a few minutes earlier, I hadn't even noticed that the car wasn't in the driveway. Now I jumped out of Bob's car, shoved my way in among fallen branches and leaf debris, and yanked open the driver's-side door.

The keys were in the ignition, and nothing looked damaged, but a pink plastic barrette lay in the passenger-side footwell. It was one of the pair Ellie had been wearing when she left my house.

Leaning in, I snatched the barrette up along with my keys, got back into Bob's car, and slammed the passenger door a little harder than was strictly necessary.

But that was nothing. By then I was so mad, I could've ripped that car door right off and thrown it off the end of the breakwater.

"We need to go straight back to my house right this minute," I told Bob, and it must've been the look on my face that made him obey without questioning.

On Key Street I raced into the house and hurried to the parlor. The daybed was empty, and Dory's few things were gone. Cursing myself, I turned at a faint sound from behind me and found Sam standing in the hall doorway. He was already wearing a jacket and a wool cap, and his face said he was not about to take no for an answer.

He held out my own heavy jacket. "I heard Bob say Ellie's gone missing. I was just about to come and find you."

And that, in a nutshell, was my son, now a grown man. I nodded wordlessly at him, and two minutes later we were back outside, in Bob's waiting squad car, with Sam in the rear seat, behind the perp screen.

He patted the worn black leather affectionately. "Just like old times," he said wryly, meaning all those many nights in the past when Bob drove Sam home drunk and disorderly instead of taking him to jail.

"Where now?" asked Bob grimly as we pulled away from the curb.

The car's passenger compartment smelled like the tree-shaped air freshener that hung from the rearview mirror, along with, faintly but surely, some whiffs of other things, which I didn't want to think about.

"We should try Babs's place," I said, because Dory would have to take Ellie somewhere, wouldn't she?

And that had to be what happened. And as for the girl not being able to drive a stick shift . . . Suddenly I wondered how much of what Dory had told us was lies.

A lot, probably, and she'd put it all over on me without even breaking a sweat, hadn't she? *And that's what pride goeth before . . .*

"But how's Dory keeping Ellie with her?" Sam wondered aloud. I'd brought him quickly up to speed on our way out of the house. "I mean, I can see Ellie getting in Mom's car, not realizing who was driving. But once she found out—"

"For that matter," I said, cutting in as a new wrinkle occurred to me, "what's Dory driving now?"

If they'd been on foot, Bob would almost certainly have spotted them when he drove around Eastport, looking for Ellie the first time.

But then I got it: Gene Wilson's work truck, gone from its usual spot. Gene left the keys in it,

I happened to know, in case one of the guys from the boatyard needed it when Gene wasn't around.

Back at Moose Island Marine, Bob slowed the squad car. "I'm going to Babs's place," he said. "You take the Fiat, go home, and stay there until I call you, understand?"

Sam and I got out, just as he'd instructed. Standing there in the darkness, with the foghorns still hooting poignantly out on the dark water, I watched Bob's taillights disappear over the hill.

Sam was already pulling branches back from the Fiat and brushing off the top. After joining him, I pulled the driver's side door open and got behind the wheel. When I turned the ignition key, the engine coughed twice, then fired up like a champ as Sam hopped into the passenger seat.

Finally, I dropped the transmission into reverse and floored the gas pedal. The car hurtled backward through the evergreen branches and swung out onto the street. Shoving it into first gear before the rearward skid had even finished, I tromped on the gas pedal again, and the feisty little vehicle leapt forward with a gratifyingly evil snarl.

And that, friends, is why I adored the little Fiat. Anyway . . .

On Washington Street we zoomed past the old Lutheran church, the art supply shop, and the (summers only) gardening center. Next, we cruised sedately for a mile or so, mindful of the homicide cops, who were almost certainly still here in town, past Bay City Mobil and around the long turn past the new Baptist church.

And then . . .

"Go home," Bob had said. "Go home and stay there—"

Yeah, right.

And then I wound that Fiat's engine right up to a power-producing whine so high only dogs could hear it, and let 'er rip.

"I thought I said sit tight," Bob Arnold growled a few minutes later, scowling up at me from the foot of the cellar steps at Babs Littrell's place.

Of course he would be here. Great minds, and so on. Peering down, I spied Richie Perrone's jeans-clad left leg still sticking out from beneath the steps.

Bob nudged the leg with the toe of his shoe. "Did you know he was here?"

I nodded, looking away. Gene Wilson's pickup sat in the driveway, but Perrone's yellow Jeep was gone. Dory must've switched vehicles.

"We were in kind of a hurry," I said defensively. "Dory called, said that Babs had called her and implied she might kill herself. Then Perrone showed up, raging, kicked the cottage door in, and attacked Dory. She pushed him, and he fell."

Simple, straightforward. Just one thing wrong. Bob eyed the leg again. "He did, huh? Kicked the door in? Wearing those?" On Perrone's feet were a pair of worn moccasins. "Kicked it right in," Bob said musingly. "Left a print, too, I noticed."

"I guess she lied," I said weakly, smacking a mental hand to my forehead, because he was right. Something about that print on the door had bothered me, too, and now I knew what.

Sam went down past me and peered at Perrone. "The fancy key fob from his belt is missing," he reported.

Bob turned to him.

"Got rid of the Fiat," Bob theorized. "Came here in the work truck. We'll find that driven into the brush somewhere around here, I'll bet. Got the Jeep, took off again . . ."

"Why switch vehicles again, though?" Sam squinted around at all the weaving and yarn-dying tools and equipment.

"Gonna be a no-holds-barred island-wide search for that work truck of Gene Wilson's tomorrow morning," Bob answered, not looking away from what Richie Perrone's face had been turned into. "Gene doesn't play nice with truck nappers," Bob added. "Nor do his friends."

But Dory didn't know that, I was willing to bet. Still puzzled, I wandered over to Babs Littrell's loom, which still held the last piece of heartrendingly lovely fabric she would ever create. The polished wooden shuttle set neatly to the left of the work, as if she might pick it up again any minute, made the sight all the more poignant.

But it was another thing that was wrong somehow. I picked up the shuttle. Its satin-smooth shape felt warm and fit perfectly in my hand.

My right hand.

"What?" Bob demanded, seeing my face.

I put the shuttle very carefully back where it belonged, resting atop the taut, colorful fabric stretched out on the loom.

Resting on the left side, because Babs was left handed.

"I know where she's taking Ellie," I said. "And I think I know why."

Bob and Sam followed me out of the cottage and up the trail by the beam of Bob's monstrously bright flashlight. Out in the driveway I leaned against the Fiat while Bob approached his own vehicle.

Good, I thought, because if there was ever a time for lights and siren, this was it.

"Sam, you go with Bob," I said, "and I'll take . . ."

But before I could finish, Bob jumped angrily out of the squad car again and slammed the door hard before stomping over to me.

"Thinks she's cute," he fumed, holding up something small and silvery. It was the head of a broken-off key. Not Bob's key, which was still on his belt. "Other part's still jammed in the ignition," he said sourly. "Hammered in with a rock or something."

So Dory had come back, or no, she'd been here all along, I realized as now from the end of Brad Fairway's long driveway came the squeal of tires as someone pulled fast out onto the road.

Sam came over to Bob. "A needle-nose pliers might get it."

But none of us had one.

"Listen," Bob said quietly to me. "Just one thing I'm a little worried about. You're sure Babs Littrell was dead when you left her . . . right?"

"Yeah, Bob. I'm sure." I was not going to describe the gunshot wound for him, I simply was not. Seeing it had been enough. "But believe me, she was."

And that satisfied him, which I thought was a little odd, too. By all rights, he should've been reading me the riot act about my recent activities, then tossing me in the clink.

But instead, he wanted only to help. Meanwhile, I thought again about the loom in Babs's cellar studio, her last work unfinished on it and the shuttle laid neatly aside, as if she might return.

"Get in," I told both men, sliding behind the Fiat's steering wheel myself.

With Sam's help, I unfastened the convertible top's latches and shoved the top back. No way Bob would fit in that decidedly non-roomy bucket seat otherwise.

Sam climbed into the rear. "Where we going?" he inquired mildly.

"Back out to the lake," I said, turning the ignition key.

The Fiat started roughly, but it started. I hit the gas and tore back out the driveway and onto Route 190, toward the mainland. The black, star-pricked sky overhead was so vast, I felt I might sail right up into it.

"Bob, you have your sidearm, pepper spray, all that?"

"Yeah," Bob growled from beside me. In the dashboard's glow, his round face looked troubled. "You want to give me an idea of just how I might be called upon to use all this fancy gear?"

He was still mad about the sabotaged squad car. But he didn't seem mad at me. An unlikely thought occurred to me; I brushed it away.

"Dory's got Ellie," I said. "She's on her way back out to the lake where Babs's body still is, and next, she'll come after me and Sam."

Once you've learned how to drive the little Fiat—the trick of it is to let speed and momentum be your friends, and don't fear the accelerator pedal—it's no fun driving other cars. At the corner we zoomed onto Route 1, then out Shore Road and around the uphill curves like this was the Indy 500 and I was Mario Andretti.

Now the trees opened up to a vista of sky and dark water, with a long flat field sloping downhill from the road on one side and the brush-clogged track leading in to the lake on the other side.

Pulling over onto the gravel shoulder, I let the car roll up and over a slight hill, then parked at the very start of the downslope. From here I could see that although the earlier fog had pulled away here, too, the clear sky wouldn't last much longer.

Just offshore, the murk was rolling back in again even as I watched. But never mind that; better weather was another thing we couldn't wait for.

"But once Ellie gets convicted of murder," I said, "she'll be no threat to Dory anymore. Unlike us." I gestured at Sam, then at myself.

"Wait a minute," Sam objected. "You think Dory killed Fairway, Perrone, and Babs? That's crazy. Why would she do such a thing?"

I'd been thinking about it on the way out here. "Sam," I said as I got out of the car, "I know that at your age, so many things can be all about feelings."

I locked the car, even though if you wanted to get in, you could just use a penknife on the canvas top.

"But this wasn't," I said. "This was strictly business."

Meanwhile, it just about killed me to leave the Fiat so vulnerable, just sitting by the road. If Dory tried getting out of here in the Jeep, she'd just bash my car aside and keep going.

Still, no sense making it easier for her, that is, if I was right and she was really here. Firmly, I turned my back on the car. Time to find out.

"If what you're saying is true, she'll want to kill me first," Sam said as we pushed through between the weeds and brush. Bob and Sam both had flashlights; I didn't, which allowed me to stumble, flail, and trip through lots of broken branches and recently ripped-out brambles.

She'd driven in here, all right. Or someone had.

"Why?" I asked Sam as Bob bulled his way forward ahead of us. "Will she want to—"

"She doesn't like rejection," he interrupted flatly. "I mean, like, not at all."

A light bulb flashed on in my head. "So . . . you mean Dory has been pursuing you? In a romantic way?"

Sam snorted softly in the gloom. "Yeah, you could put it like that, yeah. She made it pretty clear a few times." He turned to me. "And before you ask, of course I told her about Mika and the kids. Showed pictures, even. But Dory wouldn't—"

A muffled yell came from somewhere up ahead. It was Ellie's voice. Bob's pace quickened. Mine too.

"Wouldn't take no for an answer," Sam managed as we hustled along. "Got my cell number from somewhere, kept on calling me. It got weird."

"But why didn't you tell me?" I asked as my hair caught in a tangle of rose thorns. I yanked free. Ahead, Bob Arnold shoved his way through the last of the underbrush into the clearing, and light from his flashlight reflected suddenly from the surface of the lake.

I imitated him as best I could, first tripping in a weedy tangle, then face-planting into a mass of something squirmily insectile. Things with legs swarmed leggily up my hand; then something bit me.

"Yowtch!" I said, or something like it, only with more profanity. Wiping my hand across my pants leg, I hoped I'd crushed the little bastard as I scrambled out into the clearing.

"Look," Sam said, pointing, and as soon as I had, I decided that now probably wasn't the time to cross-examine him about Dory.

Under the dim pole-mounted light at the lake's edge, two figures struggled. A dozen yards away on the beach, Babs Littrell's body still lay where it had fallen.

Ellie broke away, but Dory caught her by the hair and spun her around. Bob started toward them, and Sam was right behind Bob.

But Ellie didn't need them. Watching her clenched fist draw back was like seeing a car crash as it happens, the long, time-slowing-down inevitability of mass and energy at last meeting Dory's jaw.

The smack of Ellie's knuckles against flesh was so satisfying, it was almost worth seeing Ellie cringe away afterward, cradling her hand. I hurried toward her as Bob reached for Dory and caught her as she staggered and started to fall.

But then suddenly she sprang away from him and sprinted down the beach toward where Babs lay.

"Stop her!" I yelled, but she caught Sam by surprise. When he tackled her by the ankles, she went down but yanked her feet away and kicked back hard, smashing him in the face.

If she got to the gun, which was still lying there, gleaming darkly, by Babs's dead hand, we were toast. Or even if she didn't, maybe. Her face, so twisted with rage and fright that it was nearly unrecognizable, said she'd tear us apart with her hands if she got the chance.

Because, I thought, we'd spoiled her plans. Now I meant to spoil this last one. She hadn't seen me, and in all the commotion I thought she must not have heard me, either.

Or at least she gave no sign that she had. Glancing back, I saw Ellie crouched next to Sam. Bob had stopped by them, too. There seemed to be a lot of dark blood dripping from Sam's nose, but otherwise he looked all right.

Dory didn't. Breathing hard and holding her jaw, she limped on down the narrow beach toward Babs Littrell's body, as if she were on a mission, oblivious to anything else.

I thought any minute she might collapse. Nevertheless, I took the precaution of charging her from behind, and while I am not a very sizable person physically, momentum was on my side, and also I was mad as hell.

Lies, I thought furiously. *Straight to my face.* Not to mention bird-dogging my son until she'd even managed to trouble his marriage.

And not to mention murder. Thinking this, I hit her with my shoulder in the middle of her back, and we slammed down onto the sand together. And may I just say right here that the whole "soft sandy beaches" thing we Mainers hear so much about from our Florida friends is dead wrong, at least in the softness department.

For a minute I thought every bone in my body might be broken, not to mention my most favorite internal organs punctured. Lots more stars were in my vision than were in the sky suddenly, too.

Then Dory shifted beneath me. She'd gotten slammed even worse than I had. *Good,* I thought meanly, keeping a firm grip on a handful of her hair while I started to get up.

By then, Bob stood over me with his sidearm out, his feet planted in firing stance, and a *Don't you mess with me* look on his pink, plump face.

"Nobody move. Everybody calm down. We don't need to have any more problems here."

Behind Bob, Sam was on his feet, guiding Ellie toward the picnic table under the big trees.

"Jake," Bob said, sounding every inch the experienced police officer who is holding a gun on someone and knows just how to use it. "Jake, I want you to get up and back away. Dory, you stay put." *If you know what's good for you,* his tone added.

"Bob," I began, "I don't think that's such a—"

Just as I expected, she jumped up and took off the very instant I loosened my grip on her. I staggered and lost my balance.

"Damn," Bob sighed, snatching at her as she went by but grabbing only thin air.

Also, she'd slugged me as she got up, and while I do think the taste of lake water is lovely, this time it was also damned inconvenient. Sand went up my nose all the way to my tonsils, and by the time I could see again, Dory had reached Richie Perrone's Jeep.

She'd decided she had to get rid of us all before she could do anything else, I realized as the engine roared to life, the headlights glared menacingly, and the transmission emitted a deep *thunk* as it dropped into low gear.

And then the Jeep *erupted* across the grass at us.

"Stop!" Bob bellowed, getting off a shot that obliterated the Jeep's driver's-side mirror, but the vehicle kept coming.

He shot a tire; it blew out explosively. The Jeep veered left, then corrected course, the headlights like white, dead eyes out of a nightmare as the Jeep closed the gap between us.

"Jake," Ellie cried, grabbing my sleeve, breaking my paralysis. "Come on. We've got to run."

"Oh, Ellie." Her face was bruised, and her lip was split, and if I'd been angry before, I was incandescent now.

Also, I was damned if that murderous little twit was going to chase me around in a freaking Jeep, of all things. So I did run, but not the way Dory expected. Instead, I returned to the picnic area, where I thought swerving among the big trees might slow her down.

It did, but not enough. Desperately, I threw myself at the thick brush near where we'd entered the clearing. The Jeep kept coming, its front grille slamming into the undergrowth right behind me.

But there it stopped, and although getting the vehicle through here would be relatively easy— after all, she'd gotten it in here in the first place— doing it fast was another story.

While the Jeep's engine roared behind me, I wormed, squirmed, and wiggled my way forward, noticing unhappily at last that I'd gotten off the road somehow. And have I mentioned how dark it was out here?

Dark and full of tiny, hungry bugs called blackflies, this being summer in Maine and me being the tastiest morsel that any of them had seen recently. The rising hum of bloodsucking insects gathering for a feast was drowned out only by the angry roar of the Jeep, still behind me and still making headway.

Finally, I found the road again and hurried the rest of the way down it as best I could, another fifty yards or so to the Fiat. I got in, shoved the key in the ignition, and turned it.

A fast, click-click-clicking sound came from under the hood. Nothing else happened. *Oh, come on,* I thought at it and tried again.

Nothing. The Jeep's bright white headlights were coming on fast down the road toward me. Another try: this time the clicks sounded much less eager. The car's battery was running down.

That, however, was why I'd left the Fiat parked so the front of it was aimed downhill. Not that popping the clutch always worked, and you really got only one shot at it unless you wanted to push the car all the way back uphill and try again.

Crossing my mental fingers, I hopped out, ran to the rear of the car, and gave it a shove. The Fiat was a light vehicle, and it moved easily once I got it going. In fact, as it began rolling away from me, it occurred to me that catching it was my real problem.

After flinging myself wildly onto the trunk

lid, I inched forward precariously while the Fiat gained speed. Scrambling up over the convertible top without crashing right through it was tricky, and getting both feet around and in through the fortunately open window on the driver's side was trickier.

And then I got stuck: legs inside, everything else outside. And have I mentioned the gaining-speed part? Bumping along faster and faster, the car stayed on the shoulder, but it was heading for a ditch alongside the road, and the ditch featured a metal culvert, which would probably cut my head off if the car flipped when it hit the ditch.

Which it was going to do, so I tried steering with my feet, but that didn't work, either, and finally there was nothing I could do but hang on ferociously to the Fiat's convertible top and try yet again to pry my own wedged-in backside out of the car's window opening.

And that was when the latch that held the top down on the driver's side snapped open. Suddenly I was clinging to a thing that wasn't fastened to the car anymore, but the window opening got bigger all at once, too, and suddenly I slid through, slamming the back of my head on my way in and scraping pretty much all the skin off my spine, as well.

But that wasn't the end of it. The Jeep's headlights filled the Fiat's rearview mirror with a murderously bright glare, and I hadn't even started the car yet. So . . .

Ignition. Clutch. First gear. The Fiat still rolled briskly, just not toward the culvert anymore. Holding my breath and silently imploring the car to cooperate, I let the clutch out fast and felt the small lurch of the transmission catching.

And then the engine caught, firing up with a throaty growl.

"Good Fiat," I whispered. "Excellent Fiat."

But the Jeep was there. I cut the headlights, stomped the gas, hit the brakes, and yanked the steering wheel, spinning the Fiat around 180 degrees.

Wow, I thought as the car skidded to a halt. I'd never done that before. Then I waited as the Jeep approached.

It stopped about a dozen yards away. Between us, the fog I'd seen coming back in thickened noticeably, each rolling gray billow blurring the Jeep's lights a little more.

Maybe I could get to her before she spotted me. I needed only a few seconds: hop out of the Fiat, get to the Jeep, jump in—surprise!—and put Dory out of commission, clobbering her if I had to.

That was my plan, anyway, and I thought it would work. So imagine my surprise when, as I got out and stepped away from the Fiat, a small, hard something pressed painfully into my ribs and a small, hard person kept jabbing it there viciously and repeatedly.

"Walk back to the Jeep," Dory Sloan said thickly.

It sounded as if her jaw was broken. Ellie had already done some clobbering tonight, I recalled now, and although she might be delicate looking, she's got a wicked left hook.

"Okay, okay," I said irritably. Gosh, but I was tired of this horrible girl.

"You're not at all like I thought you were," I said, taking slow, halting steps forward. I didn't know what she had in mind once we got to the Jeep, but I was sure I wouldn't enjoy it. "I thought you were an artist. A decent person," I said, "who we all enjoyed having around."

She made a sound of contempt. "Oh, good. So glad I had your stamp of approval," she replied sarcastically. "You know, you people are so easy to fool that it's almost not fair."

We approached the Jeep. Her gun kept stabbing my ribs. "Where did Babs ever pick you up, anyway?"

Maybe if I could get her talking, she'd quit jabbing.

"In an art class she was teaching," Dory replied after a pause.

"Where? In prison?" I said, taking a guess. Leo Montaine said Babs had taught in underserved communities, and considering the side of herself that Dory was showing now, a community behind high walls and bars seemed a not-so-wild guess.

"Psych ward," Dory said. "Well," she amended, "it was a prison psych ward, but still. I was crazy enough to get myself transferred out of general population, if you know what I mean."

I could figure it out: unlike inmates who actually suffered from all too real mental or emotional illnesses, Dory had faked unwellness to get better food and surroundings, plus thera-peutic activities, like art classes. One of which Babs Littrell had taught.

Dory shoved the gun in my ribs again. "Oh, Miss Littrell," she lilted mockingly, "thanks so much for seeing my true potential." She pushed me at the Jeep. "Right. I'll show you potential. Get in. Start the engine. Then wait."

I climbed behind the wheel while she stood aiming the weapon at me. The Jeep started easily and idled smoothly.

"What's to keep me from peeling out of here right now?"

If I could get her to move around behind the vehicle somehow, I'd put it in reverse and hit the gas pedal, and that would be that. But instead, she waved the weapon toward the brush-filled track that led to the lake.

"I'm going to go in there and find them, and if you're not here when I get back, I'll kill all three of them. How's that for a reason?"

I put my hands up in surrender. "Fine. Whatever you say."

I reached over and pulled the driver's-side door shut but didn't latch it. "But before you go, Dory, just tell me one thing. Why'd you kill Brad Fairway?"

She eyed me in amazement. "Are you crazy? I wouldn't kill him. Fairway was Babs's meal ticket, and that made him my meal ticket, too."

I must've looked confused. "He used her import licenses to bring in all that electronic stuff you saw in his basement," she said.

Import licenses . . . Like the kind she'd need to bring in fabric from Japan, I realized.

Dory went on, "He paid her each time, and so did a few other people he knew."

Other people. Something cold and unpleasant shifted in the pit of my stomach.

But I didn't have time for that now. "Okay," I said. "Something went haywire, though. Somebody killed him. And after that, you . . ."

She exhaled impatiently. "Okay, look. First"—she held up a finger—"once Brad got killed, Babs got scared. She'd already told me she was going to quit renting out her permits and so on to crooks." A frown creased her forehead. "That meant less income for her, so she couldn't afford me anymore."

And, presto, there went Dory's cushy job. "And?"

She faced me defiantly. "And I'm not going back to that crappy club I worked in before I got caught selling . . . well, never mind what I was selling."

But it had gotten her sent to jail, and that was where her luck turned a corner.

"Babs fixed my clothes and my hair, taught me stuff . . ."

Had behaved as a friend, in other words. And look what it had got her.

"So now I'm who I would've been," Dory went on, "if I hadn't grown up with a bunch of dopers and losers, broke as a joke in a slum that was basically an open sewer."

Hey, I had a few childhood stories that I could've told, too. The one about my mom getting murdered and me ending up on the street while my dad went on the run, for example. But I doubted she'd want to hear them.

"And now I'm not giving any of it up," she asserted "I can handle those import licenses just as well as she could."

By letting Fairway's criminal pals use them, she meant, for a fee. But if the criminals were who I thought they were, soon she'd be doing it for free. They could be persuasive, these guys that I was thinking of.

"So you killed her. Maybe she was scared after Fairway got killed, and you convinced her to come out here and lay low for a while. After that, you pretended that she was missing?"

It would keep Babs from telling the cops about the scheme to falsify import documents that she and Fairway were involved in. That way, Dory could basically inherit the whole illegal business.

Dory's smug look now said I was right.

But it wasn't enough for Babs to hide; sooner or later, she'd have to be gotten out of the way permanently. And how much better would it be to have Babs threaten the act first, then actually go through with it in front of witnesses?

"Finally, once you had everything set up the way you wanted, you got us out here to see it happen. You killed her with the weapon she'd brought along with her in case she needed protection." I took a breath. "But it didn't go quite the way you planned, did it, Dory? And letting Ellie get blamed, that worked out for you, too."

She smiled, not pleasantly. "It did turn out pretty convenient, didn't it? Everybody all of a sudden was focused on her." Her tone turned icy. "Except," she finished, "for the two of you."

Yeah, I could see how we might've been getting on her nerves. Now she was on mine. "Want to tell me how you got hold of Ellie's handgun? I'm really curious about that."

I had been all along, and I still hadn't come up with a solution.

She shook her head. "Forget it. I'm going to go round up your pals. Ellie first. I can use her for a shield."

I thought using Ellie for a shield could backfire on Dory. Last time someone tried that, she stomped down so hard on his foot that she broke it and it had to be put in a cast.

Just to be sure, though, I stuck to my own plan, straightening behind the Jeep's steering wheel, bracing myself as best I could.

"All right. You might as well go get them, I guess," I said. "But, Dory," I added, "there's something you should know first." I leaned my head out the Jeep's window. "You've got a big problem," I whispered.

She took a suspicious step. "What?" she demanded.

"Well," I began confidentially, "your problem is . . ."

I waited until she'd walked up to the window, looking annoyed.

Not as annoyed as you will be, I thought, and then I reared back and *shoved* that unlatched driver's-side door open as hard as I could.

The impact knocked a surprised *whoof* out of her, sent the gun flying, and landed her on her back. An instant later, I landed on her front.

"Help!" I yelled as she struggled like a wildcat beneath me.

Around us the fog drifted even more thickly than before, the Jeep's bright white headlights bouncing back from what looked like an impenetrable gray wall.

"Help!" I yelled again, because my trick with the truck door had worked, but now it was like what the old-timers around here say about shark fishing: It's not the catching 'em that's hard. It's what comes later that can get a bit strenuous.

Which it did when one of Dory's bony knees caught me in the gut. Pain, nausea, and the strong wish to die that very minute exploded through me as I doubled over helplessly.

Dory rolled from beneath me. Somehow, she'd gotten the gun back. Struggling up into a crouch, I felt the world tilt crazily as nausea washed over me and darkness closed in from both sides.

More fog, too. I couldn't even see where Dory's feet were, but I took a wild guess and flung myself forward just as Ellie, Sam, and Bob emerged from the roadside thicket.

"Gun!" I yelled as my arms wrapped around Dory's ankles and she went down kicking and scrabbling. This time the sole of her shoe slammed the bridge of my nose.

I am, I thought clearly through the huge mess of blood and tears that resulted, *going to need plastic surgery for this.*

By now Bob and Sam had figured out what was happening and begun running toward me. Dory twisted wildly and finally sat up, with my hands still gripping her ankles.

And then suddenly the small, dark hole at the

end of her gun's barrel was all there was in the world.

Aimed at me. Her trigger finger tightened.

Well, I'll be darned, I thought. *This is it. Unless . . .*

Then all at once a game that my grandson loved playing popped into my head. He liked playing it on a nice, soft mattress, but . . .

Scrambling up fast, I let go of Dory's ankles just long enough to grab her feet, then lifted them both very forcefully and suddenly into the air.

Surprised, Dory fell backward, the gun flying from her hand. Bob Arnold saw this and moved to advance very swiftly on her from one side, while Sam rushed toward her from the other direction.

Desperately she scanned left and right for the lost gun, then glanced around in search of an escape route. Only the dark asphalt road that we'd come here on stretched emptily away a few yards in both directions, then vanished behind the wall of fog.

And then the last thing happened: This late a car might not pass by out here for hours. But now suddenly a faint yellow glow brightened hazily, and then headlights appeared.

Coming fast, but either Dory didn't see them, or she didn't care. As Sam and Bob closed in on her, she cried out and ran.

Ellie appeared from behind the Jeep, wielding

a tire iron she'd found inside it. Seeing Dory, she dropped the weapon and ran, too.

"Dory," I cried, "wait! There's a—"

Appearing out of the fog, it was an older American-made sedan, black or dark blue, I thought in the moment before its lights blinded me. The driver must've spotted Dory's shape in the road; brakes howled, and the stink of burning rubber bloomed in the night air.

Then came a thump. Nothing very dramatic, just . . .

Yeah, I don't want to think about it. The car swerved to a stop, ended up crossways in the road. The dome light went on as the door opened. In its faint glow the driver got out and staggered toward us.

"Oh my God. Oh my God." He reached Dory's sprawled body, sank to his knees beside it, and began to cry.

Otherwise, there was silence.

Sam found me and put his arm around my shoulders. "You okay?"

I answered with quick little nods of my head, unable to speak.

"She jumped right in front of him," Sam said.

A few yards away, Bob Arnold crouched by the man who had hit Dory Sloan with his car. The man had put his face in his hands.

"Now what?" Ellie wondered aloud. The welt

on her forehead looked very much as if the butt of a handgun had imprinted it there.

Rage welled in me until I remembered that Dory was dead. "I don't know," I said. "Let's let Bob tell us."

Then a wave of exhaustion seized me. The next thing I knew, Bob was driving the Jeep, I sat beside him in the front seat, with the seat belt fastened across me, and Ellie was in the back.

Sam was driving the Fiat home, I guessed, but I didn't have the energy to ask. Outside, the brightening sky turned the fog to drifting wisps like the remnants of tattered sails.

After a while, Bob spoke. "I'm going to go talk to those homicide cops from Augusta as soon as we get back to town."

And you're not talking to anyone, his tone implied clearly. He'd called in the accident, asked the dispatcher to send out a deputy, an ambulance, and a tow truck.

Ellie leaned forward to murmur to me that the guy driving the car had turned out to be a surgeon on his way to the hospital to start his long day. He had stayed behind with Dory and would remain there until the ambulance arrived to collect her body and Babs Littrell's.

I leaned back tiredly in the Jeep's front seat. Sam might think Dory had gotten hit deliberately, and I wouldn't contradict him. It didn't matter. But I could still hear her chopped-off cry of dismay when she realized that this was it, that this moment was the very end of her life.

I hoped that someday I would stop hearing it.

Bob pulled the Jeep up in front of my house in the lightening gray dawn. "Don't forget, now," he said sternly. "Do nothing until you hear from me. Understand?"

For the second time that night, I put my hands up in surrender. The idea of doing anything at all felt hilarious to me, but I knew if I started laughing, I wouldn't be able to stop. Or crying.

Ellie leaned partway out the Jeep's little rear window and said something I didn't hear. I shot her a quick thumbs-up. *Talk to you later,* I told her with the look that accompanied the gesture, and she nodded, getting it.

So we still had that going for us, at least.

Sam came in right behind me. The kitchen was still in darkness, except for the little fluorescent bulb under the cabinets and the night-light glowing dimly in the hall.

I walked over to the fluorescent, snapped it off, then turned it on again. Thoughts and feelings were slopping all over the place in my head, and none of them felt good.

Sam leaned in the kitchen doorway, silent.

"There had to be some better way," I said.

"Nah." He shook his head regretfully, looking down meditatively at the cuticle he was worrying with his thumbnail. "Not that I'm glad it happened. But you know she'd never have quit."

I looked at the coffeemaker, decided against, got a can of Sam's cola from the refrigerator instead, and touched its icy side against my nose, which I was still pretty sure was broken.

Ouch.

"You don't know that," I began. "She might've . . ."

What? Reformed? Changed her mind? In, as Bella would have put it, a pig's eye. Sam was right. Dory had killed two people already, and from that there was no going back.

Then Sam put the cherry on top. "Also," he said, pulling out his phone, "what I said about her bird-dogging me? Even after I flat out told her to lay off, she kept calling me and texting me." He held the phone's screen out to me.

"Hey, here's a new one," he said, thumbing the device. Squinting at it, he looked a little sick suddenly. "She must've sent it while we were . . ."

I took the phone from him. Judging from the time stamp on the text, it'd been sent only a few minutes before Dory died.

Come with me. We'll be together, it read.

I handed the phone back.

"She was desperate, Ma," Sam said. "I know she'd have killed you. Ellie too. But I still don't understand why, what made her so . . ."

Right, I thought. Desperate, like I'd been

352

once. But maybe she'd inherited a tiny bit less resilience than I had, or maybe a few more bad things had happened to her.

More and worse, maybe a lot worse. But one thing was for sure: I understood not wanting to go back to the bad old days. Standing there in my safe, warm kitchen with Sam, I understood completely.

"Ma," he said, "I'm going back to my house."

I looked up in surprise.

He shrugged. "Just feels like the right time."

His glance invited me to ask him about this, but I didn't, and in that moment my not asking was okay with him, too, I could see.

"Isn't your truck still way over near Ellie's place, though?" I asked. He'd have to retrieve it, I meant.

He turned, halfway out the door. "It was, but it's out there in the driveway now. I guess someone brought it back."

But it was too late for any more mysteries tonight, so I let him go. When I got upstairs, Wade was just getting out of bed. It was past four in the morning.

"Everything okay?" he wanted to know.

And I wanted to tell him, too, but he'd be on the water soon, outward bound on the pilot boat to meet up with a cargo freighter and bring her in, and he needed to be focused on it.

So I didn't say much or let him see my face.

Now that the shock of it all was wearing off a little, my nose felt like I'd stuck it in a meat grinder set on puree.

Instead, I waited until he'd gone downstairs before I undressed and eased myself into bed, where I sat up just long enough to swallow some ibuprofen and steady an ice pack across my nose.

And then, astonishingly, I fell asleep.

But even in my dreams, Dory Sloan's final cry of despair went on haunting me.

It haunts me still.

Fourteen

A week later, at Bob Arnold's request, we all crowded around the kitchen table at my house: me, Ellie, Wade, Sam, Bella, my dad, and Bob.

"I wanted you to hear it first, and from me," Bob said. "I'm resigning from the police department."

Wade's bushy eyebrows rose in surprise, Bella's mouth dropped open, while Ellie and I just sat goggle-eyed.

I'd wondered about this. But I had never really believed he would do it.

"My ex-wife and my kid, you know, they're in Arizona. Kid's got a lot less trouble with her asthma there," he said.

I knew that, too. Bob's daughter had been crippled by breathing troubles here in New England. He'd been all in for the move, getting a new job all set up out there and doing it for six months. But by then they'd been well on their way to a divorce.

"I'm going out there tomorrow. Maybe stay a week. Get the lay of the land."

See if his womenfolk wanted him back, he meant. As I thought this, his eyes met mine.

"Soon as they hire somebody else here, I'm gone," he said.

Silence hung in the room, but there wasn't a soul here who didn't think it was a great idea, not for us, of course, but for him. Without his little girl and the woman he thought of as his wife, he remained a great police chief. But he'd become the loneliest guy in town.

"Now, about this other business." Fairway's murder, he meant. He eyed me and Ellie. "You two might have noticed a few unusual tactics on my part during that episode."

Right, things like tipping me off to the fact that Ellie's house would be watched by those homicide detectives, alerting me to when Bob would be there and when he wouldn't, and (I was pretty sure) leading those detectives on a goose chase around the island to get them off our track. Then there was not calling in Richie Perrone's suspicious death the minute he learned of it, and . . .

"Which you're going to shut up about, now and forever," Bob said flatly. "That clear?"

He looked around the table, but he needn't have worried. We were all nodding so hard already, we looked like bobblehead dolls.

"Good." He smiled beatifically, as well he might. If some of his "unusual tactics" came to light, he'd be heading out not to Arizona but to a cell in the Maine State Prison.

"Thank you, Bob," I said.

"Yes," said Ellie. "Thanks."

"Now," he replied, turning businesslike. "You've got questions—I know that—so how about I cut to the chase? The FBI is investigating Fairway's murder as organized crime related."

My stomach dropped like a lead weight. So it was true, what I'd feared. Somehow my past must've caught up with me.

"They had a time getting the state to stand down," Bob went on. "State homicide cops didn't want to hear about any New York–to–Maine mob connection." Bob turned his pale blue gaze on me. "After all, they had their suspect all lined up."

Ellie, he meant.

"And I guarantee you, nobody could've told them it was a what-do-you-call-it, a mob hit, instead. Heck, they don't believe it now."

So telling them about my checkered past wouldn't have changed anything, Bob was telling me, and I didn't quite float up off my chair in relief, but it was close.

"So Babs took Fairway's death as a hint that maybe she should get out of the rent-a-license racket before the same happened to her? And Dory had other ideas?" Sam asked.

Bob nodded. "Boiled down, that's it. And maybe Babs thought that whoever killed Fairway might come after her next?"

I was already nodding.

"And Dory probably encouraged her in that idea," Ellie put in.

"Dory was in the perfect position to give Babs scary updates, too, ones that weren't true. To keep her isolated and scared."

My dad had listened quietly to all this. Now he said, "How's this Dory person been getting around, though? From all I've heard so far, it's you people who've been driving her everywhere."

Bob looked wise. "She had Babs's car all along." He turned to me. "Remember all that firewood with the tarp over it at Fairway's?"

Of course. "More than firewood under it?"

He nodded.

Then Ellie spoke up. "What I don't understand is why Dory attacked people after they'd talked with us about Babs. I mean, what good could that possibly do her?"

"To discourage anyone else from doing it?" I suggested. "Next one we asked, they might say no if they'd heard about the others."

But that sounded weak even to me. Bob made an "I got nothing" gesture, and no one else had any suggestions, either, until Sam cleared his throat.

"Punishment," he said.

We all looked inquiringly at him.

"She was into it," he explained. "Like, at the arts center, a volunteer asked Dory not to handle some flyers that had just come out of the printer, in case they smeared." He frowned, remembering. "Later those flyers were found with a lot of ink spilled on them, and no one knew how. Then there was a thing with some wall hangings that the kids did going up in place of one of Babs's tapestries. Dory didn't say anything about them."

He looked at me. "But the next day, those wall hangings were gone, and no one's found them yet," he said.

Sam sounded sure of himself, and I was suddenly very glad that he was no longer in Dory Sloan's romantic crosshairs.

"Richie Perrone's dead, though," I pointed out. "Kind of extreme punishment, even for her, don't you think?"

Sam looked at his hands, clasped in front of him on the red-checked tablecloth. "Unless that was the punishment," he said quietly. "You ask me, Perrone dying was no mistake. It was the other two she screwed up on. She'd have meant to kill them all." He looked up. "That's my sense of it, anyway."

"Why'd this girl want in on any of this at all, though?" Bella put in. "It all seems like something that a sensible person would run away from, not toward."

Bob chuckled mirthlessly, looking around the table. "I hate to speak ill of the dead. But I did a little cop research on our friend Dory, and it turns out she's got an exciting history." He ticked off on his fingers as he said, "Forgery, embezzlement, fraud, bad checks . . . Oh, and I almost forgot. Assault with a deadly weapon."

He got up. "Babs Littrell got Dory out of a six-month sentence for theft. Not her first incarceration, by any means. Getting involved in fraudulent documents probably seemed like a promotion to her."

He moved toward the door. I got up and followed him.

"Bob, how come no one's even called us?" I asked.

The state cops were gone, as if they'd never even been here, and no federal ones had gotten in touch with Ellie or me.

"It's like they're waiting to pounce," I complained.

Probably I should've counted my blessings that the cops weren't interested in us anymore. But not even being asked about it all was unnerving, like they still could show up any minute.

Bob stepped out onto the porch and I followed him. Behind him the maple tree by the front walk shed a shower of pale green whirlybird seeds, which twirled down onto the grass.

"Yeah, I meant to talk to you about that." Over his head, a fat robin perched in the maple, chirping its little head off. "I'm hearing that the Feds' working theory about Fairway's murder doesn't involve you or Ellie at all," he said.

I let out a long, relieved breath; maybe there

was such a thing as coinky-dink, after all. Maybe Fairway's sudden arrival in Eastport, followed by his murder, had nothing to do with me. Maybe I'd nearly put myself in the middle of it by mistake, by jumping at shadows that didn't exist anymore.

It was a thought to ponder, all right, but right now Bob was moving toward his car, pulled up to the curb across the street.

"Phone records say Dory called Richie Perrone at eleven ten on the night he died," he said over his shoulder to me. "Coroner says death probably occurred no earlier than midnight."

I followed him down the front walk. "So you think she lured him, first by smashing his pottery, then by telling him that Babs had done it? And maybe by pretending Babs was there at the cottage, too?"

I could see it happening. The smashed pots would have been enough to send Perrone into a rage, one Dory had made look worse by bashing in the door and faking the boot print on it herself.

"Yup," Bob said, looking up at the robin. "The injuries to his face didn't come from a fall. Somebody hit him with something. More than once."

Oh, man. And I guessed I knew who, too.

"As for Leo Montaine," Bob went on, "he's feeling okay. Even getting up and down that ladder of his."

Dory Sloan had been the part-time employee

361

helping Leo with the houseplants and the gardens, of course. It was the side job she'd mentioned, I realized now, as I recalled his place and hers, both full of such exuberantly healthy greenery.

She must've been trailing Ellie and me already by the time we visited Leo, and it must have been a tricky task, too, staying out of sight. But she'd done it, I thought with grudging admiration, and she'd been somewhere close behind me when I visited Perrone's country place, as well.

What she'd meant to do about our bodies, I didn't know, but I doubted her plan included headstones and funerals. Stuffed into one of those culverts on Shore Road in the dead of night, more likely.

"What about the pig?" I asked Bob suddenly as a mental picture of Perrone's porky pet rose in my mind, razor-sharp choppers and all.

"Who? Jillian? She was on a truck the next day," Bob replied. After Perrone died, he meant.

"Oh, Bob, don't tell me they're going to . . ."

She was big and bristly, and I don't care what anyone says, I'd known just by looking at her that given the chance, she'd be carnivorous as hell. But I still didn't want her turned into bacon and sausages.

Bob turned to me. "Nah, she's landed in a good spot. Gonna be the mascot for a kids' hockey team up north. The Allagash Tuskers."

"Oh, good." At least someone had come out of

all this relatively unscathed, even if that someone did have four legs and an oink.

Bob opened his car door. "Anyway, Leo looks fragile, but he's got a hard head," he said approvingly. "I think just possibly I misjudged that young fellow." Behind the wheel, he settled himself and buckled up. "Probably he could handle getting his cat back now, by the way."

Darn. Poor Bella. She'd gotten attached to the animal.

"I'll take care of it," I promised. "But, Bob, just one other thing . . ."

He nodded slowly. "Yeah. Hadley Owens."

It wasn't what I'd meant, but he was right. The fabulous old white-haired painter had also talked with Ellie and me about Babs Littrell. But in Hadley's case, the attack on her had come before we visited her, not after.

So it couldn't have been punishment. She hadn't done anything yet.

Bob sighed and let his chin fall down onto his chest. Then: "I don't know. It's a dangler, all right. Doesn't make sense." He looked up at me. "Too bad we can't ask Dory."

"Yeah." I walked up to the car. "Yeah, I guess that's right. But, Bob, what I wanted to know about was the gun. Who took it from Ellie's locked car and used it on Brad Fairway?"

Bob thought a moment. "You know," he said finally, "sometimes people's pasts come back to bite them. Sometimes even their distant pasts, when they least expect it." He glanced up pointedly at me. "When everything," he said, "is going good. And I don't want to create that kind of past for someone now. You get me?"

"Uh-huh," I said slowly.

He meant he thought he knew how it had happened, and he'd decided that it ought to be let alone. That he was going to let it alone.

He reached out and gave me a fist bump, and a picture of Sam popped suddenly into my head: drunk and stinking to high heaven. Wade had been away working, and Bob had helped me muscle my grown son into the bathtub, where Bob had wiped Sam's face with a wet washcloth while I'd poured warm water over Sam's hair.

"Anyway," he said now. His lips pursed briefly. "See ya."

Yeah. The Maine way of saying it.

Back in the kitchen, Bella scraped congealed chicken fat off the top of a pot of soup she'd begun making the day before. Wade and Sam stood at the sink, washing cups and glasses; my dad was at the counter, fixing himself a liverwurst sandwich; and Ellie . . .

Ellie sat at the kitchen table, drinking my dad's Moxie, looking as if the weight of the world had just been lifted from her shoulders.

She looked up at me. *It's over?* she mouthed silently.

I nodded. *I think so. I really do think so.* But it wasn't.

Not quite.

That night we all went to the arts center for the display and reception that the artists were putting on to celebrate the fair's conclusion. Sam, Mika, and my two grandchildren came along, too, mostly for the refreshments and the fireworks on the waterfront afterward.

George and Ellie and their daughter, Lee, were already inside, where from the high white walls of the gallery hung watercolors, oil paintings, photographs, intricate collages encrusted with shells and sea glass, pencil sketches, pastels, and thin-glazed ceramic masks with inscrutable looks on their faces.

A Richie Perrone urn was there, its smooth, gleaming bulk and dizzying height still as exciting and unnerving as when I'd first seen it in his barn. Babs Littrell's loom was on display, as well, with the beautiful, multi-hued tapestry still on it, permanently unfinished.

While I was gazing at it, Ellie took my hand and drew me away. "What's with Bella and your dad?" she wanted to know. "I thought they had settled their disagreement."

In the gallery's refreshments corner, an

enormous cut-glass punch bowl held a couple of gallons of ginger ale with a block of pink sherbet foaming merrily in it. I always hate the stuff until I taste it, and then it's delicious. I poured two cups and handed one to Ellie. "They had," I said. "Made up their quarrel, that is. It was set, they were going, but then Bella changed her mind."

"Again?" Wrinkling her nose over the punch cup, she watched her newly teenage daughter cross the room.

"Again," I said exasperatedly. "Now she says she'll move into an assisted living place when we carry her there, not a moment before."

Ellie refilled our cups. "But he's still going? Your dad?"

"Uh-huh. It's infuriating, and he's so stubborn! So we can sell the house, he says. Buy someplace smaller. Easier. Less to heat."

Movement caught my eye as Ellie's daughter was seized and guided by her friends to one of the small tables near the buffet. For her birthday celebration today—the arts center people had invited her to hold it here, Ellie had informed me proudly—Lee wore black leggings with fur-trimmed ankle boots, a gray Yale T-shirt over a hot-pink leotard top, and a blue tunic-length hoodie.

Also, her smile looked as if you could light up the whole East Coast with it. While we watched, her dad, George, wandered casually over to sit with her. Soon more pals of hers joined them.

Then a hand touched my arm. "Hello, dear," said Hadley Owens, who had appeared suddenly right beside me.

"Oh! Miss Owens, how are you?"

The elderly painter still had a small bandage on her forehead but looked otherwise okay.

"We're so glad to see you," I said, admiring the bright floral tunic she wore over a black T-shirt.

Ellie greeted her, as well.

"I'm glad to see you, too," Hadley Owens replied. "Because I have something to tell you."

Just then a pair of arts center volunteers brought a pie from the refreshments area's kitchen and placed it before the birthday girl.

Thirteen candles, each one stuck through a toasted marshmallow, flamed on the pie. Brown-edged bits of shortbread peeped through the whipped cream on top, and although nobody knew it yet, the pie also had a base layer of marshmallow cream–infused chocolate mousse.

"Ohh!" Lee breathed, beaming, and blew out the candles. "Oh, it's just what I wanted!"

As the singing began, Ellie turned to me. She'd resigned herself to putting the pie off until next year, when things might be calmer.

"Thank you," she said as across the room, George clowned happily for his daughter and her friends. "But, Miss Owens, you were saying?"

Hadley Owens watched, too, clearly enjoying the youthful clamor, then turned to us again. "I wasn't saying yet," she corrected kindly. "But now I will. I wasn't attacked. No one hit me."

"Really?" said Ellie, not looking convinced.

Me neither. The painter saw our faces and explained, "One of my arts center students came by that evening. We had wine and snacks and then some coffee."

Laughter erupted from the birthday girl's table across the room. Ellie wanted to go, I could tell. But she wanted to know, too.

"Not much wine," Miss Owens added hastily. "I took the dog out afterward."

I cringed at a mental picture of that dog on those stairs. But probably it was used to them.

Unlike me.

"After that, I couldn't remember what happened until you two arrived," said the painter, "but this morning it all came back to me in a rush."

She looked across the room at the youngsters again, this time a bit wistfully. "I got back upstairs, I put our few dishes in the sink, I went back to the living room . . . and then I got dizzy and fell." She didn't seem to like admitting this. "So simple and stupid. My pride's hurt more than anything. But I thought I ought to tell you. I hope I didn't cause you any trouble."

We assured her that she had not.

"Only," Ellie asked a bit shyly, "if you could

tell us about the student." Who'd been there, she meant, before Hadley Owens fell.

The older woman eyed Ellie curiously. Then she understood. "You want to know it wasn't her, don't you? I can see you must have a reason, too. That poor Dory didn't—"

Even now, nobody else knew what poor Dory Sloan had really been. It just seemed better not to talk about it, so we hadn't.

"That's right," Ellie said, waiting, and after a moment Hadley Owens pointed across the room at a tall, sixtyish fellow with wild gray hair, a big, beaky nose, and an engaging grin.

"He's a poet," said Hadley. "We're very . . . compatible."

I'll bet. You can't always tell by the cover, of course, but from here the guy looked like a catch.

"You go, girl," I told Hadley Owens sincerely, and the three of us laughed comfortably together before the artist went off to the refreshments area to, as she said, wet her whistle.

We started across the increasingly crowded room toward the birthday table, stopping only for a moment by Babs Littrell's forlorn-looking loom.

"I wish she could see all this," Ellie said.

On the room's small stage, a trio of local high schoolers picked up electric guitars and began playing "Wipe Out."

"Me too," I said. Not that Babs was any angel

herself, but none of it seemed fair, and especially not to the ones who'd gotten caught up in Dory's treachery.

Hadley Owens hadn't mentioned it, but according to Bella, who'd learned it on her most recent visit to the assisted living place, the elderly painter wouldn't be returning to her lofty crow's-nest apartment. She'd recovered from the head injury, all right, but she still couldn't handle the open-air flights of stairs. So the artist was moving to assisted living herself, Bella had told me.

"Want to go see the fireworks after this?" I asked Ellie when we finally made it to the celebration table.

Dark haired and elfin faced, Lee looked ecstatic with her pals all teasing and giggling around her.

"Sure," agreed Ellie as George helped the girls cut into the pie, which, by the way, turned out to be a smash hit. Even I enjoyed a small piece, marshmallows and all.

Then when it was eaten and our good-byes and thanks were all delivered, we headed for the exit.

"I used our usual chocolate cream pie recipe," I told Ellie as we stepped out into the mild evening. "With," I added, "a few tweaks."

Ellie looked impressed; she was more often the recipe developer of our team. "It was scrumptious," she said as we approached the arts center's front steps.

She went ahead of me to join George and Lee across the street. I stayed back, waiting for the rest of my own gang: Wade and Sam, Bella and my dad, and Mika and the kids. And it was while I was waiting that a man I didn't know—well-tailored gray suit, short hair, expensive tie—stepped up to me and spoke.

"Hi. Are you Jake Tiptree? I'm Barry Mulligan, Ellie's attorney."

He offered his hand, and I shook it, noticing his turquoise-and-gold cuff links, which would have seemed flashy if they hadn't been so flat-out beautiful. He was quite a lot younger than I'd pictured. Midthirties maybe.

"Nice to meet you. Thanks so much for all you did for Ellie," I said.

For one thing, the state homicide cops had quit hounding her almost at once after the night Dory Sloan died, and I doubted that this had happened by accident.

Mulligan nodded, accepting my thanks without a hint of false modesty. I liked that about him.

"But that's not why I'm here now," he said. "I have a message for you." He took a deep breath. "While I was researching Ellie's case, I heard from someone whose name came up in connection with Brad Fairway. And also very distantly with you."

I braced myself for whatever came next. The only trouble with my past, I'd decided, was that it kept refusing to stay in the past.

"The message I was asked to deliver is that you shouldn't worry," Mulligan said. "That if they wanted to, they would have."

I got the sense we both knew what we were talking about: me, and the fact that you didn't just walk away from those guys the way I had. Not unless you had permission.

Which no one ever got, except now it seemed that maybe I had. Mulligan must've read the look on my face.

"And before you ask, I don't know who the sender is. It came by a kind of back channel."

Yeah, right. "You're the one who called the Feds," I said. "I'd been wondering how they got involved so fast."

He shrugged. "Dug a little into Brad Fairway's background, and pretty soon it was obvious what Ellie'd gotten snagged up into somehow."

"But I shouldn't worry," I repeated, still stunned.

"Right. I also understand that there's some money involved? You can go and get that now, is what I'm told. You won't have problems with that. And that's all of it."

Of the message, he meant. I blinked a few times; what I'd just heard from Mulligan seemed to have knocked any further power of speech right out of my head.

"Nice meeting you." Mulligan stuck out his hand again. It was dry and warm, and his smile showed white, well-kept teeth.

"Wait," I said as he turned away. He'd finished his work with Ellie, so he'd obviously come all this way from Portland to deliver the message he'd brought me.

That, or he really enjoyed smoked salmon on a stick.

"Do you want to join us for the fireworks show? On the waterfront? We could find you some dinner, too, if you haven't had any."

It was getting dark. Wade and Sam came out behind me; Bella and my dad were still chatting with people in the arts center lobby.

The lawyer waved thanks, shaking his head. "Next time," he said.

Moments later he was driving away, and most of my family was herding me along with them down the steps and to the waterfront, only a block distant. I didn't see Mika anywhere, though.

My four-year-old grandson, Ephraim, gripped my hand. "Gramma, do flying fish have wings?" he wanted to know, gazing up at me with wide, guileless brown eyes.

So I told him that yes, they did, big, gauzy ones that shimmered a hundred different colors when the fish flew through the air.

Ephraim's little red sneakers quit stomping along beside me. "Are you *sure?*" he asked. But his next words saved me from replying.

"Because *I* am," he declared confidently. "I'm completely sure."

Soon thereafter we found Mika at the park bench by the fish pier.

"There you are," she said, hugging me warmly while reaching down to take Ephraim's hand. Her blunt-cut black hair glinted raven's-wing iridescence under the streetlamp.

All around us, people had gathered with lawn chairs and blankets for the fireworks show. In the dark, little kids ran with sparklers and cans of Silly String, while their older siblings grouped together, giggling and jostling one another.

By contrast, Bella and my dad sat on the park bench facing the bay, not speaking to one another. Sam sat between them. He was saying something to both of them, it looked like, and Wade and George stood right behind him with their heads bent, listening.

"You'd better come and hear, too," Mika told me, tugging at my sleeve.

So I eased in beside Wade behind the bench, while Ephraim went with his mother. Wade dropped an arm over my shoulders.

"A little brother or sister," Sam was saying, gathering Ephraim in between his knees.

I looked at Mika, who nodded in smiling confirmation, patting her middle with one hand while rocking her sleeping toddler, Doreen, back and forth in her stroller with the other.

"But," Sam said, "there's no room in our house for three kids."

True. As it was, I'd always thought they were lucky the walls of their adorable but teeny dwelling hadn't simply exploded outward, the place was already so full.

"So we were wondering . . ." Sam glanced up at Mika, who nodded for him to go on. "If moving back in with you guys for a little while might be possible," he said. "While we find a bigger place."

He looked over at me. "And you know, maybe I could help you out with some repairs around the place while we're there."

Out on the water, in the darkness, I could make out men moving on the fireworks barge. They'd be starting soon. I took a deep breath.

"Of course you can come," I said. Wade was already nodding agreement. "All of you, for as long as you want."

My dad said nothing, but he looked triumphant. Never mind the repairs. The younger generation's presence would give him even more of a reason to move out, and to take Bella with him if he could.

That is, he must have thought it would until Mika spoke.

"The thing is," she began hesitantly, "there's one more problem to solve." She turned to my stepmother-slash-housekeeper. "Bella, do you think maybe I could hire you to help me with the kids?"

Out on the barge, a match flared and went out.

"I mean, I'd be there, too," Mika went on. "I wouldn't leave you with them. I'm mostly working from home for the summer."

Mika was an adjunct instructor in the Hospitality & Food Service Department at the area technical college.

"But sometimes I'd be busy, is all," she continued. "Conferences, evening meetings. Sometimes they run late, but if you were there . . ." She turned sweetly to my father, whose face had gone dour. "And you, of course. They love it when Gramps puts them to bed."

The poor guy had never been a match for Mika's charm. At her words, my dad softened in spite of himself, and when she leaned in to kiss his cheek . . . yeah, that clinched it.

"But how will we all fit?" he wanted to know, but in a helplessly happy way, which I thought boded well for the whole arrangement. He was right, though. We couldn't very well stuff two adults and what soon would be three kids into the attic of my big old house, even though it had been remodeled into a studio apartment.

Meanwhile, the steps up to the studio apartment were too steep for my dad and Bella nowadays and too narrow for another stair chair. I took a deep breath, hoping Wade would agree this time, too.

The cash Mulligan's news had freed up for

me made quite a lot of things possible suddenly. "An addition would solve the problem," I said. "Out to the side where the driveway is now. Bedroom, bathroom, a sitting area with maybe a woodstove . . ."

Wade turned puzzledly, read my expression, and shrugged assent. The cost had always stopped us before, but if I'd found a way, he was fine with it, his look said.

Bella's face, though, said she'd just seen into the future, and it was heaven. She leaned past Sam to look over at my dad, who was just then leaning forward to look at her, too. Wordlessly he reached out, she took his hand, and the two of them got up and walked away together, conversing intently.

A clamp around my heart relaxed its pinch somewhat. "Until it's ready, though, we'll do the best we can," I said as just then from the barge there came a *thump* and a flare lit up the night.

Black water, black sky . . . and a fiery chrysanthemum flaring across it, the boom dying at length to a sizzle.

"Ooh," crooned little Ephraim around the thumb in his mouth. His earmuff-style hearing protectors made him resemble a pint-sized radio engineer.

A green-and-gold pinwheel shed sparks; then a flame ball shot up, spiraling dizzily, and a blue rose dripped fiery petals. The show went on brilliantly until at last it ended with a series of loud bangs that, I could only assume, were meant to rupture our eardrums.

Luckily, as a firearms guy, Wade made a point of having sound-canceling earmuffs to fit almost anyone, and he always remembered to bring them.

"So," he remarked later, as we walked home, "you come into some money?"

To build the new addition to the house, he meant.

"Something like that." Then I told him what Mulligan had told me. As he listened, his arm tightened around my shoulder.

"Good," he said when I had finished. "We'll take a field trip to pick up the cash." And that was Wade: solid, practical. Unflappable. "Sounds like the money will come in handy," he added.

We walked on past the old redbrick Frontier Bank building, the Happy Crab restaurant, and Peavey Library, with its high green cupola and the War of 1812 cannon on its front lawn.

At the top of the hill, my house appeared: three full floors, three redbrick chimneys, forty-eight old double-hung windows, each with a pair of park bench–green shutters.

"Wade, would we have sold it? I mean, if Bella and my dad moved out, and Sam and Mika didn't want to move back in, and . . ."

Leo Montaine's cross-eyed Siamese cat greeted

us with a yowl as we climbed the porch steps and went inside. Wade got himself a bottle of beer out of the refrigerator while I began heating some coffee in the microwave, then gave up and just started another pot.

"I mean," I said, "if we did sell, we *could* just buy a different house."

Wade drank from the beer bottle and put it down. "That what you want, though?"

Footsteps climbed the porch steps outside. I'd painted that porch twice, plus all forty-eight pairs of wooden shutters; I'd scraped forty acres of wallpaper off the walls and fixed the plaster afterward, too.

Heck, I'd even named some of the horses whose hair thickened that old plaster, and I don't even want to think about the wallpaper glue.

"No," I whispered to Wade. "I want to stay here."

Forever. Or as close to it as I could get.

"Then that," said Wade with a shrug, "is what we'll do."

After that he went to help shepherd them all inside. Mika, Sam, the children, and my dad each had some errand that urgently needed doing, so the hall resembled a cartoon fistfight for a little while, all of them wrestling off jackets, beelining for bathrooms, and grabbing excited, over-tired children and hustling them into the quiet parlor.

And then there was Bella, grimly hunting a lost house shoe amidst the chaos. Finally, she found it and stuck her long, bony foot into it.

"So," I said to her. "You okay with all this?"

What Mika had described might end up being a lot of work, and I hadn't heard Bella's opinion yet. But when she straightened, her rawboned old face was beaming under her frizzy henna-red hair, her delighted smile exposing a multitude of oddly aimed teeth.

"How'd you do it?" she asked, glancing around conspiratorially. "I mean, I know you said you would, but you've arranged everything so perfectly and made it so he has no idea it was you who really . . ."

Then I realized she'd believed me when I'd said I would get my dad off his assisted-living kick somehow. And now she thought I'd succeeded.

From behind her came sounds of my father opening what we called the Special Toy Box. It contained items Sam's kids were not allowed to have on all but special occasions: a drum, a xylophone, and a set of bamboo panpipes.

"That box needs a padlock," said Bella as banging, clanging, and atonal tootling erupted— so much for the quiet parlor—but her big grape-green eyes crinkled with pleasure.

"You know I didn't, though, right?" I said to her. "Do anything, I mean. It all just worked out by itself."

And mostly on account of Sam and Mika. But Bella wasn't having any of that.

"Never mind," she said. "It worked out because of you somehow, I just know it. Don't try arguing with me about it."

She turned, facing me. "You're a good person, Jacobia, and don't you ever let anyone tell you different." She eyed me perceptively. "Especially when you look in the mirror."

And I suppose that if I'd been the type who could burst into tears over kindness and good advice, I would have. But just then, more footsteps thumped up onto the porch outside, and Ellie came in with Lee.

"Oh, thank you so much!" the girl sang out, hurling herself at me. "My friends all thought the marshmallow birthday pie was *so cool*."

From the parlor came a flute-tootled fanfare, then a drumroll. A breath I hadn't known I'd been holding rushed out of me. As Ellie had said earlier right here at my kitchen table, it was over.

Almost.

Later that night, after everyone was asleep, I went out again and found the boy, Harald Gleason, on his front porch. When I pulled up, he was drinking Pepsi out of a can.

I'd called ahead to make sure he'd be there. He'd sounded about as eager as if I'd suggested he show up for a firing squad, but he'd agreed.

Now there was an unopened can of Pepsi waiting for me on the paint-peeling porch rail of the little house on the edge of town.

I took the Pepsi and sat on the rickety wicker chair next to Harald's. In the room right behind us, a TV blared, while deeper in the house, somebody was arguing loudly with someone else.

It sounded as if the quarrel had gone on for a while, and that it was heating up. I looked at Harald, whose thick hanging mop of brown hair didn't quite hide his miserable expression.

"Want to tell me about it?" I asked him gently. On the phone, I'd said I wanted to ask him about Ellie's gun. He'd known what I meant.

"Why? Seems like Bob Arnold already did tell you," he muttered. "Even if he said he wouldn't."

I took a long pull on the cold soft drink. It was chilly out here, but I had absolutely no desire to go inside.

"Bob didn't tell me anything. I figured it out for myself."

That got Harald's attention. "But if you know it was me who broke into Ellie's car, then what else do you . . . ?"

Bob Arnold had been trying to keep Harald out of trouble for nearly a year now. And Harald was the only one in Eastport that I could think of who knew how to pick locks.

Door locks, car locks . . . maybe even the lock on the box Ellie kept her gun in.

Probably, in fact. It was why Bob hadn't wanted to tell me about it; he didn't want Harald pulled into a murder case, though I wasn't yet quite sure why.

Now, though, Harald had admitted it to me. Or most of it, anyway.

"I want to know about what happened afterward," I said.

A particularly angry-sounding burst of invective erupted from inside the house. Harald grimaced.

"Bob said if I didn't mess up, he'd get me out of here," he said. "There's a locksmithing program in Lewiston, he said he'd . . ." The important phrase there being "if I didn't mess up."

"Harald, I'm not going to tell anybody about this, okay?"

And anyone else who could—and would—was dead.

The kid looked hopefully at me. "Really?"

"Really," I said, and I'm not sure if he believed me or if by then he was in such deep despair that he just didn't care anymore. But he started talking.

"It was supposed to be a joke," he blurted. "I figured you and Ellie would know it was me. I even had a note ready to leave."

He dug a crumpled sheet of lined paper from his pocket and showed it to me. On it was scrawled, *Greetings from the Lock Jock!*

"See, they call me that at school," he explained,

brightening now that we were talking about something he was good at. " 'Cause I can—"

"Right, Harald, I know. But about that night."

Behind us, something crashed against a wall. A plate, maybe. Or a bottle.

Harald's eyes closed briefly as he waited for something worse to happen. When it didn't, he went on. "Yeah, okay. So I opened the car lock. It was easy. You just—"

"Harald. Get to the point."

Someone inside was talking in a low, urgent monotone about getting back here and making it quick, or else.

Harald blew a breath out. I could see that the kid had developed some patience, and from inside the house, I could hear why. "Right," he started again, "so then I did the glove compartment. I thought I'd leave the note, then lock everything back up again."

"But?" I knew what must've happened. But I wanted to hear him say it.

"But there was a box in the glove compartment. A *locked* box. I'd just taken it out to look at it when she came up behind me." He drank from the Pepsi can. "I wanted to put it back, but she said if I did, she'd tell everybody what I'd been doing."

"Dory Sloan, this was." The Pepsi was warm, but it had caffeine in it. I'd have shot it into my veins if I could, I was so tired.

"Right. And she was watching me, so it took me a little longer that it should have. But I got it open."

Note to self: *Don't rely on a lockbox to guard against pilfering.*

"And there was a gun inside," I said.

He nodded. "Right, and she grabbed it. Told me I'd better keep my mouth shut about it if I knew what was good for me."

"And then she left? What then?"

Harald shook his head. "After she was gone, I locked Ellie's car again, the glove box, too, and got out of there," he said.

"But then Bob Arnold visited you? Like I'm doing now, maybe?"

Out of earshot from his parents, I meant, not that they'd have paid any attention, probably. He really did need to get out of there.

"Yeah," Harald replied unhappily. "He said he'd figured it was me all along, and he wanted to know what happened. Why, mostly. So I told him, just like I'm doing with you."

"And he was okay with it? Well, not *okay* okay, but . . ."

"Yeah. Bob understood. Chewed me out pretty good, though." For the first time, Harald's lips curved in a near smile.

Then he looked anxiously at me. "But d'you promise you won't tell anyone? 'Cause if the school in Lewiston found out, they wouldn't take me, I'm pretty sure."

A locksmith with a history of breaking into places he shouldn't be? Yeah, probably not. But that wasn't going to happen, or at least not on account of me.

"Harald, did Dory do anything with the gun after she'd taken it from you? Like unload it, or . . ."

Harald looked up again. In the gloom of the porch outside the awful little house, his eyes were dark pools and his face sagged with some terrible remembered dread. "Yeah," he said quietly. "She put the end of the gun barrel in the corner of my mouth and dragged it across my lips."

"Like a zipper," I said as behind us, the arguing stopped and the TV went off. The silence afterward was more ominous somehow than all the racket had been.

"Yeah," Harald said. "And I got the message, too."

A little shiver went through him. I imagined the taste of the gun in his mouth, the metallic twang like old silver.

He got up. "So I did. I kept it"—he drew his pressed-together thumb and index finger across his lips—"zipped."

"And that's how Ellie's gun wound up killing Brad Fairway," I told Wade not much later that night.

Why had someone killed Fairway at all, though? It had always been my big question. But now I knew the answer to that, too, or thought I did.

"Dory's goal was never to replace Babs Littrell in Brad Fairway's illegal schemes," I said. Instead, Dory had wanted Fairway's job, and she'd nearly gotten it.

"Because, look," I went on to Wade as I slid into bed beside him, "with Babs dead and Ellie blamed for Fairway's killing, there's no pesky further investigation of Fairway's death to possibly mess Dory up in the future. Case, as they say, closed."

Bad as she was, I had to hand it to her; she knew an opportunity when she saw one.

"It must have just dawned on her all at once when she saw the gun that she could take control of everything if she had the nerve. Which she did. She grabbed it away from Harald, and then . . ."

Then the last thing hit me. "Later, sometime after Ellie had set up her appointment to see him but before she arrived . . ."

Dory could even have been there in Fairway's office already when Ellie made the call. I imagined Dory overhearing Fairway's end of it, unable to believe her luck.

"There were no hit men here to kill Fairway that night," I said. "Any FBI guys who look into it are going to find that out, too, sooner or later."

I took a breath. "Dory did it herself, with Ellie's weapon, and left it for the police to find. She shot him, then wiped off the gun."

Down in the parking lot, the fair had been closed down for the evening. I doubted the shot from inside the Choco's building would've been very loud, anyway.

"Walked right out the front door afterward," I said, "cool as you please. Nobody much was downtown anymore at that hour, and if there had been, she could have pretended that she'd just found Fairway dead herself."

After that, it had all unfolded the way she'd hoped: Ellie under suspicion, Babs in hiding, thinking she was the one who was suspected.

"But out at the lake, when she shot Babs and tried to make it seem as if Babs had done it herself, she dropped the gun by Babs's right hand." I took a deep breath. "But Babs was left handed. That's why Dory was so hot to get back to Babs's body—to move the gun before it got seen by anyone else. Anyone who would survive, I mean."

Wade opened his eyes. I'd thought he was sound asleep. I'd been talking to myself, really, just sorting it out in my own head.

"You," I said, "were not supposed to hear all of that." The part about Harald Gleason breaking into Ellie's car, I meant. I'd promised not to tell anyone.

"Hear what?" Wade asked, quick on the uptake, and he was the best secret keeper I'd ever met, so I let it go.

He changed the subject. "What I want to know is, why'd Sam move to our house alone and make us all worry about him and Mika?"

I'd wondered, too. Now I relaxed into the pillows. "Wade, he's had his own place for a while now. Wife, kids, the whole nine yards, all pretty much his own way. His and Mika's."

"So?" Wade eyed me over the reading glasses he'd fallen asleep wearing, or at least we'd decided to pretend that was what he'd done.

"So I think that on top of being worried about asking us if they could come back here at all, Sam wanted to be sure he could stand it himself before he floated the idea."

"But will we be able to stand it until the addition gets built?" I asked. "The noise, the confusion? A crying baby?"

Wade chuckled. "Guess we'll find out. We'll have to try to ignore them." He rolled over and threw an arm around me. "In fact," he said quietly into the side of my neck, "what do you say we practice ignoring them right now?"

I nodded wordlessly.

"Just to make sure we still can," Wade whispered, his breath warm in my ear. "Ignore them, I mean."

And as it turned out, we absolutely could.

Recipe

Chocolate Marshmallow Gingerbread

This makes a big pan of gingerbread! You can cut the recipe in half and use an 8-inch square baking pan if you wish.

<u>Ingredients:</u>

2 cups molasses
9 ounces unsalted butter, plus butter for greasing
½ cup brewed coffee
4 Macintosh apples, peeled, cored, and sliced fairly thin
4¾ cups all-purpose flour
2 tablespoons dark brown sugar
4 teaspoons ground cinnamon
4 teaspoons ground ginger
2 teaspoons ground mace
2 teaspoons ground nutmeg
1 teaspoon ground cloves
1 teaspoon ground allspice
1½ teaspoons baking soda
½ teaspoon salt
1 pint (2 cups) sour cream
2 large eggs, beaten
1 cup semisweet chocolate chips
1 cup miniature marshmallows

Whipped cream or vanilla ice cream (optional)
Chocolate syrup (optional)

Preheat the oven to 350°.

In a medium saucepan, whisk together the molasses, butter, and coffee. Cook, stirring constantly, over medium-low heat until the mixture reaches a boil. Set the molasses mixture aside to cool.

Grease the bottom of a 9-by-13-inch baking pan with butter. Spread the apple slices over the bottom and set aside.

In a large mixing bowl, mix together the flour, brown sugar, spices, baking soda, and salt until well combined. Set aside.

Next, fold the sour cream into the reserved molasses mixture until well incorporated. Pour the sour cream–molasses mixture into the reserved flour-spice mixture and mix thoroughly. Next, add the eggs and blend well. Stir in the chocolate chips and marshmallows.

Pour the batter over the reserved apples and bake in the oven for 40 minutes, or until the gingerbread sets. Remove from the oven and cool for 15 minutes.

Cut the gingerbread into squares and serve apple side up. Garnish with whipped cream or vanilla ice cream, if desired. You don't have to drizzle a little chocolate syrup over the top, but you could!

Center Point Large Print
600 Brooks Road / PO Box 1
Thorndike, ME 04986-0001 USA

(207) 568-3717

US & Canada:
1 800 929-9108
www.centerpointlargeprint.com